CLIQUE

CLIQUE

A novel by Jim Ernst

To George,
I hope that you enjoy the books.
Jim Ernst

Writers Club Press
New York Lincoln Shanghai

CLIQUE

Writers Club Press
an imprint of iUniverse, Inc.

For information address:
iUniverse, Inc.
2021 Pine Lake Road, Suite 100
Lincoln, NE 68512
www.iuniverse.com

ISBN: 0-595-25696-1 (pbk)
ISBN: 0-595-74172-X (cloth)

Printed in the United States of America

To my family, in the order they came into my life.

Anna Mae—My Wife
Charles—My Son
Susan—My Daughter
Marla—My Daughter-in-law
Cameron—My First Grandson
Taylor—My second Grandson
Fred—My Son-in-law
Sarah Marie—My First Granddaughter
And to any more who may come our way.

He drew a circle that shut me out—
Heretic, rebel, a thing to flout.
But love and I had the wit to win.
We drew a circle that took him in.
—EDWIN MARKHAM, Outwitted

ACKNOWLEDGEMENTS

To the members of the Morningside Writer's group, whom without their encouragement and support this book would never have made it past the first three chapters.

When I lost heart for the task that lie ahead, they offered me reasons to achieve the end.

When I fell, they picked me up, and promptly kicked me in the seat of the pants with their verbal challenges, lest this book that I was creating not be as good as I could possibly make it.

When I needed a helping hand and friendship with people dedicated to creating the written word properly, they welcomed me into their group, and they taught me.

Thank you, one and all, dear friends. You came through when I needed you.

CHAPTER 1

Early January

Two young people with backpacks, wearing hiking equipment, out for a stroll in the crisp mountain air. So it would seem to anyone closely watching. They approached the entryway to the top of the western side of a huge earth dam that stretched out 200 feet in front of them. For the past five minutes they were chatting about everything and anything. It was late in the morning and the sun was shining.

They were about to put into motion a plan to murder twenty-five hundred innocent men, women and children...They didn't have the slightest idea that they were the one's who were going to do it.

She was twenty-two, and he twenty-three; a year was a nice separation of age between them. Her blonde hair, usually worn at shoulder length instead tied in a ponytail. It bounced under her cap as she walked. Earmuffs attached to the cap were tied at the top. She felt it important to hear what he said. Strutting along beside him, using her long legs to keep up with his pace, indeed completely attentive to every word he was saying. They were in love; at least they thought they were. As with many young people being mixed up between love and what they consider exceptionally good sex is an easily acquired emotional flaw. They fell into this category. She was about five-foot-nine, not too tall, but then again not too short either. And she was what anyone would call very pretty.

Good looking, actually handsome in a rugged sort of way, he wore his dark brown hair close-cropped. Well over six-feet tall, he had a body frame supporting broad shoulders and complementing his well-muscled arms and legs hidden under his clothing. Hair on his chest showed at the top of his open collar. He sported a thin Van-Dyke beard.

They passed the guardhouse located about thirty-feet from the entrance to the black-topped pathway leading over the top of the dam. The guard stationed on the far side of the dam was looking the other way. The moment they stepped on the path a transformation took place. Whimsical banter ceased, and immediately they went into what seemed like an automated routine. She stopped walking, eyes stared at some distant point, but failed to focus on anything. He moved directly behind her; he also performed the mechanics of what he'd been programmed to do. Opening her backpack he took out a five pound rock. An ultra-thin, but exceptionally strong wire had been attached earlier, as an anchor. He tossed the rock just off the black top and into the dirt at the base of the hip-high wall.

The wall, made of large flat stones that were cemented together, was about eighteen inches deep. It was the same on each side of the pathway, twenty feet across. At best it was a feeble attempt at protecting anyone who crossed the path from falling over either side of the dam. If you fell off the earth dam by the side where the water backed up, you would only fall about fifteen feet. However, if you fell in and didn't get out of the water in less than five minutes, hypothermia would set in. The water remained extremely cold as it was supplied from the melting mountain snow-runoff.

It was kept at this level and away from the walkway, with sluice openings fortified with concrete spaced thirty-five feet apart. There were five of them and the water flowing through was vigorously controlled. The water level never came even close to the top for fear that it would erode the top of the dam and thus cease to hold back the water built up behind it. Children, who had at times been seen horsing around and climbing up on the wall, had been known to fall in, and then suffer a quick death when they exhausted themselves attempting to climb out. There simply was no place to grab hold. On the other side of the dam, where the sluices emptied, was a drop of more than seventy-five feet into a slow-moving stream. Funny thing, but no one ever fooled around on that side. It would seem even the kids had a little common sense after all, but only a little. Or maybe it was because most people were afraid of height.

He slid the rock, using his foot, to a place that set it against other rocks of roughly the same size. Then he pushed his companion slightly in the back, and she began her journey, slowly walking over the top of the dam. Ten feet of dirt-colored wire emerged from her backpack. He pulled out something that looked like a rock, although a somewhat smaller one. It only looked like it. Instead, it was a two-pound chunk of high-intensity plastique explosive called C-4. And of course, it was attached to the thin wire. Having been molded to look like a rock, similar to others lying on the side of the pathway, it was painted to look genuine. With each step she took more wire emptied taken backpack. Every ten feet there was another piece of this combustible material that he carefully lifted out and threw to the side of the path. Nineteen explosive charges were placed across the earth dam in this manner.

When the two finally came to the end of the walkway, the last piece of wire came out of her backpack. The end of the wire was split in two, providing for easy attachment to the trigger device, which hadn't yet been placed on the walkway. But it was not their job to do this. They finished their part. The moment they stepped off the macadam, they returned to the previously interrupted banter, unaware of the part they played in causing the death of many innocents.

She remarked to her companion that her pack seemed to be so much lighter, now that they had crossed over the dam. They headed up another path through the snow that would eventually lead them about five miles back up to the mountain chalet where they had been shacking up for the last two weeks. It had been all expenses paid compliments of their good friend, Wally. They didn't have a care in the world. Sex, since they left school in France, had been great, often, and uninhibited. They couldn't wait to get back to their love nest, where they could indulge themselves.

* * * *

The element of the plan to effect a final outcome was with a man now leaving his home in the town of Piôcc, Croatia. This town was located at the end of the mountain range known as the Diharic Alps, which separates Croatia from Bosnia-Herzegovina at its southern-most point. The town of Piôce sat at the base of the earth dam, where its controlled water supply was used to grow crops and take care of livestock. It had been created sixty-two years earlier, and alleviated a continual flooding condition in the town proper. It eventually emptied into the river and flowed into the Adriatic Sea. However, the real use of the dammed-up water was for the people living on the high water side of the dam. The water was the very lifeblood of many towns bordering its shore.

Stefan Valdic didn't know the reason why he had to leave his home earlier that evening, but at exactly 4:30 he grabbed the package he had been given, put on his winter coat, and headed out the door. He didn't say anything, but his wife was sure he was heading to the bar to drink himself into oblivion. He had been in a testy mood when he came home from work early with the strange looking package he carried in a small shopping bag. She was actually happy to get him out of the house, as he had been yelling at her and the children since.

He walked up the mountain trails almost three miles before he came to the guardhouse on the opposite side of where the other two had started. The trails leading up from the town were a series of switchbacks, some of them rather steep. He was winded when he approached the path leading to the dam. When he passed the guard without even a greeting, all the way to his first step onto the edge of the black top, he too became autonomic. Looking to his right he saw the end of the thin wire he'd been programmed to find, even though it was hard to see. He shoved each end of the wire into two separate holes in his package covered with brown paper. It was starting to get dark. Anybody coming across after him would hardly notice it unless you were looking for it. He laid it off to one side, and turned around and started heading back to his home down below.

Less than ten minutes later the earth dam exploded at nineteen separate points, and the water it was holding back cascaded directly down upon the town of Piôce. Out of a town of approximately 3,000 hard working farmers and tradesmen, there were to be only thirty-four survivors. There was a strange mixture of people who lived there. Croats, Serbs, and Albanians, who had migrated there over the years, had lived in relative peace with each other. When the ethnic wars boomed around them to the north and over on the other side of the mountains, these people escaped all of that misery and lived in harmony. They actually depended upon each other.

One of these people was Stefan, but he was unaware what he had done to kill his family and all of his friends. It was a shame none of the people who died this day were the designated targets. They were only the fodder in someone else's plan.

When Stefan returned to what was now the remnants of his home not washed away, he finally and despondently accepted the loss of his family. He searched the ruins for his gun so he could take his own life and join his loved one's. He couldn't find it. As it turned out, it didn't matter in the scheme of things still to happen. A stranger came up behind him and put a bullet in his brain, as he was searching the debris field that was once his home.

Somebody had paid to cause this terrible destruction, which would have a drastic effect on the people at the other side of the great earth dam. For the people who masterminded and engineered it, it was business as usual. Life meant little to these men. They called themselves,

The Camorra; they were a murder for hire organization; one that would go anywhere and do anything for money.

This closed out one of the elements responsible for implementing the plan, which could make trouble for the people causing it to happen. The red-haired man who had just assassinated Stefan thought to himself. *That's one down and two more to go.*

* * * *

Set into the side of a mountain, the chalet was ringed with an assortment of huge blue spruce and towering pines. Recent snowfall had caused their branches to be heavy and drooping, adding to the beauty of the background. With this type of architecture it looked as if the house had been transported from Switzerland. The house, painted bright colors with dark-brown corners and shutters, with a roof made from light-brown wood shakes, was indeed beautiful to look at.

They had no sooner entered the place, which had been their home for the past two weeks, when they started taking off each other's clothes even before they could get to their bedroom. They were *hot to trot* after their long trek up and down the mountain, yet they were still unaware as to their part in the damage they had set in motion.

It was only later when certain parts of what they actually did while they were on their walk started to creep through into their conscious memory. They started to remember doing something on the walkway over the dam. As the hours drew on, more and more of their real memory returned.

Sex was the magic element that kept them going. They spent all of the next two hours exploring and savoring each other. Finally they got out of bed, slipped on their underwear, and headed into the kitchen. It seemed strange to them that Wally wasn't in the house. He usually was sitting around somewhere reading a book. The pickings left in the refrigerator were lean at best.

"Where the heck is Wally," chirped Marta.

Pieter joked, "What do we need him for? There are lots of things to eat here. Why don't we make ourselves a ketchup or mayonnaise sandwich, and have some ice water for our drink?"

"Wise ass." Marta retorted.

Then he found some eggs. They were just what were needed. Marta scrambled them, and they feasted. "Don't worry, Pieter, I'm sure that Wally will completely re-stock the place when he returns to the chalet. Look, he left his book on the table. He must have just gone out for awhile. Maybe he went shopping?"

Soon after their somewhat creative meal they headed back to the bedroom and once again engaged in sex. It didn't take much in the way of protein and carbohydrates to rejuvenate these youngsters. After the final moment of passion had passed, they fell asleep, a sleep crowded with nightmares. They were both very unsettled, especially after a booming sound from a distance entered the confines of sleeping minds. However, the noise failed to wake them, although it did add to their restlessness. The deep programming was wearing off.

As the sun broke the horizon the next morning, they woke from a troubled sleep feeling startled and agitated. Some of the events that had taken place came back to them, but they only knew they had planted a string of attached rocks on the crosswalk over the earth dam. Yet they felt that something terrible had happened, and even worse, they were a part of it. While discussing what they surmised had happened, they heard noises coming from the living room.

It had to be Wally returning. A red-haired man suddenly burst into their bedroom. It was Wally all right, but he wasn't wearing his usual smile. It was more of a smirk. He threw an English-language newspaper at them. It landed on the bed and they could read the headlines.

> January 3, 2001 (AP)
> THOUSANDS LOST. EARTH DAM LOCATED ABOVE PIOCE, CROATIA DESTROYED BY EXPLOSIVES. WARRING ETHNIC GROUPS BLAMED FOR INCIDENT.
> The town of Piôce was literally washed off the map as the result of

> an unknown number of explosive charges planted on the top of the dam's walkway. It took off the top twenty-five feet of the dam, and water followed over the dirt washing it away rapidly. More than 2,500 people are feared dead. Rescuers searched throughout the night for survivors. Only 40 people were found alive. Ethnic dissidents suspected. No one has come forward to claim responsibility.

It wasn't necessary for them to read details of what happened. Their minds filled in all the rest, once they read the headlines.

Wally demanded, "You two, get your naked asses out of the bed. We're going to be making a little trip into the woods. Don't pack your bags, you won't be coming back." Pieter jumped out of bed and charged at Wally. He almost made it to him, when a shot rang out from somewhere outside the door. The bullet hit Pieter in his temple, passed through his head and dragged gray brain-matter out from his body, before lodging into one of the bedposts. The momentum from his lunge carried his body forward, and he banged into him before he fell to the floor with a thud. Wally turned and screamed at the man who had fired the shot.

"You stupid Shithead?" he yelled at the man who had fired the shot. "I told you that I didn't want to leave any evidence in here that could be traced back to me, since I'm the one who rented the place. Now I'll have to call in a clean-up team to scrub the chalet. Do you know how much this is going to take out of my profit for this activity? Our bosses will make me pay dearly in other ways if any of this gets out, since I'm the one in charge of this assignment."

Then Wally turned his attention to Marta, who had pulled the covers over her head, as if this action could protect her from what she had witnessed, and what lay in store for her.

"Okay you little oversexed acrobat. You think I haven't seen how you two go at each other. I've been looking at you perform, courtesy of that video camera I had set up in the corner of the room, and the observation monitor located in my room. Get some clothes on and we'll be on our way. We have a lot of territory to cover before you're going to meet your maker. Who knows? I may even sample some of your wares along the way, and if you treat me real good, I'll make it a painless death. How's that? I'm offering you a deal."

Since she read the threat of rape as real, and the fact it often was used as a weapon in that part of the world, Marta quietly did as she was told. She didn't say anything to him, but secretly she wanted to gouge out his eyes. She was too scared not to do what he said. Instead, she braced herself for what was coming.

The death of Pieter was devastating, but she knew she had to put it behind her. Feeling deep sadness for her lover, she rationalized there was nothing anyone could do to help him. She knew she had to do something, anything, to get away from Wally and his henchman. She planned to look for an opportunity when they would let down their guard and then she would escape. She dressed herself warmly, and decided to put on her ski boots rather than her hiking boots. She knew if she could get on a pair of skis, no one could catch her. It was the beginning of a plan. It was all she could think of. Wally was too busy trying to clean some of Pieter's blood off of him. He failed to notice her simple subterfuge.

Wally used his cell phone, then grabbed Marta abruptly by the arm and steered her out of the chalet. The guy he called Shithead, it was the only name that she heard Wally call him earlier, was left behind to direct the activities of a clean-up crew. Marta thought to herself. *Now I've only got this pig Wally to worry about. I'm going to find someplace where I can ditch him and the sooner the better. I won't stop to take my revenge now, but you can bet I'll get him later, and he won't be a pretty sight after I've finished.* Her bravado and her hatred were the only things keeping her moving, lest her legs buckled while she engaged in some form of self-pity.

They walked more than a mile when Wally stopped and decided he had to relieve himself. He held on to her arm with his left hand tightly around her wrist, and used his right hand to get under his heavy jacket, unzip himself and take out his penis. He was vulnerable and pre-occupied. Marta saw this as her chance, perhaps her only chance, to escape. She stretched his and her arm out as far as she could. He was busy making a stream in the snow.

When she was standing about three and a half feet away she swung her left leg at him with all her might, while she pivoted her body on her right foot. This provided her with the most leverage. Her heavy ski boot with metal edging crashed into his hand, which was now holding his flaccid member. The follow-through of her leveraged strike careened off his testicles, and somehow he peed on her boot. She thought her fleeting eyes had spotted some blood, but that was too much to hope for. Wally fell to the ground in excruciating pain. As he doubled up into a fetal position he gripped his private parts. She wondered what good he thought it would do for him. He began screaming a barrage of four-letter curses.

She made her chance to escape, and now she ran away in the direction of where she thought the closest ski slopes were located. She had heard they still had one slope open amid all the ravages of war that surrounded them. She felt it was the only chance she was going to get. But now, her ski boots were heavy that she found it difficult to run with any speed. She kept muttering out loud as her mind raced in different directions searching for a defined plan. *"My best-laid plans aren't worth a damn. What the heck am I going to do if he catches up with me? Think, think, damn you,"* she coached herself. *"I need another plan."* And she kept on running at the fastest speed she could manage. She did not look back, fearing every second counted and it would slow her down. She didn't know he wasn't up to chasing after her, and he wouldn't be for a long time to come, if ever. Her boot had done quite a job on Wally's genitals. It had damn near severed his penis, and the follow through had given him a rupture.

Worn out to the point of near exhaustion after her run of about two miles, she came upon the ski resort where she stole a pair of skis. They looked like they would fit her boots, and she started her downward trek. She selected long skis, from a rack located outside of a refreshment area, and these afforded her plenty of speed down the slope. She didn't really know where she would end up. She only knew it would take her away from Wally.

At the landing at the bottom she saw a large sign and discovered she had crossed over into Bosnia-Herzegovina. Her first stop was to a phone booth, where she placed a long distance collect call to her uncle in the States, who she knew worked for someone in the U.S. Government. It took awhile to get through. She was lucky. The operator spoke English.

Her words to him, as he woke up at six because of a six-hour time change, were short and simple.

"This is Marta. I've become involved with a massacre of more than two thousand people. My boyfriend was murdered before my eyes, and now the bastards responsible are trying to kill me. I don't know how long I can stay out of their hands. I'm in Bosnia in a town called Liubuski. Can you help me, Uncle Kevin?"

Her uncle's name was Kevin Winslow, and he did in fact work for someone high up in the government. He reported directly to the Secretary of State, and personally had an immediate clearance through to the President. He'd been authorized in this position by a small tacked-on addition to an appropriation bill, which had been passed through Congress with a bipartisan majority more than ten years ago. During this time he worked for three different presidents and six secretaries' of state. His job was to oversee an undercover arm of the government. He worked specifically on projects classified as illegal if assigned to either the FBI or CIA under their charters. However, both of the heads of these organizations were aware of what he did at only the highest level, and they had been sworn to secrecy. Occasionally the heads of each organization were involved in decisions this man made and acts he'd authorized.

"Stay on the line while I work on a way to take you into protective custody." Putting her on hold, he called on another line.

"This is Kevin Winslow. I need your help immediately."

The man answering was Rick Banyan, a private detective working out of an office in Morristown, New Jersey. He also had additional separate offices located in the United Kingdom, Spain and Italy. All four locations were branches of an international collection of investigative companies called "The Purple Feather Group." Rick was half American Indian, and to anyone who asked where he got the name of the company from, he'd say it was a tribal thing. He was just getting out of the shower when he picked up the phone and heard Kevin's voice. He was one of three principal operatives who worked undercover for Kevin. He was known by the code name CONSPIRATOR.

"Kevin, you're not using proper protocol. I assume you don't want to activate me, and this call is of a personal nature."

"You got that right, Rick. My niece is stuck in a place called Liubuski in Bosnia-Herzegovina. I need to get her out of there before someone kills her. I'll give you the basic details and fill you in later. Do you have any contacts in or near that area you can use to get to her? From what she told me her life is at risk."

"Hang on a moment. You know I've got Aldo Frondzi in Rome. All of my office managers have a satellite phone. I can reach them anywhere on the globe. Let's see if we get lucky." He kept him on while he pressed the speed dial. The pickup was almost immediate.

"Pronto, Aldo here." Aldo worked for Rick and managed his company in Italy and also worked undercover for the CIA. It was Kevin who introduced them while Rick was on another case. Kevin knew he was someone who could be trusted.

"Aldo, this is Rick. Where are you? How far away are you from a place called Liubuski in Bosnia-Hercegovina? Looking at the map I know it's a town located across the Adriatic Sea."

"You're in luck, Rick. I'm actually all the way over on the east shore of Italy right now. I'm at Termoli, which is a port town right on the Adriatic. What do you need?"

"Do you have any assets over there? Can they be used to locate a person in this town called Liubuski, and get someone out of there real fast? Someone's trying to kill Kevin's niece."

"Yeah, my brother Vito is over there pulling a stint with the United Nation's Peace-keeping Force. I was just talking to him on my cell only a few minutes ago. Wait a minute, I'll call him back. He's stationed in a town called Mostar. Stay on the phone." Aldo used his speed dial and was connected quickly.

"Vito, it's me again. Listen carefully. Do you know where Liubuski is, and equally important, how fast can you get there? A young girl needs your help. I'm told it's a matter of life and death."

"No problem. It's actually right down the road. Can't be more than 25 kilometers. Should take me tops fifteen minutes to get there."

"OK, I'm going to see if I can get a multi-party conference call going so you'll know who you'll be looking for. I'll try to get you to talk to the girl who you'll pick up."

Kevin was still in a wait mode when Rick told him to put his niece back on the phone. Soon they had a five-way conversation going across an ocean and covering three countries. Marta was able to talk directly to Vito, with the other's listening in on their conversation. Vito got right into it. "Marta, exactly where are you located?"

"I'm at a phone booth outside of a restaurant. Sorry, its sign is in a language foreign to me. I can't read the name. There's a bombed out building directly across the street from it, and it's near the entrance to the ski lift. Is that any help? Please hurry. There's this guy who's after me. I think I may have only slowed him down, and he's got to be madder than hell because of what I did to him. And I know he's not alone."

"Keep cool, Marta. Tell me now what you look like."

"Well, I'm tall, blonde, with my hair in a pony tail. I'm wearing ski boots, a blue ski jacket and a black hat with earmuffs tied up in the center. And if my quivering voice doesn't give me away, I'm terrified. How will I know you?"

"I'm six foot, black hair, and I'll be in a jeep with UN markings. I'm wearing the uniform of a Captain in the Italian Army and a UN arm-band. Tell you what, I'll ask you if you want one of my cookies. I don't think that anyone else will ask you that." He then tried to lighten up the obviously stressful moment she was experiencing, by adding. "And you already know I speak English with a heavy Italian accent."

"I'll be waiting for you. Hurry! Please! Uncle Kevin, I'm so scared, can I hang up now? I feel conspicuous standing here in a phone booth. I want to mix in with a lot of people who are mulling around the restaurant. That way he won't be able to find me easily."

"Okay honey, don't worry. We'll get you out of there. If Vito hasn't picked you up in a half-hour, I want you to call me back. Hang up now." She dropped off the line and Aldo spoke.

"Where in the hell did you come up with the cookie thing?" He chastised his brother.

"Sorry, It was all I could think of at the time. I'm hanging up now to go fetch her. I gotta' get moving."

Only three of them were left on the telephone connection.

"Kevin," Aldo said. "Can you arrange to get me a medivac helicopter out of Bari, Italy. It should be a safe transport vehicle. Nobody shoots at aircraft with a red cross painted on them. At least, I hope not. That place has a lot of people with guns. The chopper has to be one big enough to be able to carry enough fuel to travel about 275 kilometers across the Adriatic and return to Italy. I don't think I can get any petrol there. I can fuel it up back in Italy and drop her off where ever you want. Once I get into Italy, unless you think otherwise, I'll take her to my home in Rome. I'll also need somebody to be ***'Opening Doors'*** for me when I cross country borders. Do you think you can arrange all that, Kevin?"

"Leave that all to me. You head to the heliport in Bari now. Thanks. Let's hope this plan all fits together, and your brother gets to her in time. Call me once you get her on the helicopter." Aldo hung up.

Rick spoke. "Kevin, I'll call ahead to Europe and have my gal, Sênora Manuela Morales, fly into Rome to meet with Aldo. She was manager of his subsidiary, Conquistador Investigations, in Spain. She'll take her off Aldo's hands. I'll be catching the first Concorde I can get to Europe, and I'll meet up with Manuela in Spain. Then I'll debrief your niece. I'm going to put her where no one will ever find her until we can settle up this mess she's got herself into. Rest assured, I'll take care of her.'

Meantime, the guy referred to only as Shithead had completed his assignment back at the chalet. Pieter's body had been disposed of, and the place was cleaned. Starting to follow the trail Wally and Marta had taken only an hour ago he came upon Wally still groveling in the snow. There was a lot of blood. Without hesitation, he drew the .380 he'd used on Pieter earlier, and shot Wally through the head; easily rationalizing he was only following general orders from his boss. It stated, *If someone was down and out on your team, take them out permanently. Don't leave anything that can be traced.* Wally met all the elements of the criteria, so Shithead shot him. Besides, he knew it would mean more money for himself.

Running to track down where Marta had fled, he came to the same ski resort. People were talking with a policeman. They said they had seen a young woman steal a pair of skis and take off down the mountain. Renting ski boots and skis allowed him to take off after her. He judged he was only about 20 minutes behind her now.

Searching started in the heart of the town, and smartly focused where there were a lot of people gathered, spotting her sitting at a table in a restaurant. She saw him at the same time, and took off running. But she couldn't run fast enough with ski boots. She actually was lucky. There was a problem running with his boots too. Catching up eventually there were other things on his mind when he grabbed and dragged her down a bombed out alley. Figuring he would have time to rape her first before he killed her, he tried to get her out of sight. A Jeep pulled up at the curb and spotted them. Appearance of the army vehicle changed all that.

Shithead pulled his gun holding Marta with his other hand, and she began squirming to get away and thwarted his aim. The Italian Captain was too fast for her attacker, and released a leg kick to the face immediately flattening his adversary. Then he calmly walked over, and promptly dislocated both shoulders of the unconscious man. His brother taught him that little trick whenever they wanted to incapacitate someone. It was a fitting hurt to be applied to anybody who took advantage of women. Vito was unaware he'd given the man a death sentence because of the general order that had been issued by the head of the Camorra.

Marta threw her arms around Vito and wept uncontrollably. He helped her into the jeep, then asked. "Can I offer you a cookie?" She smiled weakly at him when he used the code word. They headed back towards Mostar to rendezvous with Aldo. She was safe...at least for the time being.

When calling ahead to make arrangements he learned his chopper was specially rigged for in-flight fueling, and extra petrol would be on board. It took Aldo three hours to arrive in the medivac helicopter at Mostar's makeshift helipad located in the center of the UN Peacekeeping Troop Complex. On the flight over Aldo used the time to familiarize himself with the operational controls of the large machine. He already knew how to fly a small helicopter. The pilot explained differences, and Aldo absorbed the information. He said: "Never know when knowledge about how to fly one of these will come in handy."

Normally the large Sikorsky was used only, when heavy ground action and fighting was taking place, to evacuate wounded to the closest field hospital. After initial treatment, wounded personnel were transported to the regular hospital by ambulance. For this reason they carried enough fuel to make limited flights of no more than 600 kilometers. Space usually required for fuel tanks had been ripped out to provide more room for additional wounded.

No one at the landing site was surprised when the large helicopter, with a red cross on its side, landed. Aldo had no time to leave the chopper before Vito rushed Marta out to the doorway of the awaiting helicopter. Before boarding she planted a big kiss on Vito's lips and left him some words of encouragement. "Vito, remember, I want to keep in touch. Now that you've rescued me and saved my life you're responsible for me. That's the way it is where I come from."

After all, they had five full hours to get to know each other…a lifetime in a war zone. Vito was actually sorry to see her leave. He liked her, and the feeling expressed was obviously mutual. The helicopter, on the ground all of two minutes, lifted off the pad heading back across the Adriatic towards its destination of Bari, Italy.

Early into the flight the pilot told Aldo. "I believe we have enough petrol in the tanks to make the return trip. However, if we hit a strong head wind we'll be in some serious trouble."

Aldo decided to use the special fuel-loading device to load 25-litre petrol cans into the regular fuel tanks from inside the helicopter. It wasn't easy, but with the help of the rigging fashioned beforehand, he managed to pour five cans into the outside fuel tank. After completing a complicated refueling process, he introduced himself to Marta. Only then was he able to get first hand information on what occurred to bring them to this juncture.

The trip took just under three hours. As the big machine eased itself downward in a direct vertical-landing trajectory, Aldo nudged the pilot's arm and spoke loudly, after his eyes had scanned the landing site.

"I think I just spotted a reflection off the barrel of a gun protruding from the doorway in the hangar. We may have some trouble awaiting us here."

No sooner had the helicopter landed than a hail of bullets, fired from an automatic weapon at a sharp angle, cut across the door of the chopper and glanced away. It was a good thing Aldo hadn't opened the door fully. He saw impressions appearing in the door, but none penetrated. Sensing a lull in firing for reloading he reacted. He drew his weapon with a fluid-like motion. It was a nine-shot Luger. He pulled open the door and emptied it in the direction of where he'd seen the protruding gun barrel. At the same time he nudged the pilot again and yelled instructions. The pilot couldn't hear the sound of the gunfire because the helicopter made so much noise.

"Get this chopper back into the air as fast as you can. There's someone out there shooting at us. We can't stay on the ground. We're going to have to route ourselves directly to Rome. That sniper must be out to get this little lady."

As the chopper started to rise, another stream of bullets coming from directly below tore into its bottom. The pilot jolted, and the helicopter shuddered. It was not because they'd been hit in a vital mechanical area, but because the pilot reacted to taking a slug in his leg.

"Christ, I'm hit. Take the damn controls before I crash." Aldo quickly slipped into the co-pilots seat and took over, while the pilot pulled off his belt and began tightening it around his leg to make a tourniquet. Blood spurted.

"It's pumping out like a son-of-a-bitch. Must have hit an artery; got two holes here, one in and one out."

"Do you think you can hang in there, and coach me, while I fly us to Rome? Or should I be looking for an alternate-landing site? The hospital in Rome is located close to the airport."

"Yeah! Let's go on to Rome. Now that I stopped the bleeding I think I can, as long as I don't go into shock. Beats staying here. We can always find another place to land, if necessary."

"Okay. I want you to know I'm not going to call in a revised flight plan across Italy. I'll ask for landing instructions only when we approach thirty kilometers of the airport. If they don't know where we're going, they can't set a trap for us as they did here. Somebody had to leak the information about whom we were going into Bosnia to pick up, and we don't even know his or her identity. But we'll find out, you can bet on it."

"But what about the young woman we picked up?" Asked the pilot.

Aldo glanced over at Marta. She was just sitting there, pale and frightened, staring into space. She was holding her arm; there was blood running down it.

"Oh my God, Marta, are you hurt badly?"

Chapter 2

"Gentlemen. Let's quiet down while I bring this meeting of the CLIQUE to order. His speech is about to begin. You all know I hate the President of the United States. This man won't open protected environments for oil drilling. My company's current leases are running dry, which means we're teetering on losing a lot of money. When he's finished talking each of you will get your chance. Then we'll discuss a plan of action to take."

The meeting was being held in the boardroom of Whitman Oil, Inc. Tobias Whitman, principal owner, Chairman and CEO of the company inherited from his father, beamed at all the attention. His tight smile and cold eyes roamed the group, searching for their respect. He was their leader, at age fifty-eight, standing six-feet four-inches tall, with bushy gray hair, and weighing in at a paunchy 223 pounds he presented a commanding figure. His underlying reason why so much hatred existed was for a very personal reason, and no one else knew about it.

Eleven of them in all were present, representing a wide variety of different types of businesses. Most of these wealthy and powerful men had come into money from family, except Thaddeus Thiebold. The only black man in the group headed a Union representing 120,000 low-skilled auto assembly workers in Michigan. His Union members were mostly uneducated and therefore filled only lower level jobs on assembly lines of the Big Three automobile manufacturers. Born in Detroit and growing up on the street in a tough neighborhood was an inherited part of life for this man. Despite being a product of what is referred to as the *hood,* the man had graduated from high school at the top of his class. A natural athlete, playing baseball in college to get a scholarship, and carrying broad shoulders on a six-foot one-inch frame, there wasn't an inch of fat on his body. Now at sixty-three, and about to retire and turn Union leadership over to a hand picked successor, he felt that attending this meeting was a must.

Thaddeus's wealth came as a Lotto winner, having won twelve million after-tax dollars. Using this money and making risky investments brought about net worth in excess of eighty million. An only son chose a career as a Sergeant in the Detroit police force, joining the force directly after completing law school. He also disliked the President immensely. Every time the Union attempted to interrupt operations of the three major automakers with selected strikes, designed to bring the Union more attention the big man always interceded in some way. Thaddeus wanted to be in a position to push for more benefits and wage hikes for workers. His people couldn't get ahead of the wage and price curve, no matter what.

All attendees had one thing in common; they held deep-seated hatred and dislike for the President of the United States. They hated him with passion, each for what he considered his own important reason. Not surprisingly, was the fact there weren't any women in this group.

Another of the men in attendance was Martin Longfellow. Short, fat, and most times seemingly jolly was his nature. It was the guise of a bald-headed cutthroat bastard, who was playing at being CEO/CFO of a national restaurant chain. Not jolly looking tonight though, he hated the President because the man maneuvered Congress into raising the minimum pay by a dollar. This action played havoc with his company's bottom line. Shareholders were talking about replacing him.

Next was Peter Rogers, who stood only five-foot three-inches tall, with thinning gray hair and a pencil-thin stature. CEO of a family business that made aluminum pots and pans, he recently saw most of this business head south, literally and figuratively, into the Mexican low-cost sweatshops. He couldn't compete with labor costs. He blamed it on NAFTA. The only problem was that the previous President pushed it through Congress, not this one. This was a guy who had to hate someone. Tag, the President was it. The oldest of the group at 70, he was also meanest of the lot.

Seven other powerful and wealthy businessmen present were, in order of their ages:

Anton Williams 39—Majority Shareholder-Automotive Parts
Larry Gelbhart 43—CFO-Spice Importers
Harry Hanson 44—President-Independent Tobacco Co.
Abhend Ibsen 48—CEO-Computer Software Manufacturer
Bear Crowell 49—Owner-Specialty Fabric Producer
Joseph Polking 49—Owner-North West Lumber
Justin Active 51—Independent Film Producer

Calling themselves the CLIQUE they believed in an Oligarchy, where the few and powerful control the masses. To add fuel to their fire, last November the President had been reelected with less than a majority of the popular vote. It was a far cry from the same ticket winning the election four years earlier, by garnering 60% of the popular vote on a law-and-order plank in their platform.

The ticket had since lost public favor, with a good chance it would be unseated once the opposing candidates were nominated. However, the independent candidate siphoned off just enough votes to upset the election in favor of the incumbent, who barely received enough electoral votes to be re-elected. This fact twisted them deep inside, one and all. The President carried all of the large States, as he very smartly had already written off all the smaller ones and spent little time in them during the political process preceding the election. Members of the

CLIQUE had each spent thousands of their company's soft money to elect his opponent. All was for naught. As far as they were concerned, the man they despised had lied his way back into the Presidency. It was true, simply because they chose to believe it.

Not being elected for the first time, the end of January was the usual time for President Germond Faller, age fifty-eight, to report to everyone in the nation what he saw for the future. Historically, sitting Presidents claim all sorts of progress from their first term. This evening was the State of the Union speech. Both houses of Congress met in the House of Representatives. As was the practice, at least one hundred seats were added to the gallery to provide for the Senators and seventy-five more seats for selected attendees. The hall would be packed. Invitee's included Justices of the Supreme Court, the Cabinet, the President's wife and children and the Vice President's (she was a widow) children. There were fifty more special guests who were personal friends of the President. As usual security was high. The place had many Secret Service agents present all busy doing their usual thing.

* * * *

A large projection television screen sat in the far corner of the boardroom. All eyes were focused on the man, as the applause from the congressional floor quieted down. The President began to speak. Whenever something he said was thought to be profound and precipitated more hand clapping, many in the boardroom disagreed and yelled displaying their anger. This happened just about every time applause started, immediately after the President made a particular point, or had emphasized something important. There was no pleasing these men.

After sitting through a speech lasting seventy-four minutes, it was time for the men in the room to conduct their business. It was the reason they had gathered here this evening on a cold New York night. Most were ready to create a plan to oust the man by possibly mounting a recall vote; all agreed it would be no small task. At least, a recall plan was what they thought they wanted to do.

The television was switched off. The meeting was brought back to order by Tobias Whitman. Smartly, the man solicited remarks from around the table.

"As I said earlier, I want to give each of you a chance to vent your built-up anger. Don't be afraid to speak up, you're with friends"

He wanted them frenzied. Only then could he drop a new plan on them. He wasn't disappointed; they were livid after the speech. One by one they voiced their diatribe. When it came again to his turn to tell them more complaints about the President, he really shocked them, one and all. It was best described as dropping of a *bomb*.

"As I said earlier, I hate him because of what he's doing to my business. He's impacted my personal wealth. Because of this..." He savored hearing himself say the words that once said, could never be retracted..."I plan to have the man assassinated exactly one year from tonight. It will take at least that long to set it up."

He paused for maximum effect. "But there's more, much more. I want you men to help me by sharing the cost of bringing this about. I can't do it by myself."

Subtly he switched to using '*We*' instead of '*I*'. "We can have this expertly done by a professional group. One such group has already guaranteed me they can do the job without any of us reaping repercussions. They'll keep us out of it completely...guaranteed."

The first one to comment was Thaddeus Thiebold. He almost fainted as the blood drained from his head in shock. "Are you out of your fuckin' mind. I don't like him any better than you do, but this is an absurd thing to be talking about. You're speaking treason, man. Have you thought it out? The Vice President, A. C. Expon, will become the President. She isn't much better; in fact, she could be worse."

"Don't worry, Thaddeus," Tobias countered, "I've been assured the Vice President can be handled."

He lied. The vice president was devoted to the president. They were close. She was an ex WAC General, and a lawyer for the Civil Liberties Union, before she jumped in to run with the president. Nobody could get to her; she was untouchable. It was all false bravado, said in order to support his point.

Thaddeus thought it unlikely that any of the others supported his point of view, since none of them uttered a word. He shouted at them before he stormed out and slammed the door.

"Count mc out. You people are crazy if you're serious about this."

Tobias replied with a shout of his own, "We don't need the likes of your black ass in our group anyway. Go screw yourself."

The initial shock of what Tobias said was already wearing off. The rest of the group bantered with each other; he encouraged them.

"Talk it over. I'm sure that you'll see my way is the only way to get rid of him. His death will open voids throughout the government. Many of you will be asked for advice on how to make this country great again. After all, you're the real patriots."

Seeing many heads starting to nod yes heartened him. But he needed them all. It would be their contributions to the cost of such an endeavor, which would make the contract work. It would help achieve his goal. Lying once again, he addressed them.

"Look, guys. It's going to cost one hundred and sixty-five million dollars to get this done. Since we can't count on Thaddeus I'll start it off with thirty million of my own money…That will leave only fifteen million from each of you. A bargain price for this kind of an action, believe me."

Quiet for a moment, pausing to let what was said sink in, he added.

"What's the good of having money if you can't spend it to get what you want? It'll take a lot of planning, and many professionals to pull this off. This organization I've contracted doesn't work cheap." He was subtly saying they were already commissioned to do the job.

It didn't take too much cajoling. Telling them they were patriots fanned their ego's just enough. By the end of the evening all of them agreed to put in fifteen million each, all of it up-front. Of course, he was only going to put in fifteen million. If he had gotten Thaddeus to contribute he would not have put in anything. The cost negotiated was one hundred and fifty million, not one hundred and sixty-five million. The men filed out of the boardroom at one-thirty AM. As soon as the last one left, Tobias went to a small anteroom.

Victor Salvetti, head of the Camorra, the secret international criminal and terrorist organization, which first dominated Naples early in the 1900's, was the man who Tobias had contracted to kill the president. He had heard it all and was now smiling and shaking the offered hand of Tobias Whitman. Victor was dressed in a $2,500 suit and was neat in appearance. He was the same height as the man who hired him, and being in superior physical shape, although sixty, looked years younger.

(Ed.Note: The organization called the Camorra, which this man represented, is not to be confused with the Mafia, also called Cosa Nostra, out of Sicily. It was less well known, and worked mostly in the international scene. But it also operated ruthlessly, maybe even more so than the better-known group.)

"I think you handled it very well tonight, Tobias. Now, let's get down to the business at hand. You'll pay me by wire transfer. I'll need half up front, seventy-five million ASAP, and the final seventy-five million the day after he's dead. You know, it's a brilliant piece of work on your part, making them think you are putting up an extra fifteen million." Now he was fanning Tobias's ego. "Here's the plan. When I get the first payment you won't see me again until after it's all over. I'm not going to tell you how it's going to be done, but I'll give you monthly progress reports by phone. It's the way we usually handle dangerous contracts."

Victor saw Tobias grimace. He wanted to make the bitter pill more digestible, so he thought he'd throw him a bone.

"Tell you what Tobias, I'll take care of that guy, you know, Thaddeus, right away. It won't cost you another dime. You see, I've got to keep all non-participating parties in that room quiet; you get my drift, don't you?"

Victor dialed his cell phone to call for the hit. He stated he wanted it done, now, smiled and came right back to the point.

"Plan to make the down payment in ten days. I believe it provides you with enough time to transfer the money to my account in the Cayman Islands. Here's the account number." He handed him a card with a number. "Let me suggest you get all the money from your buddies up front, and have it put into a secret account known only to the two of us. This way you'll be in position to make the final cash transfer immediately after the contract's complete."

The way it was stated was an order, not a suggestion.

Victor's organization would be responsible to plan and execute the job. But Victor had another agenda. Actually there were two agendas, and they were already worked into the plan. Using the occasion of having someone pay to kill the president provided an opportunity to have someone else pay him to do the same job. There was another important person. Someone else, who Victor was sure would be present that particular night and would be killed during the attempt. It would be under the guise of collateral damage. It was the real reason the contract was made. Victor had an old personal score to settle; a family blood debt needed to be paid.

* * * *

Thaddeus Thiebold had somehow gotten past Victor's henchman. It took the thug until six AM to track down the hotel where he was registered. After coming out of the office building Thaddeus hailed a cab. He never told the cabbie the name of his hotel, opting out of the cab only two blocks from where he was picked up. He decided he wanted to walk for awhile and clear his head. When he met his wife back in the hotel late at night he was agitated and pensive. He didn't tell her much.

"Something frightening was brought up at the meeting I attended. It really upset me."

"What's the matter, honey? You can tell me."

"I'll tell you tomorrow, after I think about it and get a chance to cool down."

As Thaddeus left his hotel room the next morning, a man stuck a gun in his ribs and pushed him into the alley next to the hotel. "Don't give me any grief now; I'm only going to rob you. Your life isn't worth your watch and what you've got in your wallet, so don't try and make like a hero, okay?"

Once he got him into the alley without causing any trouble he shot Thiebold in the head. He searched his body and took his wallet and watch, trying to make it look like a robbery. The killer wasn't aware Thaddeus was visiting New York City with his wife. She had left the hotel earlier in the morning as she planned to meet with a relative.

Thaddeus never had a chance to tell his wife what it was that had him so concerned.

Two days later at the wake being held in Detroit, a Camorrista soldier assigned to cover the funeral overheard the wife saying to a relative her husband told her something shocking was said at a meeting he attended. A day after Thaddeus Thiebold was buried, her son, Sgt. William Thiebold, found her in her garage, sitting behind the wheel of her car with the engine running. The thug who attacked her had used a Martial Arts nerve pinch, one that left no mark, to render her unconscious. Bill was able to get his mother out of the car and out into the fresh air. As he cradled her in his arms, she started to revive and whispered to him. He could barely hear. He pressed his ear close to her mouth.

"Your father...he was...he was killed...killed because of something he knew...something said at the meeting he attended. Find out what he knew, Billy. Do it."

That's all she said, quietly lapsing back into unconsciousness and then, she died. The coroner's office, decided she was despondent over her husband's death, declared the woman a suicide. There was no evidence to prove otherwise, despite what her son told them. Once they rejected what she had said to Bill, he thought it wise not to press the subject any further. He couldn't change their minds anyway, and had ideas of his own to pursue.

It would seem the Camorra didn't only use a shot to the head to solve their problems. Sometimes they used more unconventional ways to murder someone.

The day after his mother's death, Bill Thiebold was determined to see his lieutenant; a man named Mario Amati. When Bill appeared in the squad room later in the day the lieutenant offered his hand in condolence, and immediately motioned him into his office when he saw the look in his eyes. In the confines of the Lieutenant's office, Bill Thiebold laid it all out.

"Boss, I need time off to do some investigating. My mother died in my arms. She didn't commit suicide like they're saying. I don't want to let anyone think I'm questioning what the coroner's reporting, but I know it's all wrong. Just like I know my father didn't die by an accident during a robbery. She told me with her dying breath; 'Dad was killed because of something he knew.' Well, that means I've got to get to New York City to see what I can turn up. But first, I have to bury her. I'm not sure I can go back to work until I get some answers. There's some weird conspiracy going on, and it has taken the lives of both of my parents. I owe it to them to get to the bottom of this."

"Look, Bill. I understand the pain you're in. I'll put you on a three-week leave-of-absence. If you need more time, you'll have it. While you're at your mother's wake, I'll call a friend of mine I met during the Gulf War. He's an international detective and the best in the business; works out of New Jersey; I'm sure the New York City Police will cooperate with him. I'll have him find out what he can about your dad's murder. If anybody can dig up some hidden facts, trust me, he's your man. I'll call him today."

"You'd do that for me, Boss?"

"You bet. I think you may be on to something. After you've buried your mom, call him up and see what he's found out. His name's Rick Banyan, and his company is called 'The Purple Feather Group'. He has four separate offices, three of them located in Europe." Mario wrote Banyan's cell phone number and handed it to Bill.

Sergeant Bill Thiebold left his lieutenant's office with somebody else solidly in his corner. It gave him a feeling of confidence he would find out who and why his parents had been murdered. But for the moment, he had to concentrate on putting his mother to rest. He mused to himself. *This detective could give me a head start on my personal investigation.*

Mario dialed Rick's number as soon as the sergeant left his office.

"Hey there, Red. (Nickname for Rick because of his American Indian heritage.) I need a favor."

"Don't I at least get a hello, Pinkie (his nickname for Mario from their days in the Gulf). How the hell are you?"

"I've got no time for small talk, Red. I told you, I need a favor. We'll say nice things to each other later, okay? I've got an officer in my squad, a real fine man. His father, an important Union leader out here in Detroit, was shot to death during an alleged robbery on the morning of January thirtieth in an alley outside of a Manhattan midtown hotel. His wife says, the previous night when he returned to his room, he told her that he knew something both important and dangerous."

"That's not much to go on."

"I know, but he didn't give her any details. Then they find him dead the next morning, while the wife's out visiting a relative. His watch and his wallet are missing. It's quite possible they were taken as cover for the murder."

"Wait, there's more. His mother supposedly is so distraught she kills herself right after the father's funeral. The coroner says her death was caused by self-asphyxiation, but the son is sure someone knocked her out and put her in the garage while the car's engine was running and the door was closed. It all sounds like a crock of shit, and I agree."

"So who's the guy I'll be working for?"

"His name's Sergeant William (Bill) Thiebold. His father's name was Thaddeus Thiebold. He was in town to attend some high-powered executive meeting. It's all the son's got to go on. Oh yeah, and he's a black man who's pretty well-heeled."

"This is gonna' cost you, Pinkie."

"Okay, so what will it be?"

"Steaks for me and Brownie (another buddy from the Gulf, Raymond Abdul) the next time I'm in your neck of the woods. You pay for the tickets for all of us for whatever sports event is playing in the Silverdome at the time. Besides, do I have to remind you that I paid the last time we met up there?"

"Deal! Get on it right away, will you? My guy will be calling in about four days." The conversation ended. They both hung up.

Rick called the chief of detectives from the Midtown Precinct in New York City. They became friends when Rick helped to solve a murder a few years earlier. He also shot the man who was going to kill the detective. The perp got the drop on him when he went to arrest him for murder. After Rick's timely intervention, Phil Baxter would be his friend for life.

Phil recognized the phone number on his call box as he picked up.

"What can I do for you, Rick?"

"I'm on a case where a man was killed in an apparent robbery on the morning of January thirtieth. What can you tell me about it? I understand it happened in your precinct."

"You know, Rick. It's funny you called about this specific case. One of my guys pulled the jacket out of the file and was just looking at it.

He did this because they found the wallet with money intact, and the watch, in a dumpster four blocks away from where the man was killed. This murder is now being reclassified as a class one homicide, and our investigation will take a different track. It's quite obvious it was a professional hit. But here's what's funny about it. There's nothing in the file; its been cleaned out. We're going on memory as to what happened on this one. It's a good thing it's still fresh in the minds of the detectives who took the call that morning, and we can recreate what was in the file, even though it's not much."

"Tell you what, Phil. I'm going to start nosing around the city on this one. I'll be sure to keep you posted if I find anything. Meantime I'd appreciate it if you tell your boy's I'm on the case and I'd like anything they come up with as well. I'm heading into the city now, and the first place I want to look at is where he was killed. Then I'm going to check out the hotel where he and his wife were staying."

"You know that you're gonna' be on a cold trail?"

"Yeah, I get that. Got no choice.

"Their son, who incidentally is a sergeant on the Detroit Police force, say's his dad went into New York to attend a meeting with other wealthy executives. See if your guy's can turn up anything about who else attended that meeting. Another thing, this guy's wife is found dead, supposedly a suicide in her car, immediately after her husband's funeral. The sergeant's coming into your town next week after he buries his mother. Any information we can have ready for him will surely be appreciated."

"No problem, Rick. He may be from out of town, but if he's wearing a shield, it makes him one of ours. We'll be glad to help in any way we can. I'll be talking to you; I've got your cell phone number."

A rainy and dreary sky greeted Rick upon arrival in New York. Remains of an earlier snowfall were now black and ugly in the alley where Thaddeus Thiebold was murdered. Five days passed since the tragedy, indeed it was a cold trail. A street person was rummaging through a beat-up garbage can, looking for somebody's discarded junk he could claim as his treasure. Rick started up a conversation with the man; at least he tried to. Then he held out a five spot and the man became talkative, very talkative indeed. When he spoke his breath was obnoxious. The man reeked of a sour smell of stale alcohol. Rick tried to hold his breath as the derelict spoke directly at his face. His whole body smelled.

"Were you anywhere around here a few day's back when a man was killed in this alley?"

"Yup! This here's my territory. I'm the one called it in. I told everything I saw to the policeman. I wuz a first-rate citizen. But that stinkin'cop didn't offer me any money, even after all my trouble."

Rick gave him the fiver, and then took out another. When the street person saw it his tongue got even looser and he continued.

"Of course, I wasn't actually the one who found him. It was this here friend of mine, a fellow called 'Georgie Boy'. He's the one who actually discovered the stiff."

He stopped talking, for fear he was getting his friend involved. Rick gave him the second fiver, and then took out a ten-dollar bill in order to keep him talking.

"So what was Georgie Boy doing when you came upon him and the murdered man?"

"He's not gonna' get into trouble, is he?"

"Not if he didn't do anything wrong, he won't."

"Well, he didn't get the chance to do anything wrong. He told me he saw the guy that off'ed the stiff, and that the killer already took the watch and wallet. There was nuttin' left for him to take. He don't want to call the police. I told him that maybe the police would drop a few bucks on the one who reported it. He told me I should do it; he don't want to get involved. I promised to keep him out of it. Now you forced me into telling his secret. I'm in trouble."

He snatched the ten-spot out of Rick's hand and attempted to run away. Rick reached out and grabbed him by the arm.

"Whoa, where do you think you're going? You've got to give me a description of Georgie Boy, and tell me where he hangs out. If I can't find him then I'm coming back after you. Are we clear?"

He took out another ten-spot, and dangled it in front of the bum. He knew he'd sell his soul for money and a chance to warm his belly with a fresh bottle of hootch. With the money Rick had already given him he'd be in a drunken stupor for a month. Rick knew he had to get the information out of him immediately. He looked at him menacingly, speaking sternly through his teeth.

"Tell me what I want to know, *or else*. You can guess what *or else* means."

"All right, Mister. Georgie Boy hangs out by the dumpster on the next street over. That's his territory. Please don't tell him it was me who fingered him, will ya? He's about my height and build. He's a black guy with only three fingers on his left hand. It's all I can tell you, really."

Rick gave him the last ten-spot. He had gotten a lot of information for only thirty dollars. He decided to talk to the clerk on duty and the manager at the hotel where Thaddeus had stayed, before searching for Georgie Boy.

"My name's Banyan. I'm a personal friend of the son of the man who was killed in the alley outside the hotel. Since he was staying there with his wife on the night before he was killed I'd like to talk to the desk clerk and the person who cleaned his room. Did you see the man, when he checked in or when he checked out of the hotel?"

"What make's you think I have to tell you anything? I spoke to the police on the morning he was reported killed. That about covers all the people I have to talk to, and I told them everything I knew. So, go away."

Rick took out a fifty-dollar bill. The manager sneered at it. "Really, do you think you can show me a measly fifty-bucks and I'll tell you everything you want to know. If you really want information out of me put some real money on the counter, say three big ones?"

Rick was the last person anyone should try to shake down. He reached across the counter and grabbed the manager by the front of his shirt, squeezing his tie in his fist, and dragging his face along with the rest of his body across and over the top of the desk. He pulled the man in front of his face and scowled when he talked.

"You'll tell me everything you told the police; after which, you'll let me talk to the desk clerk who was on night duty, and then you'll go upstairs to the room with me and introduce me to the lady who cleaned the room. If you do, I'll give you the fifty. If you don't, I'm going to punch you in the face. That'll maybe break your nose and crack off a few of those pretty store-bought teeth. You won't be so pretty looking after that. Choice is yours, Mac, either way."

The manager was terrified. Even though he reasoned the man couldn't just hit him, but then, suppose he does?

"Let me go. I'll tell you anything you want. Actually…I never saw the man. The desk clerk told the cops he remembered checking him and his wife in after six. He told them he spoke about the other executives. If they didn't want to discuss legal steps to take as a group, he was going to leave the meeting early."

He straightened himself out. Then took him over to the day desk clerk that was on-duty when the man checked out.

"This is Clarence. Ask him anything you want. Clarence, tell this man whatever it was you told the police."

"Well, Sir. I remember when the gentleman left the hotel in the morning, he asked how long he could keep his room; said that his wife was visiting with someone in the city."

"So he didn't check out yet that morning. Did he say anything else?"

"He said something as an aside, not really a statement directly to me. He muttered at no one in particular. It sounded like he said 'There's a bunch of crazy people with a lot of money running around the place.' He pointed in the direction of Mr. Harry Hanson, who was in the process of checking out. He apparently knew Hanson, but he didn't even wish him the time of day."

"Didn't the police get interested in this man?"

"No, not really. I guess they were absorbed in finding out only the basics about the man who was killed in the alley."

"Can you give me the address of the man who was checking out; I think you said his name was Harry Hanson?"

The clerk looked at the manager, who nodded. He then looked up and wrote the man's address and his listed business information on a piece of paper and gave it to Rick. Harry Hanson was from Winston-Salem, NC. He listed himself as the president of a small tobacco company.

The manager grabbed a key and they headed to the elevators. He took Rick to Room 615.

"You know, the police went over the room right after the murder in the alley. They didn't find anything at all. What makes you think you'll find anything at this late date?"

Rick ignored his comment and walked around the room, checking the closet, looked under the bed, anything, which could give him a lead; nothing leaped out. Then he met with the cleaning lady.

"All's I did was clean the room two days after the police were here. I didn't find nuttin', other than a messy room after the police finished."

Rick gave the manager the fifty he promised, and set off to find Georgie Boy. Something he'd been told kept nagging at him. He knew it was important, but he couldn't get his arms and thinking around it, yet. He knew he would, eventually. He was sure he would drag some little fact out of the recesses of his mind.

It was easy to find Georgie Boy. His hand, minus fingers, was barely holding the rim of the dumpster while his other hand scratched at the contents in a searching motion. Rick couldn't see his head but was sure he had the right person. He was bending far over into his own private garbage storage, when Rick came up behind and called him by name. The man fell in, and Rick had to pull on his legs to get him back onto the ground. This guy smelled worse than the other one. Rick tried with a five-dollar bill, like he did with the other street bum. He was thankful he was not downwind of him.

"So, what you want me for?"

"Tell me about the dead guy you found in the alley."

"What about him? I found him dead; didn't have anything worthwhile on him anyway."

It was the way he said it that made Rick press further. He gave him the five-spot and took out a twenty.

"What did you lift off the body? I know you took something." It was a guess. "I'm buying it from you for twenty bucks. You won't get any more from a pawn shop."

"How do you know I found his recorder? It was stuck in his overcoat lining. He had a hole in his pocket and it fell through and was down in the lining. The guy who killed him took everything else. He didn't even leave anything for me to make some money on. After all, the dead guy didn't need it anymore." He handed a small tape recorder to Rick. It was the type used to make notes for someone's secretary.

"Tell me who killed him. Describe him."

"Do you want to get me killed?"

"I'll kill you myself if you don't tell me what he looked like." Rick threatened.

"He's tall, over six-foot, dark black hair, wore a black leather jacket; forced him into the alley. Next I know he put a gun to his head and pulled the trigger, that he did. The gun didn't make any noise. It didin' look like he was trying to rob him at first. He just ups and shoots him. I think he planned all along to kill him. He searched the body and took everything he could find. It's all I saw Mister, I swear."

"I'm going to give you an extra twenty. Tell everything you told me to the cops. They'll be looking for you, after I speak to them. Can you identify the guy if they show you his picture?"

He could read the skepticism on his face. It was in Georgie Boy's eyes.

"Don't worry, the police will keep you safe." He tried to assure him.

"You sure of that, Mister? I don't trust them guys at all. They don't like street people.

Rick called Phil Baxter to advise him he'd made a lot of progress. He went to the precinct and updated him and the two detectives assigned to the case. He told them to pick up Georgie Boy.

They listened to the tape made by Thaddeus Thiebold right after he came back from the meeting that night. It was only a few words. As it turned out, the federal authorities would take over the case simply because of what had been recorded:

"The crazy bastards want to pay someone to kill the president. I didn't want any part of it and I told them so. I think they'll try to kill me."

* * * *

Rick put in a call to his contact, Kevin Winslow, at the State Department, and gave him the full report. He would contact the right person in the Secret Service. It became their responsibility once a plot to kill the president was detected. The local police would pick up Georgie Boy and hold him for the Fed.'s. While he was talking to Kevin he realized what had eluded him.

"Kevin, Thaddeus Thiebold never checked out of the hotel, yet there was no luggage found in the room immediately after the murder was reported. The wife didn't come back to the hotel until after noon and she never checked out either. I'm sure someone searched the luggage looking for anything incriminating. They had to do it after taking the luggage to someplace where they could be thorough and would not be detected. It had to be a professional who perpetrated the crime."

Shortly, the police became sure of that as well. It was made very clear to them when they went to pick up Georgie Boy, and found him in a dumpster with his throat cut. The Fed.'s would find a cold trail as well

Rick didn't wait for Bill Thiebold to call him. He got a phone number from his friend Pinkie, and then called Bill at the funeral parlor where he was sitting at his mother's wake. He wanted to save him the trouble of the trip into New York City. He also wanted to keep him out of the way.

"Bill, sorry to bother you, but I wanted to get to you before you left for thc city. Here's' what I found..." Rick filled him in on all he discovered.

Then he placed another call to Kevin Winslow.

"Kevin, I just finished speaking to Sergeant Bill Thiebold. I told him everything I knew, and the Fed.'s are going to pick up the trail of whoever killed his father. He's not buying it. He's going to go after the killer(s) himself. Can you get him off the track somehow? I'm afraid he may muddy the waters. See what you can do, will you?"

Twenty minutes later Kevin called him back and gave him the news.

"Bill Thiebold had been offered a position in the FBI. He was on a waiting list, so it had been easy to get his appointment moved up. Actually they were just about ready to make him an offer anyway but were holding it up because of the deaths in his family. He wasn't satisfied with what they offered. He was still determined to make his own investigation. Then somebody from the Secret Service got on the line and assured him they would never rest, until they bring the persons responsible for his parent's death to justice. They agreed to keep him updated on progress. It wasn't an easy sell. They didn't want him in their way either. After a lot of cajoling he finally accepted the FBI's offer.

"He gets three weeks to straighten up his affairs back in Detroit; you know, resign from the force. Then he starts immediately in a six month training program. The FBI has nothing to do with a case involving a presidential death threat. That's the Secret Service's job, so he has effectively been set on a shelf. The assignment will keep him out of everyone's hair. And the government gets a pretty good man entering their ranks."

CHAPTER 3

Three Weeks Earlier

Rick arrived in Spain, catching the Concorde to Paris, then caught a short flight to the Madrid airport. He had moved fast shortly after receiving word from Aldo that transfer from his control of Marta to Sênora Manuela Morales had taken place. She met Aldo with her own helicopter at the Rome airport. He had called ahead to get her into motion when he knew he would be landing there.

"Rick, this is Manuela. By now Aldo has told you I have Marta. I'm taking her to the place near Castille where we met you and Kitty. I thought you'd like it because it's desolate."

The meeting place was located about 150 kilometers south of Madrid. Aldo told Rick that Marta had a slight flesh wound, and he'd taken care of it, but that she was more frightened from her ordeal.

Once Rick knew where Marta would be taken, he called his chief operative in the United Kingdom, Kitty Grahme, responsible for his subsidiary, Grahme Enterprises.

"Kitty, I want you to turn all active cases over to your second in charge. Then head to the meeting place in Spain to meet up with Manuela and me. You'll need to pack a bag with clothes to last at least three weeks; you can buy a bathing suit where you're going. You'll be on a working vacation with someone for whom you'll be providing protection. You'll pick her up there after I make some arrangements. By the way, you're going to have to hone up on your Italian. I heard you speaking it to Aldo and his brothers."

Rick finally met with Marta and she told him the complete story. Manuela had found a doctor to check her general health. He was quite surprised at the job Aldo had done stitching her up with needle and thread. There was no apparent infection, but to play it safe he gave her an antibiotic. Kitty arrived while Marta was telling Rick and Manuela what had happened.

"I remember when Pieter, that's my boyfriend who was killed in the chalet, and I were standing outside of school in France, where we were both attending. A man bumped into us. I felt a prick in my arm, as if someone had given me a shot. Next I knew I started to lose consciousness. I remember being pulled into a van, and then everything went black. Same thing must have happened to Pieter, because we both woke up on a strange bed, in a room neither recognized. We jumped out of bed and ran to the door. To our surprise, it was open and led to the living room of what we later found out was a chalet."

"We were even more surprised when a man with red hair, calling himself Wally, greeted us by name. He said when he first met us in France we told him we wanted to ski during the break, but didn't have any money. He offered us use of his chalet. He said we were located in a peaceful area of Croatia on the side of a mountain. The kitchen was fully loaded with gourmet food, enough to last for weeks. It was beautiful at this place. And he was letting us stay there free. He apologized for the method used to get us there. Stupid as this may sound, we believed him when he said he was doing a study of college students and their behavioral patterns while not in school. He explained he would only need an hour a day of our time. We were to be hypnotized so he could collect data. It was first day of a school vacation supposed to last three veeks, so we foolishly agreed. For twenty days we let ourselves be hypnotized, never knowing what was going on when we were under.

"He never had enough time to take us away from the chalet and have us practice what we were eventually going to do. Yet, I haven't got the slightest idea how he trained us to do anything. All we knew was we felt great every time he brought us out of hypnosis."

"It turns out that he'd been teaching us to plant explosive devices on a great earth dam located not too far from the chalet. He made us think we were placing decorative stones on the bridge, and while under hypnosis, we believed him. But I don't think, in fact I'm sure, we never went down to the dam until that fateful day. We hadn't any idea we were doing anything wrong. I guess that's because we are basically good people, and he could never make us do anything that went against our will or personal beliefs. At least I heard that much about hypnotism. But Wally had somehow disguised exactly what he had us do. As it was, we only did a programmed portion of the operation, which killed all those people. It was only after we saw the news report of what happened, that we fully came to our senses about the part we played in the tragedy. You pretty much know the story from the point when Wally's henchman killed Pieter and I made a break away from him and called Uncle Kevin."

Tears rolled down her face. None present had asked any questions while she spoke. After she completed her statement Rick let her vent her built-up emotion, until there were no more tears left to cry.

Then he explained to Marta and his associates what he believed would be next.

"It will not be too long before the people who want Marta dead will find out she's in Spain, because as far as I can see these guys are professionals. I can't confirm who they are yet, but we'll soon find out. They don't leave any loose ends, and you, Marta, are a loose end. So we have to set up a diversion for the time after they kill you."

Marta winced when he told her she was about to die and he was going to let it happen. Manuela and Kitty smiled, and waited for the rest of the boss's plan to unfold. Rick continued speaking directly to Marta.

"At least they'll come away from here thinking they killed you. When they attack, and you can bet it will happen soon, probably tonight, they're going to shoot you. They will see you bleeding and lifeless. Kitty will see to that. Immediately after confirming your death, you'll be going with her to a place in Sicily, called Licata Resort. It was originally owned by the Mafia, but was bought by a private resort company after the Mafia fell into some bad times I had a part in a few years back. I keep a suite of rooms there in the name of my company 'The Purple Feather Group'. It gives me a place to spend some of the money earned in Europe, since I can't transfer all of it to the States. The people who work for me have access to it, and I hold meetings there with staff operating in Europe. It's the ideal place to stash you; especially if it's the people whom I think are tracking you. They don't ever operate in the land of their competitor.

"By the way, Marta, how's your Italian?"

"I took three years of it in high school and two more years in college. But I'm a little rusty. Why?"

"Because you're going to be placed in the Italian army. You'll have to come up to speed in the language fast. You'll only be staying at Licata for three weeks at most; that is, if I can get Kevin to pull strings. Then you're going to live like a normal person doing something useful for the next thirteen months, or at least until I can close this operation."

It was after midnight. Rick had sent Manuela into town on an errand vitally necessary to his plan. Her success would depend on what they would be able to do to protect Marta. Kitty stayed in the upstairs bedroom with her. She had been coaching Marta how to act once an assailant came into the bedroom. Rick waited downstairs for the attack they were sure would come. He carried the .380 revolver Manuela had given him, but he thought of it as a toy and preferred to use a bone knife his Indian grandfather had taught him to make when he was a boy. It was very sharp, never lost its edge, and weighed only half the weight of a knife the same size made of steel. He kept it strapped to his leg, and because it was made of hardened animal bone it never triggered airport security alarms. Kitty also had been given a .380 to protect Marta. She probably wouldn't have to use it because they wanted her to be killed.

There was a sound from outside the front door; Rick looked out the window. There were two of them. One of them entered the downstairs area of the lodge. The other thug stood guard outside. He would only come in if needed. They had communication devices attached to their shoulders so that they could speak without having to use their hands. The room was dark except for the dim moonlight coming through the flimsy drapery-covered windows. The gun he carried was equipped with a silencer. In the light of the moon Rick was able to see the gun that the man was carrying. It looked to him to be a nine-millimeter Beretta. He was familiar with this type of gun, owning one. This was good; he had plenty of that type of ammunition available to him, his version of it anyway. Now he had to get his hands on this man's gun and be able to make the switch. Manuela had provided him with many different types of ammunition, just in case. They had to get a little lucky. He'd made an educated guess; only one person would come inside the house to make the hit.

As soon as the man closed the door Rick charged and they struggled. The man outside heard noise from within and spoke softly into his communication device. "Gunter, what's going on? Do you need me to help?"

"No. He's a tough one, but I'm sure I can handle him. Stay where you are and keep my rear covered."

Once Rick heard him speak to his partner assuring him, he could move to immobilize him. They were rolling around on the floor when Rick's bone knife came up to the man's throat. Their eyes met. Gunter relaxed the struggle aware the man attacking him could cut his throat if he continued fighting. Rick rendered him unconscious by pressing on his carotid artery. He quickly changed the bullets in his gun with blanks, and dragged him to a corner of the room. Rick carelessly turned his back and started walking toward the front door.

The man regained consciousness and saw him walking away. He saw his gun on the floor. He picked it up and without any hesitation shot Rick in the back. **Pfft.** It hardly made any noise. The bullet spun Rick around, and he put another bullet into his heart. **Pfft.** He clutched his chest and blood spurted from the wound as he fell to the floor. Gunter looked down at the man he killed, and smiled.

"Gunter, are you OK?" His partner called to him after he heard more noise from within.

"Ycs I'm finc. This big guy got thc drop on mc with a knifc, but I got the better of him. I'm going upstairs to take out the girl now."

When the assailant entered the bedroom he could see a red headed woman standing in the corner of the room pointing a gun at him. He whirled and dropped to one knee, shooting twice. She was slow to move, and it cost her. **Pfft. Pfft.** The woman released her gun and clutched her breast. He could see blood flowing from her. He turned to the girl in the bed. She was terrified, attested to by violent shaking.

He carefully aimed at her heart and emptied four of the remaining five bullets into her. **Pfft. Pfft. Pfft. Pfft.** As each bullet fired he lowered the gun slightly, in order to be sure to hit another vital organ. When the first bullet hit Marta, blood squirted from her as she grasped where she was shot. He thought he must have hit her in the heart because the other bullets only made her body twitch. She was already dead. He was sure he earned his commission for the hit.

He spoke over the communication device.

"Santanna, I took care of the bitch. She's dead. I also got rid of her bodyguard. The contract's complete. I've saved one more bullet for the guy downstairs. That bastard almost cut my throat, and I'm going to take great pleasure giving him the coup-de-grace."

Rick and Kitty heard what he said. This is where the plan could fall apart completely.

The assailant found Rick's body downstairs face down where he'd left him. He put his final bullet into the back of his head. **Pfft.**

Although the light was very low, he saw the head move slightly, not surprisingly, as the bullet hit him from close range.

"Call it in, we earned ourselves a bonus." He said to his partner, and they left the scene.

Manuela came back to find the three of them sitting by the fire downstairs. They were all covered with the blood-like substance she had provided. Rick had a red welt on the back of his head and a terrible headache.

"Damn, those small wads of cotton hurt like hell when you take one in the back of the head close up. But the operation went off as planned. Apparently Marta was a good enough actress when she took those shots to her body.

"Manuela, did you get what I sent you out for? We needed a body about her size and build in order to complete phase two of this subterfuge."

"Yes, I got one from the morgue. No one has come forth to claim her body for three days. My friend down there owed me a favor. Besides, now he can save the cost of cremation. She was a prostitute who recently died of AIDS. She's a little older than Marta, but approximately the same size. We're lucky, she had the same type nose and long hair so we can bleach it and tie it in the back. Nobody will notice her boobs are a lot bigger than Marta's; Of course she looks like hell. Now it's up to the undertaker I've hired to do a fantastic job on fixing her face. After all, he's got a real live model to copy."

"Rick, did they see who you were?"

"I'm sure the guy I struggled with didn't get a good look at me in the dim light. But we can't take a chance he didn't notice Kitty's red hair. Marta and Kitty will be well on their way to the Licata Resort by the time we have the wake for this poor creature. We've got at least twenty-four hours to make this substitution happen, and then be accepted by the people who know Marta."

Rick turned to face Marta with some final instructions.

"Young lady, from here on you cannot contact anyone; not a soul. Remember that your parents will be made to believe you were killed here tonight. A small mistake on your part could bring you back into danger. We've gone through too much trouble so far to let you foul it up. We'll bring you back only when I think it's safe. Do you understand? This is not a game we're playing. It's your life that rides in the balance."

Rick got on the phone to Kevin to give him some time to set up Marta's activity for the near future. Kevin said he would tell his brother, and his brother's wife, about what had happened to their daughter, Marta. They were divorced. It would be tough for him to lie convincingly to them when he tells them about the details of her murder. He would have to manage. He would also accompany them over to Spain to attend the final services for his niece.

The moment of truth had arrived. Kevin, the mother and father approached the coffin. "She went through a terrible ordeal before she died. I understand she's badly disfigured. Don't be surprised if you don't remember what your little girl looked like. They can't hurt her anymore." A quick look at the body and the mother turned away and wept uncontrollably. Kevin and the father supported her. Rick and Kevin let out a sigh of relief. Kevin's remarks had fooled the parents.

Later at the wake, a man went up to the casket to view the remains. He must have carried a hatpin hidden up his sleeve, because Rick saw him jabbing it into the dead body of the young woman. Satisfied she was dead he went over to the parents and offered condolences.

At the end of the service Marta's mother went to Rick. Kevin had told her about his heroic involvement in attempting to protect her after she called. "I want to thank you for the help you gave Marta trying to get her out of the terrible situation she found herself in."

Rick was somber in his reply. "I'm so sorry I was unable to help her. In the end, these despots got her after all. I lost two people on this assignment when they attacked the house here."

"Do you know who did this terrible thing to her?"

"I'm thinking it was somebody from the Mafia, because they were so well prepared. They acted like professionals. But I'm really not sure. Interpol will be looking into the matter. It's out of my hands."

The Camorrista soldier sent to check the body heard Rick, and grinned. He would report to his boss that the people attempting to protect the girl were searching for the wrong one's.

Cremation followed, and the ashes were placed into an urn and given to Marta's mother. It would be flown back to the States with her and buried in the family plot.

Marta was amazed when she and Kitty arrived at their destination. Licata Resort was everything Rick said it would be, and more. It was exquisite, from the entrance over a medieval-style moat set between high blue stone pillars located at each front corner of the walled-in area, to magnificently cared-for shrubbery. Flowers, plants and trees were well placed in the center courtyard, from where everything seemed to flow. Five large buildings could easily be reached from the courtyard, the largest building being hotel accommodations located directly in the center. It stood eight stories.

No cars were allowed on Licata Resort grounds. Visitors arriving by car had to leave them at the gates. This seclusion from the outside world provided a mystique and added to its charm. While they were checking in, Marta tried out some of her Italian on Kitty. They were practicing continuously during their trip.

"Are we going to get separate rooms? Rick said it was a suite with two bedrooms."

"No honey, we'll be sharing a room. I'll be very close. Get used to it. First things we have to get you are clothes, some nice clothes. This is a classy place."

As the bellman opened the door to the suite, Marta could hardly believe what her eyes saw. Vito Frondizi was there to welcome her. She was speechless. He quickly stuffed a few thousand Lira notes into the hand of the bellman and closed the door behind him. She threw her arms around Vito. He spoke to Marta in Italian. That would be the name of the game.

"Guess what? Rick called, and I was able to get three weeks leave. He must have pulled some strings. I'm officially your Italian teacher, and I might add, your constant companion for the next three weeks."

Not if I have anything to say about It, Kitty thought. *Vito probably doesn't know Marta's sleeping in the room with me.* She smiled, remembering her youth and that she was thinking bitchy.

"Boy, are we going to have a good time. Did you see what this place has to offer?" chimed Vito.

Lavishly furnished, the rooms were spacious and beautifully appointed. There was a fully stocked bar loaded with premium liquor. It was difficult to walk across deep-piled rugs and fresh-cut flowers were everywhere.

Rick joined them two days later. It was obvious Marta had a crush on Vito, and it would seem, he on her. Rick summoned them into the spacious living room.

"Listen up, you two. At the end of the three weeks, Vito, you're going back to duty at your United Nations post. And Marta, you're going with him as a Lieutenant in the Italian army. You had better have your use of Italian down pat. Before you leave here you'll be given credentials in the name of Maria Tamari. You have seventeen days to learn your language lesson, and to have Vito brief you on what a Lieutenant is supposed to do on a peacekeeping mission. He'll also work on establishing a story of where you were born, along with names of your parents, aunts and uncles, and so forth. You'll both be billeted in the same general area where Vito was stationed. Marta will be assigned to your platoon. Keep your noses clean, because you're both officers you'll have easy access to each other. Remember that you could be doing this for more than a year. All this is compliments of Kevin Winslow. It's nice to have a relative in high places, Maria. Don't you think so?"

He didn't expect an answer.

"And Kitty, while I've got you here I'd like to talk with you about the work going on back in the United Kingdom at Graham Enterprises. I hope you can remember everything there is to report. Sorry I'm giving you such short notice and you didn't have time to properly prepare. But it will save me another trip back to Europe later this month. I've already covered everything with Manuela, and I'm meeting with Aldo later this afternoon."

* * * *

It was the third of April when Rick got the call at three-thirty in the morning. He picked up the phone, his mind coming out of a sound sleep on the second ring.

"CONSPIRATOR is activated." These were the words putting him back into his country's service. He got dressed and went to a phone booth two blocks from his apartment to sign in and accept the assignment.

"This is Rick Banyan. I am CONSPIRATOR. What are my instructions?"

He was talking to a machine. A tinny-sounding female voice responded with the usual message he had heard six times before. He knew the routine. A voice-check analyzer was processing what he'd said and verifying who was making the call. He was told to hang up and to wait for the return call. It was cold this time of the year, but he was forced to wait in the telephone booth. It could take as long as thirty minutes. Fifteen minutes later he got his call. It was Kevin.

"Sorry I had to get you out of bed so early in the morning but just came out of a top-security meeting at the White House. You remember that information you suggested I pass to the Secret Service; they're taking it very seriously, so much so they have already briefed the President. He's asked the Vice President to resolve it. She ordered me to assign my best operative. She's aware that it may take some extra-ordinary and slightly illegal finessing. Catch the earliest flight tomorrow morning to D.C. I'll have a limo waiting to take you to the meeting place with the Vice President and the head of the Secret Service. We've got some serious talking to do before this situation erupts in our face."

The meeting was at the Watergate Hotel. It started at eleven. Present was the vice president, **A**gnes **C**atherine **E**xpon. Her friends called her ACE. She was now fifty-nine and was one year older than the president; a big woman standing five-foot-ten in her bare feet and weighing 175 pounds.

George Papadopilis was the head of the Secret Service. A naturalized American, he arrived in this country when he was two years old. He started his career as a FBI agent, and transferred to the Secret Service when he was thirty-two. He worked his way up, and a year ago was appointed to the position when his predecessor died of a stroke. He is a fifty year old dedicated professional, and has been married for five years to a woman who herself was at one time a Secret Service agent. It was the first marriage for both, and she resigned once he proposed.

Kevin Winslow was mostly unknown inside the White House. A little known Special Council he reported directly to the head of the State Department. Now sixty, his jet-black hair had forgone graying and fell out, leaving him mostly bald with only a halo of fringe hair remaining. Stayed in fine physical shape by running five miles each morning.

Representing the State Department at the meeting, he headed a small clandestine group of men who performed operations not authorized under the law of the land, but desperately needed by the government. The Vice President had specifically asked for Kevin.

Rick was just sitting there listening. He reminisced back to the time Kevin met him. *He liberated him out of the Levenworth Military Prison, where he was serving a sentence for striking a senior officer during the Gulf War. The officer he hit left his guys and him on assignment behind enemy lines. The bastard failed to support a lone helicopter attempting their recovery. The stinker withheld the AC 130 gun-ship he promised. It was supposed to provide a heavy field of fire during extraction. During the ensuing firefight after the helicopter had landed, both of his men were wounded and the helicopter pilot killed. Written off for dead, the three of them made it back to their lines by walking three days until they met advancing United Nations troops. Boy, they were damn lucky Operation Desert Storm had begun.*

The pilot who was killed was Kevin's nephew, and he investigated. Kevin found that the officer he hit had a prominent Senator for his father. Instead of receiving only the reprimand this situation should have called for, he was sentenced to fifteen years at hard labor. The investigation was how Kevin became aware of his dilemma and the extenuating circumstances surrounding his case. He had him released. But there was a price to pay for his freedom.

Signing on as a special agent he was freed. After his first assignment for Kevin he was put back into the service, promoted to Captain, and received an Honorable Discharge. Six assignments completed now. It's been long since the blemish was stricken from his military record, yet he still serves. He feels that he is doing what's right for his country.

Rick snapped back to the present when he heard his name mentioned. Three seconds had passed. Kevin was introducing him. "Rick is referred to only by his first name. He's a special agent assigned to my office. I'm sorry for all the covert secrecy. It's necessary. Here's some background on him, so you'll feel confident he can do a job for us. He studied law and after College went directly into the service, recruited because of his mastery of four languages; Spanish, Italian, Arabic and of course, English."

"How in the world did you find him?" Asked ACE.

"That's another story I don't want to get into now, if you don't mind." Kevin had said no to the Vice President, and got away with it. He continued. "I understand his mother traveled the world with her diplomat father and became a language teacher after his death." Another interruption broke his stride.

"What's his nationality? He's got some sort of glow to his skin."

"You're not supposed to notice things like that, George. But I'm glad you did. Rick's father is an American Indian from the Nez Pierce Tribe. Rick likes to be called a half-breed. I know he's proud of it. His bronze skin coloring's a gift from his father's heritage. He maintains that hardened physique you see by doing bodybuilding exercises. At times he was trained by his paternal grandfather, a Tribal Shaman, in ways to survive off the land. He also taught him a special mind-control trick, allowing his brain to quickly enter into a self-hypnotic trance, slowing down all bodily functions, resembling deep unconsciousness. You can conclude that that little gift has come in handy more than once in his line of work."

ACE officially opened the meeting. "I think that's enough about Rick, don't you think so, George? I'm glad he's on our side. Let's go over all the information we have."

George Papadopilis commented he had his agents contact their one hard lead, the tobacco executive Harry Hanson. "The guy flat out denied he attended any meeting while he was in New York City. He even denied knowing Thaddeus Thiebold. All he said he knew about him was that he saw his picture in the newspaper from time to time.

"Hanson said he was in town to attend an art auction. He even showed my men a painting he purchased. We checked it out; he bought it that day. We need some leverage in order to break down his story, and get him to tell us who attended the meeting. In the meantime all I can do is have him followed around the clock, and I've got a judge to sign off on a wiretap, both in the office and home. All we picked up so far is he was a neo-nazi in college. Divorced three times, he's presently single. His current girlfriend is a light-skinned black woman. Cracking him is a key to our moving further on this threat."

Kevin spoke. "Let Rick handle that assignment. He has ways to pry information out of people. How much time do you think you'll need, Rick?"

"Give me two weeks. But first, I want you to call off the Secret Service agents you've assigned to cover Harry. I don't want them around as witnesses."

"Why, what are you going to do?" George chimed in.

"Believe me. You really don't want to know; gives you deniability. I'll get the information you want, but I may have to twist an arm, literally. Once I do you'll have to put Harry Hanson into witness protection. Pull some strings and do it fast. As soon as these guys know we know who they are, they'll move heaven and earth to take him out."

The meeting was closed. The same principals would meet again in two weeks.

* * * *

Rick was able to get an appointment with Harry Hanson by telling his secretary he was a tobacco supplier with a new low strain of nicotine products. His business card said that his name was Gus Sapp. Harry, who shook his hand vigorously, offering him a drink, welcomed him. While sipping on a single malt scotch Rick casually said to Harry: "I'm afraid I'm really here to give you some bad news." *There was an implied threat in the manner he was speaking. Rick had used this tone of voice many times before. It was almost a practiced science. Harry immediately felt the pressure.* "I know for a fact that you and your colleagues met in Midtown, New York on the night the President gave his State-of-the-Union speech. I know the hotel you stayed in, and that one of the attendees of the meeting was killed the following morning. I also know a proposal was made after the speech ended to have the president killed.

"Don't just sit there with your mouth open. You know details about the meeting that I don't know, yet!"

"Who the fuck do you think you are? Are you another one of those Secret Service agents who've been following me around since they questioned me? I told them, and I'm telling you, I didn't attend any meeting when I was in New York. I'm going to call my lawyer and have him sue you bastards. You've got one hell of a nerve." He reached for the telephone.

As his hand touched the cradle Harry felt a sharp nerve-tingling pain in his right forearm. Rick was suddenly behind him, with a knife at Harry Hanson's throat. Harry lost his bowels, and the odor permeated the room.

Even with his sense of survival being threatened, he still wouldn't give up the information Rick wanted. It would call for another plan of attack he'd prepared.

"I don't know anything, just like I told you and the other agents." Then as an after thought, "If you kill me then you'll never get any more information."

"I'm not with the Secret Service. I'm a private investigator working for the family of the man who was killed. What's the matter Harry, don't you like black people? Then how come I hear you have a black mistress? I'm going to give you a little time to think things over about cooperating and providing the information I want."

Rick pressed a nerve in his neck. Harry slumped onto the couch, awaking a few minutes later when Rick was long gone. In the lobby of the building he stepped into a phone booth, and then used his cell phone because he was sure the Secret Service still had the phones bugged. He called the private number of Raymond in Detroit. He was a man he served with in the Gulf War. He'd lost a foot when Saddam's Republican Guard attacked them. The other man he wanted on the job had worked for Raymond and helped Rick before.

Rick had learned that when government agencies agreed to cooperate they rarely did so. He was betting that all they did was reduce surveillance on Harry, when he asked that they pull back and let him do his thing. The phone was answered after the first ring.

"You've reached Raymond. You had better have a good reason to be calling this number."

"Hey there, Brownie. It's me, Red. I've got a job for you and your boy, Luther. How would you like an all expense paid vacation to Winston Salem, North Carolina? It's all courtesy of the United States Government, and they won't even know what they're paying for. Gotta' be careful though, the Secret Service is bugging the mark. Catch the next flight out and register at the Radisson. I'm in there as Gus Sapp from South Carolina."

"See ya soon." Raymond said, and hung up.

* * * *

They met in Rick's room. It was an information and planning session. "Brownie, this guy I need you to put pressure on is involved in a plot to kill the president. He also may have been indirectly involved in the murder of one of the brother's who lived in Detroit. I need you to open him up so everything he knows comes flowing out voluntarily. Then he'll be stashed away in witness protection, but he can't know that up front or he'll think we're working for the government. I've been dealing with him as a private investigator. Now, as near as I can tell he has one vulnerable spot. He's got a background that had him supporting a white supremacy group in his youth, and he's now keeping a black woman as a mistress. Couple that with the fact he's a well-known businessman here in the deep south. Do you think that you can put the moves on him and get him to talk?"

"Sounds like you got something right up our alley." replied Luther.

"What's the girl's name? Asked Raymond. "And where can we meet her? Also, Red, I'll need that bone knife pig-sticker of yours in order to make the final persuasion to let him know we're serious."

"Names Lola. She's in Room 619 in this hotel."

Raymond and Luther met with the mistress that afternoon. Once he told her Harry Hanson had become involved in the murder of a brother, she was willing to help set him up. Raymond assured her he would make it worth her while because, after all, she was giving up her

Free Lunch pass. He liked spending the government's money, so he paid her in advance with a roll of ten fifties.

"Get Harry into the sack in your bedroom. Nobody will be bugging your room. Then grab him by the testicles and yell for us to come in. We'll take it from there, and you will have earned your money. That's all you have to do."

She had been fondling Harry Hanson's private parts while he lay naked in her bed waiting for her to undress, and looking forward to the pleasures he thought would surely follow. She made the call as agreed, and two sinister looking black men entered the room, but she held on to his testicles, squeezing them gently, but squeezing them none-the-less. One man who came in the room walked with a noticeable limp. The other one weighed three hundred and fifty pounds, and was shaven bald. Only light stubble could be seen on his head.

The large man put his hand between Harry's thighs and grabbed his gonads in his large fist as soon as she let go. Harry no longer maintained his manhood. "You're a *Nigger Bitch.*" Harry complained. Then he saw her smiling as she left the room, understanding he'd been set up. Too late, he realized he never should have made that racial comment.

The other man held a small tape recorder in his left hand and a large whitish-color knife in his right. He spoke in a very deliberate manner.

"You do know you have only two options. The first one is for you to tell me everything you know about the meeting that took place in New York City on January twenty-ninth. I want to know who was there, who led the meeting, and what you know about the brother who attended and was killed the next morning. I do mean everything.

"I don't know what you're talking about." Harry squealed.

The man continued talking.

"The other option is for you to decline my simple request and take your chances on what might happen to you. I understand castration is final, as opposed to just having my friend squeeze tighter until they pop. But don't worry, this knife is surgically sharp, so you'll hardly feel any cutting of the skin.

"Just think, people around these parts won't even side with you, because they'll find out you've been messing around with a black woman. No sirree, you really don't want anybody to find out about that. I'd say you're in a heap of trouble, Harry.

"Lastly, you should know I don't like people who make racial slurs, and you haven't endeared yourself to me and my friend here in any way that matters. You get the gist of what I'm telling you now, don't you?"

Raymond pricked Harry's belly with the knife, and a drop of blood immediately leaked out. He simply used a point, to make a point. Then he put away the knife and held forth a piece of paper he wanted Harry to read before he started to make his statement. He put the tape recorder up to Harry's chin and told him to begin.

He read from the note. "My name is Harry Hanson. The statement…I'm giving here…here today is…is made under…under my own free will and I am…"

"Stop!" Yelled Raymond. "For Christ's sake, Harry. Make it sound as if you're the only one in the room. And make it sound convincing. We can do this all night."

He nodded yes, and gulped in order to gather control of his voice. Raymond rewound the recorder. He started it again, Harry's monotone voice was clear. It was the best they could get out of him, under the circumstances.

"My name is Harry Hanson. The statement I'm giving here today is being made of my own free will and I am not under any duress. After I thought about my own possible involvement in a matter of grave concern regarding someone in my government, I have decided to cooperate with the authorities and tell all I know."

Raymond gave him a moment to catch his breath and to try and calm down. He took out the knife again. His eyes shone black as coal as he stared at Harry. "Start your statement."

"Tobias Whitman was the one who organized the meeting. He was the leader of our group, which we call the CLIQUE. He was the one who came up with the idea of killing the president. He talked us into giving him a draft for fifteen million dollars each as our share to pay whomever he hired to kill the president. I swear I don't know whom he hired, and I do not think any of the other eight who agreed to go in on this knew either. It was all Tobias's idea. He told us he had already contracted with a group of men who said they guaranteed they could kill him, and it would never be traced back to any of us. I do know that while we were attending the meeting, Tobias kept looking over at the small room located behind his company's boardroom. Someone was in there, I'm sure of it."

Then Harry rattled off the names and any other information about them that he could remember. There was quite a bit of facts he had to give. He continued. "Thaddeus Thiebold, he was the union guy, walked out of the meeting in a huff. I guess that's why somebody killed him. He knew too much."

Raymond switched off the tape recorder, rewound it and then played it back. Luther relaxed the grip he had on the man; Harry started to breathe easier.

"You heard what you said. Do you have anything to add to your statement? Are you sure you told us everything? You don't want us to come back."

"So help me; you know it all. When the information I put on that tape gets out I'm a dead man. You know that, don't you? You've all but killed me."

Harry started to sob uncontrollably. Raymond and Luther left the room as quietly as they had come in. They met with Rick in his room and transferred the tape. He thanked both for their help and told them that as promised, he'd be picking up all of their expenses, compliments of Uncle Sam. And they should finish their trip down south with a couple of big steaks and a bottle of good wine.

Rick immediately called a number at the Secret Service that Kevin had given him. He spoke to George, asking him to provide protection for the traitor who had confessed and gave them their first solid lead. George would be getting the tape of the confession via courier.

CHAPTER 4

Rick called his friend, Lieutenant Mario Amati of the Detroit Police Department, to provide him with an update on their case, which had been taken over by the Secret Service. He was already in the loop and definitely one of the people who had a need-to-know. He advised him Raymond had helped out. Smartly, he left out details. What he did was just a little illegal.

"By the way, how's young Bill Thiebold doing at the FBI Academy?" inquired Mario.

"Kevin tells me he's doing real fine. He's going to meet him on the weekend and fill him in. That was part of the agreement struck with Bill when Kevin talked him into taking the federal appointment. If he'd gotten himself tangled up in the search for those who murdered his parents he could have interfered with the full-scale investigation that the Secret Service was pressing."

"I'm still very involved in this investigation, Mario. Kevin wants me to identify the organization running the show. They're a very coordinated group, and widespread. We've ruled out the Mafia, not that they're not capable of an operation this big. There are indications another international terrorist group has got the contract. See what you can pick up from your sources. I'm currently in the process of running another gambit; this one's a private job involving an international group. They are definitely not Mafia, but they have one hell of an organization stretching all over Europe."

"I told you before that I heard about these guys. They're a bad bunch. Rick, look up the government files on an organization called the Camorra. They're from Italy too; I think around Naples. They're real big in the European scene. I've recently heard rumors they are trying to start up full blast in the United States. I received this information from one of my Mafia undercover guy's. The head of the local Mafia met with the head of this Camorra group. Supposedly the Mafia was assured they would be looking for new opportunities only, and had no intention of stomping on their territory. For now the Mafia is just watching; it's a quiet truce."

"Would you believe they seem to be more ruthless than the Mafia? They think nothing of killing their own people if they become impaired while on the job. We have evidence of such happenings. Mario, can you give me the name of the head of the Camorra? This would be a short cut for me in my investigation. So far the Fed.'s haven't come up with anything. They are being very tight-lipped, even when they're supposed to cooperate.

"His name's Victor Salvetti. He's no street bum, highly educated I've been told. Never trust what he says. He can lie with the best of them, if it can get him what he wants. Most important, never trust what he does; there's always an angle being worked."

"I really appreciate this lead, old buddy. Thanks, I'll keep in touch."

* * * *

From Kennedy, the first flight in his long series of multiple stops began in the early evening when the airports were filled with travelers. It was less likely anyone would pick him up, as the authorities in the United States were not aware of him…not yet, anyway. He was heading directly to Amsterdam dressed as a priest and carrying an Italian passport. Victor Salvetti, head of the Camorra, traveled coach and was seen praying on his rosary beads the entire trip. Upon landing and clearing custom's, took off the collar, and put on a suit in a rest room, where a bag with fresh clothes and identifications had been left in a locker for him. His new passport listed him as a German tourist heading home to Bonn. A few words of German were enough to get by.

After a quick change he assumed another identity and flew to Great Britain. There were three additional changes in character. Final destination was a small hotel in Paris with a great view of the Eiffel Tower. He checked into Room 921 as a French businessman named Henri Argon, owner of a small vineyard in Le Mans, located about 150 kilometers outside of Paris. The room was lavishly appointed. Opened velvet drapes in green pastel adorned the window, picturing the Eiffel Tower in its center. Furniture was bleached mahogany, and the linen was silk-embossed on velvet. The carpet was extra-plush, matching the color of the drapes. A tiled bathroom contained gold-plated fixtures over solid brass.

Accommodations were as usual, luxurious. This pleased him, especially when he thought about the back alleys and streets of Naples where he'd grown up. He joined the Camorra at age fourteen, had his first kill for them by the time he was fifteen. He caught the eye of a kingpin in the organization who later sent him to college. Victor spoke French fluently, as well as Italian and English. He had long ago worked hard to remove traces of an accent in any language spoken.

Dialing a local number the call went through quickly. "Ah, Suzette, it's me Victor. I'll be in town for awhile, and I'd like to make arrangements to engage your services."

"*Oui, Monsieur*, tonight I am on my day off, but I would be most happy to see you this evening. Do you want the full treatment? I must know in advance so I can bring the proper accouterments for our episode."

"Suzette, *ma chérie*. That will not be necessary. You should enjoy your day off. I've just arrived and have a business meeting in the morning. Why not come to Room 921 at Le Bourne Hotel, say eight-tomorrow night. I'll order an exquisite dinner and we'll celebrate, before we feast on each other. And by all means, bring everything necessary to make our evening a night for us to remember."

"*Au revoir, until tomorrow, mon amour.*"

He showered and slipped on silk pajamas. Lying back on the king-sized bed, he gazed out at the magnificent lines of the Eiffel Tower outlined by hundreds of lights only now starting to glisten in the early evening. Sleep came in only a few minutes. Traveling for twenty-nine hours had left him exhausted. He had to be well rested to meet the special guest arriving the next morning. Much money was at stake; he needed to be at the top of his game. It had taken more than three months to arrange this meeting. Middle Eastern schemers had their own protocol to be followed. There were middlemen, and then more middlemen, whose hands were to be greased with money before the offer to kill the US President would be allowed to reach the ears of Saddam Hussein.

After agreement was made to meet and discuss details of the plan, it took another month to set it up through a myriad of third parties, while secrecy at the highest level had to be maintained. He was smart enough to know there were no real secrets on the world scene. To thwart parties interested in what he was doing, Victor Salvetti used members of his organization located in many European countries to establish several false leads about a meeting of lieutenants of the Camorra with minions of Mid-East countries. The guise of these planted leads was made to seem a clandestine attempt to corner some segment of oil production, and to make huge profits by manipulating prices. He leaked this information to Interpol, and actually went through the trouble to set up several meetings, so no one would draw a bead on this encounter.

Assad Karbala, a member of Saddam's inner circle, was a fanatic follower. He had lost his wife and two children during the Gulf War, which was why Saddam had selected him to be his representative. Assad was dedicated to Saddam. He had even put his family in harm's way during the war by direct order of Saddam, who wanted Iraqi civilians positioned at or near military installations, in the hope Allied Forces would not bomb these areas. Saddam knew this would not stop the bombings. He wanted to be able to show the world pictures of how his people were being torn to pieces by attacking forces. Assad's hatred of the Americans, and his total blind allegiance to Saddam, made him the logical choice to meet with Victor Salvetti. Assad had also taken steps, similar to those taken by Victor to avoid detection as he made his way from Iraq to France. He was fluent in English, as well as Arabic.

Each man traveled to the appointment without having any accompanying aides. Assad arrived at Room 921 at precisely ten AM. It had been checked for electronic bugs by one of Victor's technicians before he arrived. The room faced the tower over one thousand meters away. Victor was sure there was no visual surveillance; he had left the drapes open.

He was wrong! It was to be a costly mistake.

Rick Banyan had a man on the tower with a super-powerful telescopic lens attached to a digital VCR camera focused on Room 921. This apparatus also contained a high-tech parabolic acoustic-listening device, which employed the use of a laser. If a person was looking straight at the recorder there was no problem recording what was said. However, if speaking while facing another direction the recorder picked up all sound as it bounced off any solid objects in the room, including the walls. It did lose some of the sound in absorbent materials, such as drapes but there were ways around that as well. The device was mounted on a tripod to avoid excessive movement, which could magnify and cause captured images to flutter. The man using it was a pro.

Subsequently, a lip-reader would put words to any missed part of the conversation made by occupants who faced the window sideways. These specialists were good; they were able to read lips seeing only half a face. Technology had jumped leaps in the last year, and the same visualization could be used to pinpoint movements of a man from a satellite 22,000 miles away. It was now available in a hand-held device. Unfortunately they didn't have a long-range microphone that would cover the distance of space. For close surveillance they used this new gadget in listening technology.

It was luck that one of Rick's people had been assigned to trail one of the would-be assassins of Marta, the one called, Gunter. He saw him putting a suitcase into a locker in Madrid, Spain. Rick's agent wisely waited to see who would pick it up. Shortly thereafter, he observed a man not known to him (Victor Salvetti) going into a restroom disguised as a common workman with a mustache. He saw the man exit as a clean-shaven French businessman, dressed neatly in a suit and tie and carrying an attaché case.

He didn't know whom he had spotted, but per instructions he made an immediate call to Rick on the satellite phone. Rick was made aware that Joseph carried his passport and had ample funds for an extended tracking expedition; he authorized him to follow the man who made the clothing/character change. Rick told him they'd meet when he arrived in France later the next evening. Joseph was to gather all the information he could. Rick would call ahead and give Joseph's boss Manuela, who ran the Spanish office, known as Conquistador Investigations, a heads-up on what he had him doing, and arrange for someone else to track Gunter.

Following him through the different countries was difficult, especially since Salvetti went twice through different locations in Spain. Fortunately, customs inspectors were busy and rarely checked previous travel dates stamped on passports. Finally, after Victor took the commuter flight from Valencia to Paris, Rick's agent trailed him to the hotel where Salvetti registered. Victor had never spotted he was being followed. It was no small feat and a credit to an astute agent who used a few disguises of his own along the way.

A few Francs to the desk clerk quickly made the room number and name he was using available. Sizing up the situation the man called a local investigation firm. It was on the authorized list of companies Rick used in France that he obtained special surveillance hardware. He also needed an agent to cover the door of the hotel room for twenty-four hours while he set up camera eavesdropping from the Eiffel Tower.

Victor greeted his guest. He offered him a drink and, even though it was early and drinking was against the laws of Islam, he quickly accepted. Assad was no stranger to a finely bonded-bourbon. They sat on the couch facing each other. Only the sides of their faces were visible to the long-range camera. There were no formalities as Victor quickly came to the point.

"I'm in a position to use my organization to assassinate anyone in the world. Because there's one country standing in the way of Iraq's prosperity and its re-entry into the world marketplace, I'm willing to strike a blow on your country's behalf. It will have repercussions around the world. I can, and will if my price is met, terminate Germond Faller, President of the United States. But of course you know that; it's why you are here."

He let what he had said sink in for just a moment when he countered with additional information. "I can make this happen when the man gives his annual speech to congress; this occasion occurs in the fourth week of January. I've done preliminary planning and assure you this date offers me the best opportunity for complete success."

"Mr. Salvetti, I've traveled many long hours to meet with you and hear your proposal. On behalf of my country, I have a number of questions concerning this possible, contract. I believe that's the proper word."

"Please, ask all the questions you have. I'm at your service."

Assad put his chin in his hand and rose from the couch and faced Victor. His speech was baffled and deflected by his hand. This situation was not good, thought Joseph, as he willed the man to remove his hand from his face and provide him with an unobstructed view of the man's lips, or at the very least, a chance to have his voice resonate from the wall. He dropped his hand to his side and began his inquisition of

Victor. It was as if he had heard Joseph's thoughts. He faced the window of the hotel room.

"How much is this going to cost us?"

"The price is one hundred million dollars to be made via wire transfer of Unites States currency to my account in the Cayman Islands. I will require half within ten days of a contract. The final payment is to be put into a numbered box at the Paris branch of the Suisse Nationale Bank. On the day after the deed has been accomplished I'm to be provided with the access numbers." Victor was talking directly to Assad and it was impossible to see his lip movement. But most of his voice was being captured as it bounced off the wall.

Assad winced when he heard the amount. He'd only been authorized to go as high as fifty million dollars. He knew he could negotiate only another ten million. Beyond sixty million he was powerless to consummate a deal without first contacting Baghdad. He felt he had to bluff from this point to be able to learn more about the proposal. He attempted bravado in the way he spoke. Victor assumed Assad would not be able to confirm a deal on the spot, especially for such a large sum, but he played along to let him believe he was dealing from a position of strength. Victor had a concern that Saddam would be toppled before he completed the contract, and he needed to be sure he'd get the final payment. One of his agents was a vice president of the bank where he directed the money be placed. A smile creased his lips as he thought of a better method to assure his being paid.

"We will get back to the amount we are willing to pay for such a service. First I will need answers to all of my questions. My superiors (meaning Saddam) made it perfectly clear on this point before I left to meet with you."

Victor nodded to him to continue.

"How can we be assured that once you attempt and fulfill this contract we will not be implicated in any way with adverse publicity?"

Steely eyes peered out at Assad as Victor rose from the couch and began to answer. He raised his level of voice and walked slowly towards the window. "Because, only if you do pay me the final payment" He stopped, turned around and faced Asssad, his face once again hidden from camera view, but the walls will listen. "will we have completed a transaction. In my trade it is a sacred bond, and to tell anyone about your country's connection would be the last contract I would ever be able to make. On the other hand, if you fail to make final payment by the time agreed, your culpability will be displayed in every newspaper in the world. Now you know where I stand on this matter; any other questions?"

"How can you make such an assurance this transaction and our relationship will be completely transparent to an ever-present press corps?"

"This is our business. If we don't want anyone to know, then they simply don't know. We are professionals; we do this sort of thing all the time. On the other hand we certainly want recognition as the perpetrators of this kill. Did you ever think of all the new business the notoriety will provide? You and your country are nothing more than a shadow in this transaction." Victor sat back down on the couch still obscuring his face from the camera.

"How are you going to kill him?"

"My entire organization will be involved. I cannot divulge the details. Be advised that there will be more than one assassin assigned." It was time for Victor to add another element. "We will require, as an integral part of this contract, someone from your country to work with us. We are aware you have several sleeper agents in the United States, and they have been in place waiting for years to come out of hiding and do something for their country. We want only one of them, and it is in your best interests to give us someone who is both expendable, and has a high-level United States Government clearance. If you have planted them deep enough, no one will be able to trace that person back to Iraq."

"But...But...Nothing has been said about this before."

"Don't look so shocked; did I not tell you I have done all my homework in this matter? Now, I realize you must return to Baghdad to discuss this proposal with Saddam, as only he can authorize meeting the terms of this agreement. I will give you ten days to make the trip home and return with the name of your undercover person, and full control of all funds. On second thought, do not plan to pay via wire-transfer. Coming from Iraq it is too easy for Interpol to trace. Pay me the first half in diamonds, and deposit the other half of the diamonds in a numbered box at the bank I've identified. You can use your ambassador to bring them here in the diplomatic pouch. Be sure to tell Saddam one hundred million dollars is non-negotiable. Also tell him I will arrange to have the bank hire an expert to verify that the quality and grade of the diamonds are equal to the stated value."

A distressed Assad sat flabbergasted. Victor was not through with him. "Take this telephone. It reaches me anywhere in the world. If Saddam needs to speak to me, tell him to use it any time, day or night. Transmissions will be encrypted, and no one else will be able to hear."

"Remember, ten AM exactly ten days from now we will meet in this hotel, but in Room 721. If you do not want me to take on this contract do not show. Your country will miss out on the one opportunity to strike a blow at the very heart of the imperialistic government of the United States. Return to your country. Make the arrangements for this agreement."

After Assad left, Victor chuckled that Saddam would be paying for a contract already in effect with someone else. He started to speak, this time to no one in particular. It was his way of thinking out loud to help collect his thoughts. He faced the window. "Is it possible I can sell this same assignation to yet another party?" He thought further on the subject. "No, I had best complete this without other considerations. Two hundred and fifty million dollars to kill a man is so much money to comprehend."

The conversation with Assad had lasted only twenty-one minutes. Joseph had filmed and hopefully recorded everything. A lip reader would put words into place for whatever the listening device was unable to capture. A computer would eventually be required to translate reverberations that bounced off walls, and to filter and improve quality of video and sound recorded.

Rick arrived in Paris and immediately went to meet Joseph. During the flight his mind had conjured up all sorts of information that Joseph would have for him. He reviewed the tape in its undoctored state. He was not disappointed. This stroke of luck in finding the head of the Cammora, and being able to film him with an Iraqi agent was more than he could imagine. He realized he'd have to get this information to the task force headed by the Vice President as soon as possible. After thanking Joseph, Rick relieved him for some much-needed rest. Then he placed a call from a phone booth to his control using required protocol.

"This is CONSPIRATOR. I request conversational mode."

The message was received and identified by voice recognition. It also stored the phone number from where he called. Kevin's location was tracked down and he was notified Conspirator needed to talk. Through encryption and multi-satellite transfer the phone located at the booth where Rick waited, began ringing. It took eighteen minutes from the time he called. He grabbed the receiver. "This is Conspirator."

"Rick, its Kevin. We're on a secure line. What have you got? I hope that it's good, because it's four in the morning here, and I haven't been getting much sleep lately."

He gave him chapter and verse as to what went on.

"Rick, get on the first Concorde and bring that tape directly to me. Sorry that you have to be the courier. But I need you and that tape here as fast as you can manage. I'll have the sound techs and computer guys waiting to finesse it. We're due to meet back at the Watergate with ACE and George in only three days. With the information you were able to get out of Harry Hanson and this tape, the investigation has leaped giant steps."

* * * *

They met at the Watergate as planned. ACE opened the meeting and introduced Peter Grace. "Peter is with the Central Intelligence Agency. He's assigned to the European Theater and is the liaison officer to Interpol. He's in town for conferences with the Director. When Kevin called to tell me the gist of what Rick's man taped in Paris, I had him assigned to the task force. Secret Service doesn't have jurisdiction outside of the continental United States. I've spent the last hour briefing him. George, why don't you start off?"

George Papadopilis began with a summary status. "Thanks to Rick we've been able to identify everyone in the board room that evening with the exception of the person, or persons, who was observing from an anti-room. Harry Hanson is stashed in witness protection. We'll be bringing him out only when we need him to testify. Each of the men identified will be under surveillance 24/7. I don't want any of them to know how much we know. We'll see what we can pick up. In addition, I'm having our forensic people do a character and personality study on each of them. Let's see what details we can uncover about these traitors' lives. We're not going to pick any of them up now. We don't want to alert the Camorra that we're on to them, not just yet, anyway. The next time they, the Clique, holds a meeting, we'll be taping."

"Kevin asked. "Has anything been done in finding the killers of the Thiebold family? I did a lot of fast-talking to get him to accept the FBI assignment. One of your agents will have to keep Bill Theibold informed. The agreement is that I'm supposed to update him. That job has to be taken over by you, George. You're closer to the overall situation, and we don't want him messing in your pudding, do we?"

"I've spoken to him already." George answered the challenge. "I've got agents working with the Detroit and New York police. They've identified the man who killed Thaddeus. The perp left his fingerprints on the wallet and watch he ditched in the dumpster. Haven't picked him up yet because the police want him to lead them to the guy who killed the mother. They're making good progress. Bill is satisfied, so far. I told him that from now on, I'll be his contact."

"Okay, so what are you planning to do to protect the president as a result of this threat?" Kevin persisted.

"Funny you should ask. Let me change the subject slightly, but still stay on the point of this meeting. I've ordered two new armored limousines from Ford. They actually farm out the post-construction of special vehicles after supplying the engines, frames and steering mechanism. These stretch-Lincolns are the latest technology, built like a tank and have so much armament they weigh 20,000 pounds. To compensate, specially designed twelve-cylinder engines power them, and the tires are solid rubber. One inch of the outside of the tire is made of a special softer rubber compound, which flattens under the weight. It makes it look just like regular tires, but a fifty-caliber bullet will be absorbed if it is hit. The glass is also armor-plated with some new-age plastic, and will deflect something as large as a twenty-millimeter shell. If any attack comes at the president while he's in his car, he'll be safe."

"Put a trap door in the bottom, in case he has to get out fast. Also, rig it to drive and operate under remote-control, like they do with that spy-plane." Everyone looked at Rick when he made the unexpected remark. Now that he had their attention, he continued. "Start construction of a series of underground escape routes near the White House and Congress, which the trap door can straddle while it allows him to evacuate the vehicle. Give him at least three places to get out of the car. You don't know what they'll throw at him. I'm telling you, these people will use new technology to their advantage, too. And while your at it, look into security clearance for all personnel at that post-construction firm, and anybody else who will be in on creating these tunnels around the city."

"That's a tall order, Rick." Said ACE, appearing shocked. It was as if he was giving orders. He was!

"You bet it is, Ma'am, but I really feel it's necessary. Take a look at this tape. Kevin's people have been tuning it, since it was taken from a distance. There will be no doubt in your minds who we're up against, once you've seen it. The principle character in this show is Victor Salvetti. He's the head of the Camorra, and the man who was in the anti-room when the pitch was made to get the money to kill the president."

ACE nodded to Kevin to begin. He lowered the lighting and let it rip no narration necessary! When the lights came back on, George led off.

"If its okay with you, ACE, I'll get the construction started immediately." Then he charged off in a different direction. After what they saw, he was becoming a bit rattled.

"Peter, what can you do to get information on what the Camorra may be up to? You know, can your people get us some details as to how they're going to go about doing it? Christ, they're going to be coming at him with multiple assassin teams. I need every bit of Intel I can get to stop every attempt to kill him."

Peter never got the chance to verbally reply, nor would he have to. Everyone present knew he would immediately bring all his assets to bear. It was why ACE added him to the team.

Kevin thought it best to simmer everybody down with some basic logic. "Let's take first things first. We've got time on our side to plan for this properly. In less than seven days Saddam's guy will be back in France with his answer. I'll bet he'll strike a contract. We need the name of the deep-agent the Iraqi's provide to this Salvetti character. Who's going to cover it? We got lucky when Rick's man picked him up in Paris. Do you want the same man to tape this meeting? Let's plan what we have to do."

Now Peter got his chance to speak. "Rick, can you have your man report to me for the near future? I can use him, and anybody else you can spare to keep on his tail. The Central Intelligence Agency will foot the bill."

"I've got investigations companies located in the United Kingdom, Spain, Italy and of course, locally in New Jersey. I'll notify the managers and they will all be in contact with you ASAP. I'll need your cell phone number. The manager here in New Jersey should probably get in touch with you, George, that is if you want to work your intelligence gathering in the States?"

"Ma'am, I think you may have to bring the Federal Bureau of Investigation in on this. We shouldn't trample on their turf."

"Don't worry about it, Rick. I'll speak to the President. He'll call the shot. Hold off on contacting your New Jersey manager for the time being. You're correct though, the FBI has the manpower, as well as the authority to do in-country surveillance. I'll let them know that your people are available. I'll have them contact you if they need more people."

"They can't contact me. I'm supposed to be a non-entity. Besides, I'm not available. Kevin already has me on special assignment."

ACE stared at Kevin. She knew he was up to something she didn't want to know about. She abruptly ended the meeting. The task force would continue to meet every two weeks. It would be the last time that any of them would see Rick Banyan, for quite some time.

Rick and Kevin had lunch in the Watergate Café. Kevin turned on a special device designed to allow them to talk without anyone being in close proximity able to hear. When he was sure it was operational, he spoke. "Do you have any idea on how you can penetrate the Camorra?"

"I've got a couple of ideas, but I'm going to have to talk to Manuela first, she still has contacts in the Spanish Police Department. I think she'll be able to help. Remember, Kevin, once I'm in, the only way you can get to me will be through her. I'm going in deep, and you won't hear anything unless I have collected information for you. I'm going to have to do some things to make them believe I'm one of them…"

Kevin was aware of the capabilities of the man he was sending undercover. All he could do was give him a few words of advice. "Watch out for the LambieDog."

"What the hell is that suppose to mean? Is that some sort of code that I'm supposed to decipher?" Kevin didn't answer him; he just smiled. Rick tucked away what he said.

"How long will it be before you'll be heading to Europe. I assume that's where you want to start from."

"You're right on that count. It will take me awhile to plan for a long-term absence. I've got to call my people and give them Peter's cell number. Most important thing I've got to do is start Manuela on creating everything needed to let me slip into my undercover self. I sure as heck have to alter my appearance. Everything I do from here on depends upon Manuela."

Rick spoke to his recently hired manager, Cameron Taylor, in New Jersey. "You're going to have to take over for me, and I do mean everything that's on my plate here in the States. Now here's what I'm working on." He recited his caseload from memory. Cameron recorded their conversation. "If you need more information, I've kept the files up to date. Beyond that, you're on your own. I'm going to be out of circulation for quite some time. It's also possible that you may get some surveillance work from the FBI. If you need more people, hire them. You run the show."

Next he called Kitty Graham in the UK, and Aldo Frondzi, in Italy on a conference call. He gave them the cell number of Peter Grace of the CIA, and asked them to call him for an assignment of the highest priority. Then he told them that he would be incognito for anywhere up to ten months. Rick had one more call to make before he contacted Manuela.

"Hey Sis, pick up the phone. It's your brother, and it's important that I speak to you. Come on, don't make me talk to a box." He heard her pick up.

"So, what or who do I owe this privilege?"

"Okay, I stink as a brother and I didn't come over for dinner last week as I promised. I'm truly sorry that I didn't call either. Don't get pissed at me. It's just that I got tied up in something important." She cut him off.

"Rick, you're a bastard. What is it you want me to do now? It's always something."

"I'm going to be out of town for quite a while. Could be almost a year, and I won't be able to contact you either. It's my job, and I can't tell you where I'll be or what I'll be doing. I've got all the bills being paid automatically from my checking account. I need you to go over to my apartment and clean out the fridge by Friday. The freezer is loaded with steaks, and they won't last. I also need you to check the place at least once a month while I'm gone."

"Oh, Rick. You know I can't stay mad at you. I hope to God your safe in whatever you're doing. Of course I'll help you. I mean it, stay safe."

"Piece of cake, Sis. Thanks." He hung up. He knew that it would be too tough to go over and see her before he went on his mission."

He dialed again. "Manuela here."

"It's me Rick. Couple of things I need you to do. I want you to call this CIA agent, Peter Grace. He wants you to assign Joseph, and perhaps some additional staff to work on surveillance of the Camorra. Specifically, they want you to track the movements of Victor Salvetti."

"And what else do you need in a hurry?" She said almost sarcastically. Oh yes, she was spunky, and gave little to any man.

Rick took her comment in stride. He liked it that she was dauntless; she always did great work. "Here's the tough part of what I want. I'll be leaving tomorrow for Spain. While I'm there I'll need a cover identity. I'll need everything, from a family, to the documents to prove who I'm supposed to be. I'm not a nice guy. In fact, I'm a real son-of-a-bitch. I need an international police record dating back at least twelve years. So, you can see, I want to get hired by the Camorra. I'm going in deep, and you'll be my only outside contact. Oh yeah, I'm prepared to alter my appearance. So don't use any picture that you may have of me for a passport photo."

CHAPTER 5

A New Beginning

The small private plane landed at Rebio airport, located thirty-five kilometers south of Castille. Manuela was waiting for Rick.

"Hello, Rick." She sounded gruff. "I guess I'm supposed to ask how was the flight, so 'how was the flight'?" She asked sarcastically.

"Don't tell me your still pissed."

"Sorry, boss. I shouldn't let it show. I've lost two employees to a rival firm. They went back to work for the police force, when they finally came through with enough money to pay the guys. Some of them had as much as ten years on the job when the layoffs began. I guess I knew that I couldn't keep them all. Damn it, they couldn't have picked a worse time. First I've got to hire replacements. Training new people will be tough enough, especially in light of that CIA guy you put me in touch with. He wants not only Joseph, but three more people as well.

"Simmer down. You'll get people."

"Where's your luggage? We're spending the next week in the Castille cottage while you learn about your new identity."

"Got no luggage, got no baggage at all, not even a carry-on. What you see is what you get to work with. You can burn what I'm wearing. Remember I'm a new person. I expect to be reborn into this world as a bad guy. I'm not joking. I'm serious about getting hired by the Camorra. I hope that you can do well by me. The cottage is a fine place to study my case history. But with this personnel shortage you're having to handle, how are you going to find the time to brief me?"

"So, we all have it tough at times. Don't worry about me. I'll survive. It's my job to make sure that you do too. The car's over here. You drive. I want to reference my notes as I start your transformation. Your papers won't be ready until the end of the week. I've got to take a few pictures of you once you assume your new identity. I need some for your criminal jacket at both Interpol and the Spanish Police, as well as for your Italian passport."

"I see you've already got the situation in hand. That's great, Manuela."

"I'll first need some earlier pictures of you for the Italian files. I've got somebody lined up that's a wizard with a computer. That's why I'm using a digital camera. He'll have to make you much younger at a few different stages of your life. I'll be spending my days commuting to the office. I'm planning on sleeping at the cottage, so we'll be going over the details of what you have to know all night if we have to."

"You're the boss, for now, anyway."

"Okay. Here goes nothing."

"Your name is Riccardo Giovanni Blanco, nickname Ricky. Your mother was an Italian mistress of a Spanish diplomat stationed in Italy. She was actually a whore he took off the street. She became pregnant with you. He gave you his name. Pissed his wife off back in Spain that he was paying for her and the bastard child. So he sent the wife lots of goodies to keep her satisfied. You were born on February 11, 1970. That was a Tuesday. I made you a little younger because you have that great body. And I made you an Italian as a cover for your bronze skin color. So you can keep your first name, almost, and it looks like your skin color comes from being born in the area near the Mediterranean."

"Where did I learn to read and write? What language do I speak?"

"Whoa, you're jumping ahead. All will be covered in good time. I estimate about a week. Then you'll be going to jail, where you'll meet up with Santanna. You remember, he's the guy outside the door supporting none other than Gunter."

"Okay. You'll spoon feed me the details, but you have to make sure that I have them all."

"You're mother taught you to speak Italian, and to be able to write a little. You hated school and were a bad student, so she kept you home most of the time. You learned English on your own, but you're not very good at it. You were always getting into trouble with the police, mostly roughing up people when you robbed them. Because you were such a troublemaker, at age fourteen you were thrown out of the house and your father disowned you.

After that your father was recalled to Spain. He couldn't leave your mother, though; took her back to Spain. You came to Spain when you were twenty-five. The reason you gave was that you were looking for your mother. You were really looking to keep away from a long prison term for attempted murder and larceny. However, when you went to look up your mother to hit her up for money, you found out your father's wife murdered her. You also found that your father was killed in an auto accident. Since he's now dead, poof, no more family in your background to worry about."

They pulled up to the cottage late in the afternoon, shortly before dusk. After settling in, they went to a market where Manuela picked up supplies while he stayed in the car. He had asked her to pick up a razor and shaving cream. He wasn't going to brush his teeth for awhile—he needed the breath. It was the last time Rick would leave the cottage as himself.

Later that night they met in the kitchen. "You do the cooking. I've got to make sure that you can manage for yourself. Also, give me your sizes. I'll get you some used clothing. That includes underwear and socks."

"You're so kind, lady."

"Don't be a wise ass. This is your idea. All right, Ricky, tell me all about yourself. Let's see what you've learned so far. I'll be leaving early in the morning, so let's not waste the night."

He did pretty well, until it came to when he was born. He drew a blank.

"It's two AM. I have to get up early to start my commute. We'll go at it again tomorrow. But let me get a 'before' picture for my guy to work on and make you look younger. There has to be a trail of you when you first started getting into trouble in Italy. After that it's up to you."

After Manuela left, Ricky decided to take the next step. He never had much of a beard thanks to his American Indian ancestry, but he had a good head of hair. He started with scissors and cut his hair as close to the scalp as possible. Now came the tough part. After soaking his head in warm wet towels he began lathering. It took the whole batch of disposable razors that Manuela had bought to take off what he thought was all of the hair. The wet towel was used to wipe the remaining lather from his head. A mirror indicated he had missed some sections on the back of his head. He would have to wait until Manuela returned. She could reach it better.

Looking at himself closely in the mirror, he could see that his skin tone made the bald look seem as if he'd not been wearing hair on his head for quite some time. This was good. He poked around the cottage to see what he could find to re-open his ears that he had pierced while in college. No luck. He took his second shower for the day in order to prepare himself for his new clothes. The underwear was European style, which he never liked and sleeveless undershirt tops. Also, she had purchased worn jeans, one collared shirt and one with a crew-neck style. She had gotten him two of mostly everything, except boots. Good thing, he thought, they didn't fit. He found one jacket. It was beat-up leather, well worn. At least he would travel light.

He had made his own breakfast in the morning as he usually did, but not brushing after he ate would be tough. While in his new *business attire* he started to perform a series of calisthenics, partly to work up a healthy sweat, but also to have the sweat stain his clothing. He had plenty of time to spare while waiting for Manuela to return, and took a five-mile run. This would become a standard procedure for the time he remained at the cottage.

"Hi, honey, I'm home." Manuela said joking. "Would you believe that I saw that in an American movie?" It was seven PM when Manuela came back. Ricky had dinner waiting. A meat loaf and mac-n-cheeze made from a package. He made a lettuce-only salad with wine vinegar, there were no other ingredients available.

"There's a case of good Spanish red wine in the storage closet. I thought you would have found it by now. You look cute in your new attire. And get a load of that hairdo. Turn around and let me look you over. OOP's, you missed patches on the back of your head. Good thing I bought an electric shaver. It's used of course, just in case. By the way, when were you born?"

"February 11, 1970. For your information, it was on a Tuesday. Let's eat first. I don't want your dinner to get cold. It's the least I can do, dear. Then we can do more of my life." They both smiled at the sarcasm.

"OK, Ricky. Last night I told you that you didn't have any relatives left alive to worry about. I forgot about your Uncle Aldo. Plan to use him as a contact back home in Italy, just in case. I think we had better bring him in on this. You really need a back up, and a woman just won't cut it. Especially one who was a former Madrid Police Lieutenant before you recruited me to run Conquistador Investigations. I want him to see you as you look now. I can bring him here at the end of the week and you can rehearse your Italian by reciting the story of your life. Sorry, but I don't speak Italian. I'm no help to you there."

"Its okay with me to bring Aldo on board; good idea. Can you get the lumps of hair that I missed off my head before I try to use the electric razor? I should be able to manage by myself once all the hair is gone. Also, can you loan me some earrings? I sorta' like those big hoops I've seen you wearing."

"I don't see any holes in your ears. But you can have them. Be careful with them, they're fourteen carat gold."

"I used to have holes there when I was young. Just plan to push-em through again."

"You smell like you had a wonderful day. I'm glad I'm sitting up wind from you. How do the clothes fit? They look okay."

"C'othes are fine. Boots don't fit though. Get them a size bigger, or get them round and not pointy. Look, can we get the hair fixed up? I used up all the razors you bought me. Also get the earrings and do the deed. Don't worry, you won't hurt me."

A few minutes later Manuela came back downstairs. "Come here, macho-man. Let's get the hair off first. I've only got this old style ladies razor for legs. I hope it's not too dull. Then I suggest you go over the head with the electric razor. That's a new battery in there. Let's see how many head shaves you can get with that thing before you have to charge it. When you're in jail you won't be able to give it a charge."

She easily found the marks in his ears. Time had healed them. He bled slightly once she punched through. She had to agree he was starting to look the part. She took fifteen different poses of him against an empty wall, and his fingerprints three times.

"What's your height and weight? Also, what's your blood type?"

"Blood type is A-minus. I'm six feet two inches, weigh approximately one hundred and eighty-five."

"That's no good, dummy. I need it in metric. You're in Europe now. I'll get my guy to make the conversion, and I'll bring you a table that you had best memorize along with everything else. Take off your clothes."

"Why? What do you want me to do that for? I thought you were all business."

"Keep your shorts on. I've got to examine your body for scars. Interpol files require this kind of information. Do you have any tattoos where I won't be able to see."

"You're no fun. I was never stupid enough to get a tattoo. Got a lot of scar tissue though. I can tell you when they happened. One-inch scar on the right side back of the head—three years ago. Got conked on the head by accident in a Martial Art's course. I weaved when I should have bobbed. My opponent had the big stick. Stab wound on left shoulder—happened last year. I was stabbed in a bar fight, and I got in the way. Three-inch scar on my left side—a year and a half ago. You really want this kind of detail?"

"You bet I do."

"Two scars in my upper left chest—five years ago. That's about it."

Before Rick could say another word, Manuela jumped all over him for being so nonchalant. "Christ, those knife wounds must have hit your heart. How the hell did you survive that?"

"I'd like to let you think that I don't have a heart, but it's actually on the other side of me. I'm one out of every three hundred and fifty thousand born that way. I'm built like a mirror image of most other people, the medical term for it is *'Sidus-Inversus'*. It saved my life when a guy stabbed me because of its location."

That answer, without a lot of detail to support what he had said did not satisfy her. But she moved on anyway. "Lastly, are you circumcised?"

"Yes! What do you need to know that for? Never mind. I think I know."

"Italian's don't usually circumcise. If anybody notices and asks, say that your mother told you your father wanted it done."

When all that business was out of the way he asked. "What part of my past do you have for Ricky Blanco to remember tonight? Times-a-fleeting."

She spent four more hours with him that evening going over small details like who his friends were while growing up, where he lived, when his parents were born, what crimes he was convicted of, etc.

The next three days went by all too slowly for Ricky. On Friday Manuela came back to the cottage early. Rick was out on his run. She had brought Aldo back with her. "Boy-oh-boy, you really look the part. Manuela told me what you're going to be doing for the next half a year or so, Rick."

"The name's Ricky if you don't mind. Let's keep the talk from now on in Italian. I'm a bit rusty. By the way, Manuela, how's my paperwork and my prison files doing? And what the heck are you so happy about?"

"Everything will be ready by next Monday. I'm having a problem with getting your records inserted into the Interpol files. The guy I knew isn't there anymore. You can't go undercover unless your file's in place."

"Call up that CIA guy whose number I gave you. He's got a secure phone. Let him know what I'm up to. He is supposed to be my government's liaison with Interpol."

"I'll go into town and call him from a phone booth. Don't cook tonight, Ricky. I'm bringing in take-out. I hope you two like Spanish food. I've had enough of food like meatloaf. Besides, it will give you two a chance to go over everything, and I've got to make arrangements for you to rob a store and beat up the owner. Hopefully we can get you arrested next week. And as to why I'm happy, I've got three retired officers who will be working part-time for me. Also, two of the guys that left to go back on the job want to continue to work weekends."

Two hours later Manuela returned. "How did you make out with Peter Grace? Can he get me inserted into the Interpol files?"

"Done deed. He told me to tell you to be careful. Then he said something strange. He said you would probably know what it means, '*Watch out for the LambieDog*'."

The dumbest look came over Ricky's face.

* * * *

The moment of truth had arrived. Aldo had stayed over an extra day and left Tuesday morning with Manuela. He had honed up Ricky's Italian. He also took his bone knife for safekeeping. They both knew it would be confiscated when Ricky was arrested. Aldo gave him a metal one about the same size. Manuela came back at noon with a passport and an expired visa.

"Why is the visa expired? Did somebody make a mistake? Passport looks okay. I'm glad you took the pictures after I started shaving my head. I notice that it has three years to the expiry date."

"You want to call attention to yourself. The picture in the passport and the expired visa will certainly do that. I checked, your friend, Santanna, also has an expired visa. The Spanish authorities won't waste time with you two after they get you before a magistrate. They'll deport you back to Italy, where you, my friend, will be put into jail for that outstanding attempted murder. Don't worry, a good lawyer will get you off. There's not enough evidence to convict you."

"I assume I'm supposed to become buddy-buddy with Santanna."

"First things first. The prison records are being planted as we speak. You are a bad person, Ricky. And yes, you and Santanna will buddy-up. You will be put in a cell with him. You could be in there for as long as three weeks. You've got to become fast friends so that he will think of you when they recruit more Camorrista soldiers. I guarantee you they will need more personnel. Peter Grace told me that Interpol is beginning to alert the nations they serve to round up many of the current soldiers in the field. Time spent here in the cottage will feel like a vacation compared to your time with Santanna."

"Okay, so who am I supposed to rob, and when?"

"Tonight. You'll be holding up the local hardware store. Use your knife. You're going to steal all the pesetas from the cash register and while you're at it, beat-up the owner. Make sure that you pull your punches; he's a friend of mine. You're allowed to hit him only four times. He will go down, and out, but not before he triggers a silent alarm. Then go to the local bar up the street. Have something to eat and drink. Drink a lot. The police will arrest you there."

"You seem to have thought of everything."

"One more thing, Ricky. If you put up a fight with the police, expect to get roughed up in the struggle. The police who come to arrest you won't be in on any of our scheming. I can only suggest you do your best not to hurt anybody. If you do, they'll make you pay for it."

"Gee, thanks a lot.—Now I really mean it. Thanks for all your help. I realize that you had to work night and day to get me to this point."

"Take care of yourself, Rick." She kissed him on the cheek and walked with him to her car. All he carried was a small bag with his clothing, electric razor, and a well-worn leather wallet containing his papers. He'd get the money he needed from the robbery.

At five thirty that evening, Ricky Blanco put his metal knife to the throat of the hardware storeowner and forced him to give up the money in the cash register. Then he punched the owner twice in the stomach, once in the mouth, and finished with the handle of his knife on the man's head. Everything he had done was captured on the store's surveillance camera.

Two hours later in the bar up the street; Ricky was arrested for robbery and assault. He seemed drunk and swung wildly missing the arresting officer's jaw, and was forced to the ground with one swing of a club to his head. Blood gushed from the break in the skin. He didn't have any hair to cushion the blow. He passed out. The bartender said the man was drinking heavily.

Ricky awoke in a dimly lit cell. He had a headache and found a bandage had been put on his scalp. Saw the blood on his fingers when he touched the bandage. Somebody was standing over him and staring. He assumed it was Santanna.

"You got to be a first class shit head. You took on two officers, and you were drunk? You're lucky they didn't take you apart."

"Where am I? Who the fuck are you?" He said in Italian.

He replied in English. "I'm Santanna, asshole. I'm your cellmate. You're in the Madrid jail, better known as the hellhole."

Ricky rolled over on his side, facing away from Santanna. "Go screw yourself. I don't feel like talking."

Santanna persisted. It was quite awhile since he had someone to talk to. "I don't speak much of the language of the old country any more. Forgot most of it since I've been out of Italy more than ten years; been hopping around Europe. I hope you speak some English or we're gonna' have a tough time talkin' to each other."

"Yeah, I speak English. I've been practicin' it. Not too good at it yet."

"Phew, man. You smell. I can't make up my mind if it's coming out of your mouth or it's your whole body that reeks. Don't you ever brush your teeth?"

"Who the hell do you think your talking to?"

Santanna wanted to keep the conversation going. "I don't have an extra toothbrush to give you. Take a gulp of this mouthwash and spit it into the toilet."

"Will you get the fuck off my ass? I told you I ain't up to talking. My head hurts like hell."

"Don't get so huffy, shithead. You'll be glad to talk to me after a week in this joint. Why don't you just try to get along with me?" Then as an afterthought, or maybe it was an attempt to keep him talking, he said. You should know they let us take showers every Friday. Make sure that you take one, or they'll scrub you down. That ain't nice to have happen."

"My head's pounding on me. Take a look, will ya? Is it still bleeding?"

Santanna pulled down the bandage. "You're still leaking blood, man. Gonna' take at least a coupla' stitches to close, if you ask me? What's your name?

"Ricky Blanco. I'm Italian, but my father was a Spaniard."

Santanna started beating on the bars with his metal cup. "Hey, you guys. Better get back here and stitch up this bozo, before he bleeds all over the floor. You guys cut up his head real bad when you made the arrest. Bunch of violent bastards, you are." When nobody answered right away he continued. "It you let him die you're asses are in trouble?"

A guard came to the cell five minutes later. He had a needle and thread in his hands. "They sent me back to stitch him. Understand he took a swing at Petro? Serves this Guinea right for what he got." He mumbled in Spanish. Ricky understood what was said but didn't let on.

The guard opened the cell and motioned Santanna to stand back. He ripped the bandage off of Ricky's scalp. Then he sewed it up in one continual stitch, not separately as it should be done. Ricky was glad that it was done, regardless. "Wash it off and bandage it now, you stupid Spic." He said in Italian. A few Band-Aid's were passed through the cell about ten minutes later. Apparently, the guard understood what Ricky had said.

Three weeks passed and the two goom-ba's sharing the cell became fast friends. Ricky had taken Santanna's advice to brush his teeth and to shower weekly. It was much to his personal delight. However, he complained every time they made him shower. He had to keep up his act.

One time a guard shoved Santanna because he didn't move fast enough for him. Ricky hit the guard with a kidney blow, for which he took a brutish whack across his legs with a club. He was then put into solitary confinement for two days on bread and water. When he returned to his cell there were still bruises on his legs. Santanna would never forget what his newfound friend had done, and what it had cost him. After that incident, it seemed they had a lot in common and were always discussing what each had done during their criminal lives. Santanna suggested Ricky take a job with a large organization when he got out. He was a cocky bastard. He was so sure he would be released soon. He promised Ricky, that when the time came he would vouch for him.

One morning they were both told to dress up in their cleanest prison clothes. They were going before the Magistrate. Santanna was first. His appointed lawyer had him take the stand. He stated he was only attempting to rob the guy; it was a simple felony, he argued. His lawyer didn't say anything. The guy he tried to kidnap testified against him. Ricky watched while Santanna was convicted of attempted kidnapping. But because they found out he had an expired visa, the magistrate sentenced him to be deported. They could have put him in jail for five years, but common sense dictated otherwise. The victim was not harmed. Thus, they reasoned, why should Spain foot the bill for this Italian, and for such a long time? He was sent back to his cell to pick up his belongings, and to change from prison clothes.

Ricky was assigned the same lawyer that Santanna had. *This ought to be good,* he thought quietly. When Ricky stood before the magistrate he was told the witness to his crime was nowhere to be found. The prosecution then asked to view the surveillance tape. It was missing too.

The lawyers chatted at a sidebar called by the magistrate.

The result, Ricky was quickly found not guilty. His tourist visa was checked before he left court and they found out it had long since expired. The magistrate decided to send this troublemaker out of the country. He was to be returned to his country of origin.

He picked up his small bag of clothing and personal items and changed into street clothes in the cell. Both he and Santanna were cuffed and boarded a van. It was a short twenty-five kilometer trip to the local airport. Upon leaving the van they were put into leg irons, and handcuffed to security guards assigned to them.

They were flown to Campania, Italy, landing at a small airport located 100 kilometers east of Naples. Ricky was transferred to the Italian authorities because of outstanding charges pending. Santanna had a lawyer waiting and was released into his custody. There were no warrants pending. As long as he had someone to vouch for him he was immediately released.

"You'll beat this thing, Ricky. You've been out of the country too long for them to make it stick. Don't tell them nuttin'. I'll see if I can get you a job with my boss. I'll keep in touch."

The lawyer frowned and grabbed him by the arm pulling him away, before he said anything more that could get him into trouble. Two days later, Ricky was released from jail, advised that the statue of limitations on his alleged crime had expired. He smiled and thought, *Manuela sure knew what she was doing.*

Once he was out he called Aldo, collect. "I don't have any money, and I want my knife. I need a place to stay. I'm hoping Santanna will be pushing to recruit me for the Camorra." They met in an out-of-the-way wine shop that evening. Aldo transferred the bone knife and euros to Ricky. They separated immediately. It wasn't safe to be seen together.

Ricky got a room in a fleabag hotel. Two days later Santanna caught up with him as he was leaving his room. They embraced. "Got you an interview with the person handling my group. I told you that they would be looking for more people. You're a natural; you've got the talent to make it big. Forget this place. You're coming with me. But first, you're gonna' get cleaned up and get some new clothes. I got me plenty of money, so don't worry. You know, I'm glad you've been keepin' yourself clean since I last saw you. It's important that you make a good impression."

Four hours later, after they drove to Naples, they entered a small but clean and neat hotel located in the tourist section. A meeting had been arranged and Santanna made the introduction. "Ricky Blanco, this is my current boss in Italy, Saila Ewe."

The woman was tall. Ricky judged her to be about five foot ten; for some reason his mind refused to translate it into metric measurements. She wore her white curly hair short, and was evenly tanned. She had definite oriental features, her eyes saying it all. Her hips were set perfectly on long-slim legs. Her face was beautiful, with a distinctive nose indicating other than full oriental ancestry, and sensuous thick lips. He tried, but couldn't guess her weight. She wore a red leather mini-skirt, four-inch heels, and a pink silk blouse, open far enough to display ample cleavage. Ricky was taken back by her physical stature and beauty. *So this is the boss of the local operation,* he thought.

Ricky was put through vigorous questioning for more than an hour. The fact that he spoke both Italian as well as English seemed to be the break he needed. Her questions led Ricky to believe a great deal about his past was already known. No doubt they had been able to review his planted criminal record even though hardly enough time had elapsed to do so. He was being vetted, much like he was being hired into a government job.

Saila waved her arm as if to say stop. "Okay, let's wrap it up. You're on trial for one month. Every soldier gets the same pay in the country you're assigned. It's certainly ample. You, Santanna and myself will take the next caper. I want to see Ricky in action. We're going to kidnap, and hold for ransom, the son of a wealthy café owner. I don't want either of you to hurt the merchandise, that is unless I say so. I'd rather collect the ransom. You two will make the snatch outside the café. I'll be driving. You do it fast and quietly using chloroform soaked cloth. I've got a stash of that stuff the boss gave me. Don't get it too close to your nose, it's potent.

"Keep him blindfolded with his hands tied behind his back. Untie him only when you escort him to the bathroom. One of you better stay with him at all times. Then you'll take turns watching and feeding him, until we get paid. If the father balks at our demands...well, we'll talk about that only if we have to."

"How are we going to identify the mark" Ricky questioned.

"Don't ask dumb questions. Of course we're going to case the job first. You'll dress in a suit and tie and you'll take me to dinner at the Café Beneventura. It's a great place for the tourists. Santanna, bring a girlfriend. Ricky, you can escort me. Tab's on me. We'll make it a foursome, just out having a good time. I hear the food is great. They have a late show, followed by dancing. The man we want takes the day's receipts to the bank depository every evening for his daddy, after the café closes. Size it up. You can grab him the following night before he makes the deposit. Keep the money he's transporting as a bonus."

Santanna brought along an older woman; she was about fifty. Classy dresser though, with a nice shape, red hair and, of course, large boobs. He had made his preferences known to Ricky many times during their incarceration. He said he picked her up in the bar at the hotel where he was staying. She was a tourist from New York and was supposed to leave for home the next day. It fit in nicely with their plan and would offer Santanna some entertainment later that evening. Most important was that she got along with everybody and didn't ask questions.

Ricky was almost embarrassed to be seen in a neat tailored suit and a striped red and blue tie. His large frame, muscular-build, and shaved head with two dangling hoop earrings made many a head turn to look at him. They were out having a good time, while less than a month ago he was transforming himself into a thug. Now he was playing a new game.

Saila was a knockout. She wore a light blue dressy-dress with a hemline above the knees. She also wore two-inch platform shoes with four-inch spike heels and was almost as tall as Ricky. It was obvious she didn't want to be matched with the much shorter Santanna.

The mark was easy to spot. He and his father greeted diners, and showed people to their tables. The kid was about twenty-two and researched to be recently out of college. The father barked orders, and the kid was expected to jump, which he did, but not willingly.

Santanna noticed that the young man had a blackened fingernail on his left pinky. He thought he probably had caught it in a car door. He called it to Ricky's attention, just in case it was dark when they had to positively identify the mark, once they snatched him off the street.

During the evening Santanna asked his date to dance. Saila then suggested that Ricky escort her to the dance floor. The moment she folded into his arms and drew her body close to his he wanted to make love to this beautiful and desirous woman. She seemed to like him as well. They danced often that night, only asking for their check when they saw the son planning to leave for the bank drop. The four followed the son, walking slowly behind for about two city streets, but keeping him in sight. They had made their mark, and plotted where they'd take him. Surveillance was a success. Santanna's date believed they were walking off the heavy meal recently eaten.

Next evening, with Saila driving a rental four-door car, Ricky and Santanna waited for the prey. The street was empty. Slowly the car came up behind the young man and Ricky prepared the potent cloth. He got out of the car first. Santanna was driven further up the street and got out. He went to a telephone stand, and started fumbling in his pockets as if he were looking for coins. Ricky came up behind the young man when he had passed where Saila was parked waiting for Santanna. He placed the cloth over the mark's face. There was a struggle, but the mark quickly succumbed, and nobody saw what had happened. They dragged his collapsed body into the back seat, where Santanna blindfolded him and handcuffed his hands behind his back.

At the remote house in the woods located outside of city limits they locked him in a windowless room with a bed, on which they threw him face down. He was never allowed to see the faces of his abductors. His life depended on it. He would have to call for one of them to take him to the bathroom. The kid was scared, as well he might be. Saila sent the ransom note. The instructions to the father were simple. It was typical Camorra procedure, having worked hundred's of time before with little problem encountered.

We have kidnapped your son. Place fifty thousand euros in a small suitcase. Put it into locker fifty-seven, located in the Naples bus depot, within forty-eight hours. Failure to meet these demands

will result in a painful episode for your son. Do not contact the police if you value his life.

Two days later, Saila opened the locker, finding it empty. "For Christ's sake, the cheapskate didn't leave the money. What the hell is he trying to pull?" She was talking loudly, and people were starting to look in her direction. She immediately became composed and closed the locker

When she returned to the house, she found out that the victim, called Tony, had suggested to his captors that they double the amount asked for ransom. He wanted them to give him a cut. To his thinking, this was all a game. It seems his father kept him in tight reign. Tony was sure his father would pay any amount for his safe return. He was wrong. The father had no intention of parting with the money. It wasn't his to give. Besides, the father thought it was a bluff.

She called the men in for a conference. "The bastard didn't pay. I want one of you to cut off a finger. I'm going to send it to the father so that he knows we're serious about this. I don't care which one of you does it. Here's a box to put the finger in."

The young man knew something was up when he sensed two people had entered the room. Ricky had soaked the cloth with chloroform once again, and rendered the boy unconscious.

"Santanna, hold his left hand tight, in case he comes to." He took his bone knife out of the leg scabbard and cut off the first joint of the pinky finger; the one with the smashed fingernail. Then he applied a bandage so that Tony wouldn't bleed too much. His rationalization for doing it was that if he didn't, Santanna would have cut off even more. He then put it into the ring box Saila had given him.

She sent the father the finger with another note.

Look in the box and you'll know that we mean business. We're giving you another forty-eight hours to comply. And the ransom is

raised to fifty five thousand euros. Pay the ransom if you don't want other bad things to happen to your son.

The man quickly opened the box and immediately recognized it when he saw the piece of the injured finger.

Two days later, Saila again checked the locker, only to find it empty. When she returned to the house she was beside herself. She yelled: "Ricky, cut off one more piece of his finger. Get me the next joint. Here's another box."

The kid almost shit in his pants when he heard footfalls of his captor's returning. Ricky chloroformed him again, and he and Santanna repeated the act of cutting yet another joint off of his left pinky, leaving now only a remaining stump.

Saila sent the piece of the finger in the box along with another note.

This is our final demand. Did you think that we were fooling? Because of your stalling, the ransom demand has been raised to sixty thousand euros. I hope that you value your son's life.

Ricky hoped the father would pay; he didn't know what he was going to do if he didn't.

The third trip to the locker produced the desired results. The papa really loved his son and finally paid as instructed. Ricky was pleased to see it come to an end.

Saila gave Ricky and Santanna five thousand euros for them to give to Tony. She felt sorry for him and what they put him through. Ricky suggested to the boy that he use the money and get away from his father's coattails as fast as he could when they released him. Making sure that his blindfold was secure they drove him around for two hours before they let him go. They dropped him outside town in a desolate area. It was in a location only two kilometers from the house where they had kept him. Saila was pleased when she got her hands on the money. She had an accounting to make to her boss.

"I want you two to lay low for the next few days while I report to the boss and transfer this money to him. I'll be returning with your next assignment."

Santanna and Ricky each purchased a bottle of their favorite booze and drank for two days.

Saila returned to Naples and called the men, asking that they come to meet with her the next day. They were scheduled an hour apart. Santanna was on first at ten, and Ricky was to follow at eleven. They were told to be on time at her hotel suite, which doubled as her office. Their summons to appear before the boss had them guessing.

"Why do you think she wants to see us separately? Jesus, she can't be upset because we didn't get the money from that café owner with the first note?" Santanna asked Ricky.

"No way she can hold us responsible for that mess. We did everything she said. It's gotta' be something else. Who knows? Maybe she wants to give us a bonus? We did bring in more money than was originally asked for. What say we just play it by ear? We've got a whole day to clean up after our binge."

Santanna looked spiffy. He wore Italian loafers, tan pants, white shirt and a brown sport jacket. He was trying to impress Saila. When he came into the room she waved him to the sofa and she sat facing him in a straight back chair. She was dressed in a cream-colored jump suit zippered in front, and had a folder in her hand.

"I saw Capo Ruffino. He wants you to know that he's pleased with the work that you've done over the last ten years, and he's happy with the job just completed." She lied about the first part of what she had to tell him. It's all here in your jacket, every caper where you've been involved. He wants you to stay working with me. I'm going to give you an envelope with cash totaling ten thousand euros."

"Gee, Saila, I never got a bonus for a job before."

"It's not a bonus. It's prep money. You're going over to do a job in the United States. You'll need the money to get a decent wardrobe. Buy what you think an Italian visiting America would wear. Just remember that you'll need cold weather gear as well as an assortment of regular clothes. Don't spend all the money, but do buy yourself some nice stuff, you've earned it. You're heading to Colorado next week. You'll also need some of this money for tickets."

"Wow! What are we gonna' do there?"

"I'll let you know the details when we meet. We're each going in separately, and will meet up at the Brown Palace Hotel in Denver. I'll need your passport to apply for a visa. It will clear, don't worry."

"Thanks, Saila. I gotta' do me some shopping."

"Send Ricky in now, would you please? Don't let on what we talked about."

Santanna looked grim when he left Saila's apartment. He couldn't meet Ricky's eyes.

"She wants you now. Go right in."

He was wearing loafers, a neatly pressed pair of blue slacks and a silk shirt. Ricky knocked first, then entered. "Sit on the couch, Ricky. I have a few things that I want to go over with you." She was very formal.

"Yes Ma'am." He sat as instructed, noticing the file in her hand. She sat directly opposite him on the chair. He looked down and saw marks on the rug indicating the chair had recently been moved closer to the couch. The aroma of her perfume reached him. It was disturbing Ricky, and Saila was aware of the effect she was having on him.

"The powers that be think you did well on your first assignment. They told me they were finally able to get a copy of your Interpol file. It cost them a bundle, but you checked out and are no longer on trial. Our next assignment is in Denver, Colorado."

"I may have some trouble getting into the country, what with all the background checks being done and all the extra security."

"It's not a problem. Give me your passport and I'll have a visitor's visa prepared that will pass muster. Here's an envelope with ten thousand euros. Go buy yourself some tourist type clothing, including something warm. We're going into the mountains."

As she reached across to hand him the envelope the folder dropped to the floor. They both reached for it. Their hands brushed. When they stood up they found themselves only a foot apart. Ricky caught the scent of her hair. It was intoxicating when combined with the other aromas emanating from this voluptuous female. He was aroused as she moved even closer to him.

Ricky took her in his arms and pressed his body closer. He could feel her nipples hardening against his chest. The embrace was returned, and they kissed. With both of their passions heightened, he pulled down the zipper on her jump suit exposing bare breasts. He took her in his arms, carrying her into the bedroom. He found the bedspread already turned down. There was no fumbling or excessive eagerness as they undressed each other. Then, they had sex…not as two, but as a single entity bringing pleasure to each other.

The moment of passion soon passed and they lay satiated, entwined in each other's arms. After a while they separated, and lay side by side. Saila spoke first. "So, how does it feel to have had sex with LambieDog? I'm more than just delighted to have you on board with me. This has been a lonely life I've had to lead."

Ricky sat up and looked at her, his mouth wide open in astonishment. "I've been told on two separate occasions to watch out for LambieDog. I should have known that calling yourself Saila was no trick of fate, since it spells alias backwards. And your last name, Ewe, it means lamb. Now I don't know if I'm supposed to watch out for you or you for me. Clue me in."

"I was told to expect an undercover man from the States. You could have knocked me over with a feather when I saw a real live *Mr. Clean* come walking in here. You do realize that's what you look like, don't you? Santanna tells me that he takes credit for you bathing and brushing your teeth. I suppose I'm beholden to him."

"Oh yeah. That was a tough adjustment for me to undergo, part of the disguise."

Saila continued, "I'm an undercover agent for the CIA assigned here to provide Intel to Interpol. I came into the Camorra organization three years ago. Would you believe, that was the last time I was with a man? Since then, I've been involved in seventeen kidnappings, made them a lot of money. I suppose you could say it's become my specialty. Lifting someone off the street goes on all the time in Italy. You can't let yourself get upset about it. Police rarely get involved, and insurance companies end up making the payoffs."

"So, then Interpol's aware of what you do for the CIA?" He looked puzzled, then thought about what he did. "I didn't particularly like what you had me do to the kid."

"It happens that the job we did together was against Cosa Nostra laundering operations. The man running the café works for them. I just received word they had to give back money, all of it, including the amount we took from the bank drop."

"Who set it up? I'm surprised they didn't know it was a Cosa Nostra operation?"

"I did, of course. It was suggested by my CIA contact that I do something to get another assignment. As part of the money-give-back agreement, the three of us have been made persona-non-gratis. We have ten days to leave Italy and never return. Hence our new assignment."

"I want to change the subject back to what we were doing. Do you think you're up to doing it again? You're a great lover…and it's been so long."

Later, as they dressed, Ricky felt compelled to comment: "I learned two things today that really surprised me."

"Do I have to wait all day to find out what it is?"

"Well, I've learned that there really is a LambieDog." A smile crossed his face. "And, I've also learned that you're really a natural toe-head."

Now she smiled. "I want to give you these to replace those oversized hoop earrings." She handed him a small box containing two small gold crosses. "No more looking like *Mr. Clean*...please. You do know that you look just like the character on the bottle of a cleaning solution."

Chapter 6

Six Weeks Earlier

The Watergate Hotel—The Vice President convened the meeting. Also present were George Papadopoilis, Kevin Winslow and Vince Green, Director of the Central Intelligence Agency. Notably absent was the man known only as Rick, and Peter Grace, CIA Agent/Interpol Liaison from Europe.

Vince Green spoke up first. "Peter Grace only comes to the States once a month. In order to maintain continuity, I'll be sitting in whenever he's not available. I only know what he told me."

"Rick's away on assignment," chimed Kevin. I really don't have any idea when he'll be back. Just trust that he's working on our problem."

"I guess I'll have to bring everyone here up-to-date." George offered. "Harry Hansen is safely tucked away in witness protection. It upsets me when I think this piece of trash will be given immunity when we need him to testify.

"They've started work on the underground escape tunnels Rick proposed we create near the White House and Congress. I now think that it's a good move for what we know is coming, and perhaps for a future president. There will actually be four places where he will be able to leave the limousine undetected."

"How are the two special armored limousine's coming?" Asked ACE. "Are they going to make them so they can be operated by remote control?"

"Can't even start doing the modifications until everybody in the auto transformation-company are vetted. The changes we have authorized must be kept absolutely secret. I don't expect it to take more than another week before they start. Ford has already shipped the stretch Lincoln Town Car frames."

"What about the results of the meeting the Camorra boss had with Saddam's man? Are you saving it for the last?" Griped Kevin.

"All in good time." George seemed annoyed with Kevin's question. "The National Security Administration, the place where they eavesdrop on all telephone and radio transmissions worldwide picked up something interesting. However, all they were able to get was the last part of a conversation. They believe it was a phone call from Iraq directly to Victor Salvetti. We knew he gave Assad Kasbala a supposedly secure telephone to have Saddam call him directly and discuss the plan. NSA only picked up the transmission because I alerted them to be on the watch. Salvetti had some pretty good encryption technology built into that phone, because by the time NSA cracked the code recognizing where it was coming from and going to, they missed the first part of the conversation. They were unable to record the earlier part of the message due to the encryption technology that first had to be overcome.

"Here's what they did get, verbatim...*service was original base. She is expendable. After Assad gives you the diamonds and establishes strongbox in bank with final payment you are to eliminate him. He's too dangerous because of what he knows. No more contact with us is to be made. Make our leader happy with results. This phone is being destroyed.*"

Kevin was fuming. "What the hell do you mean that's all you've got? You mean all we know is that Saddam himself didn't make the call, but that he did authorize the contract. We now believe they identified a female to Salvetti to use to kill the president. And what does the word 'service' mean that leads off the recorded conversation? Christ, man. That could be almost anything, including any one of our armed forces, or it could even mean Secret Service. What did you people get when you videotaped his room a few days later?"

"We were able to confirm that Saddam validated the contract and paid fifty million in diamonds up front, and deposited another fifty million in diamonds in the bank. Assad never made mention of the undercover sleeper agent. Apparently that business was taken care of with the telephone call from one of Saddam's people. We also found out that Victor has some weird sexual interests. He's got a dominatrix who provides him with his personal sort of fun. He acts the role of the submissive, which is strange when you think about his violent disposition. I don't know if we can use it against him. We'll keep it in the file.

"I'm real sorry that's all NSA could come up with. It was some really tough technology they had to break through to get what we did."

"Where do we stand with the Thiebold murders?" An exasperated ACE asked.

"New York City police just arrested the man who killed Thaddeus. He's lawyer-ed up, and won't say a word. They've got a pretty solid circumstantial case against him. Then there is the street bum that witnessed him kill Thiebold, and he later kills the only witness. Well, somebody saw him kill the street person, Georgie Boy. They're keeping him under a suicide watch. Not that they're afraid he's going to do himself in, but to keep him protected from his own people. I've already notified Bill Thiebold. He's pleased but anxious; wants the person who killed his mother brought down too. Unfortunately Detroit police still don't have a clue. That ends my report."

"I have some new information." Chimed, Vince Green. "Got word from Peter Grace that he has a deep undercover agent working for the Camorra. He's going to try and get her to transfer to the American operation. As for Salvetti, we're digging into his background. We know he had an older brother, Mario, who had moved to the United States back in the eighties. He was pretty heavy into the rackets and was in prison more than once. It seems the current Speaker of the House, Thom Crowell, was the federal prosecutor who had him tracked down, and later put him away for life, with no chance of parole. Mario Salvetti died in prison during a knife fight."

"George, don't you have any more information about the other men who were in the room that night when they hatched the plan to kill the president?"

"Sorry, ACE, but there's not much we have on any of them other than Hansen. They all seem to have the same type of backgrounds; got their money through family wealth. Spoiled, rich and lazy fits them all. They think money can buy anything. Should have more on them next time we meet. Right now we've got NSA monitoring all telephones. They call each other sometimes, but have never said anything we can use against them. They scheduled another meeting of the CLIQUE in three weeks. You can be sure we'll have the place covered with agents and surveillance equipment. Since the January meeting, Victor Salvetti has not been in touch with Tobias Whitman. He's got to be antsy to know what's going on with the contract."

ACE closed the meeting. She remarked. "I'm having lunch with the president and plan to brief him on what has been going on with this task force. Keep me in the loop if anything special comes up before we meet."

* * * *

LATER THAT WEEK

Gunter Bendt, met the man from the Ford Motor Company in the last booth at a bar located downtown Chicago. He gave Gunter an envelope containing plans for two special stretched Lincoln's, that the government had ordered for use by the president. In turn, Gunter passed him a package containing $100,000 in tens and twenties. "Mr. Gunter, I'm in a position to offer you some *special handling* of the vehicles before they ship out to the factory, where they will be customized. Do you think your boss would be interested?"

"The name's Bendt, Gunter Bendt. What is this special handling that you can do for us, and how much extra will it cost?"

"On Saturday I'm assigned to do finishing touches on the vehicles, like making sure all the welds are strong enough to hold the heavy steel plates that will be added to them. There are eight contact points, called stanchions, on the body of the car where it is attached to the roof. There are two each in the front and rear, and four more separating the doors and added seating area. I'm proposing to weaken the upper points of the supporting stanchions to allow them to take only the weight being added. At some point in the future, at your choosing, extra pressure on the roof will cause the heavy plates to drop down and crush anyone in the car."

"I'm interested. Once again, I ask; how much?"

"It will cost you another $150,000. But I must know tomorrow if you want me to do it when the guy I'm working with this Saturday takes his break. This is my one and only chance. I know just how much to cut, and where to reduce the strength of the weld. If I do the job for you, I need all that money, to be able to leave the country for all time. I don't want the Fed.'s on my trail after this thing goes down. I should have enough time to be able to disappear."

"I think we'll be interested. Assuming that I'm correct, I'll have the money for you tomorrow night. Only this time it will be in fifties and hundreds. We'll meet here, same time and place." The deal was consummated the next evening. The following week the basic limousines were shipped to the post-construction company, under a security guard. It wasn't necessary: the damage had already been done.

* * * *

The Brown Palace was a ten-story, luxury older hotel, situated in the middle of Denver. It was to be their headquarters. Rick was the last of the three to arrive at Stapleton Airport. Saila was at the gate to meet him. She had left Santanna at the hotel bar. He was hanging on a hell-of-a-drunk, and was, in effect, out of the way of what she wanted to do.

"How did you know when I was going to arrive?"

"Easy, only one flight from Naples to Denver direct daily. What took you so long?"

"That visa you acquired for me said I was coming here for a temporary job, assisting a research doctor, which was supposed to last for only thirty days. When I was questioned at the airport I didn't know that information. I hadn't talked to you since my visa and passport was returned to me via courier. I stupidly said that I had applied for an Italian tourist visa and someone had made a mistake at the American Embassy. They hung me up two days, until a guy by the name of Peter Grace finally cleared me. You don't happen to know him?"

"He's my boss. You must have the Gods on your side. I told him about you before I left. What happened to your head? Is that hair I see?"

"I started to let it grow in the day you gave me the new earrings. As long as I have to continue to wear earrings to keep up my cover, I like them better than the hoops. I sent them back to Manuela in Spain, who I borrowed them from."

"Who's Manuela?" A frown creased Saila's face.

"She works for me."

"Oh...We can catch a little time together, that is, if you want?

"Saila, I've been thinking about you night and day since we made love. Where can we go that we won't be seen?"

"Were stopping at a motel on the way to Denver. I'll brief you in the room. Santanna is at the hotel getting sloshed. Don't worry, we'll have time for a quickie...or two, as well as business."

During the first interlude Rick spoke. "I hope we're not going to blow it all by being intimate. You're a very desirable woman. You are unique, in so many ways. Where did you come from?"

"I was born in Kuala Lumpur, Malaysia. Mother was a local and father was an English Naval Officer. At the time his ship sailed for another port, my mother was unaware she was pregnant. When I was five years old, he came back to the islands, and starting looking for her. He knew that I was his from the moment he looked at me. There is a regressive gene in his family bloodline, and I've got it. I'm not an Albino, but I'm close to being one. My body hair is the only part of me that has no pigment. My somewhat brownish skin is my natural color from a blending of my parent's races. My mother was killed in an automobile accident that almost took my father as well. After being released from the hospital he took me back to England.

"I was educated in the best schools Great Britain had to offer, and returned to Malaysia after college, where I received my doctorate at the university. It was where I met the CIA agent, Peter Grace, once again. He was my father's cousin from the States, and he was recruiting. I didn't join the CIA right away, but he put Interpol on to me to tell me how I could be helpful to them if I was working undercover. A year later I accepted the CIA's offer for the greater cause. Now you know the story of my life. What about you?"

"I'm half Nez-Pierce American Indian and half Caucasian; my mother being the daughter of a diplomat. They're both dead now. Now you know why my skin is bronze-tone.

"I was married once while in college, where I studied law. We divorced and later became friends, until she was killed. I became engaged one other time, but marriage never occurred. Been in the service during the Gulf War, and since, have been working as a special agent.

"We are a pair, are we not? When this is over we could make some beautiful babies, don't you think?" That remark caused her eyelids to raise. "Is Saila really your name?"

"Would you believe that is what my mother named me? She told me that it was my grandmother's name. Now let's get serious, for a little while, at least.

"We both have to survive getting ourselves out of the Camorra first. Here's what they have lined up for us. I still don't know all of it yet.

We're to meet tomorrow morning with a Doctor Wilhem Ahrens. He's the developer of a procedure involving an injection of a special chemical he's invented. He hypnotizes the subject and inserts a mind control beta wave state; then shows special movies designed to have the subject perform post-hypnotic activities. The mind assures the victim they personally are not doing anything wrong, but they're being trained to set up certain situations, which benefits the Camorra.

"Sounds like space age technology and I suppose that's what it is. We meet with the doctor tomorrow afternoon. Then we'll find out who the mark is, and plan details. I'm told we have two weeks to get it done once we snatch him, and it has to be done eight days from now. That's all I have."

"They'll want to kill the mark after he or she does what they want. It's because the person, who performs the act, will eventually have total recall. That would expose the doctor and the Camorra. I believe I know someone who went through this process. I had to fake her death, and she's still alive."

"Better keep that 'faking-a-death' thought. It may help us to get away from the Camorra when the time comes. I'm serious about this." Once said, Saila smiled and wet her lips with her tongue.

"Let's make love again. Once we check into the Brown Place we'll have too many people watching us. Who knows when we can be alone again?"

* * * *

Kevin had been attending the by-weekly meetings since their inception. Ten weeks had now elapsed and little had been reported as of late. He was hoping this meeting would bear some fruit. ACE opened. Attendees this week were Kevin, George and Peter Grace, who was in from Europe. George was asked to provide an update.

"We have complete dossiers on all the people who attended the latest CLIQUE meeting. At the meeting they asked Tobias Whitman for an up date on what their invested money was doing. Now we've got proof that they are in on the plot. Tobias said that he received a call from a man he called 'Victor'. He said the man told him that all planning for the event they had contracted for was moving along nicely. He was lying. He hasn't heard from Salvetti since that night. We suspect he is infuriated that he has not been kept 'in-the-loop'. But, he's keeping up a good bluff to the others. The group was wondering where Harry Hansen was. None of them reported seeing him in person since they put up their money."

ACE questioned George. "Have you been able to identify the person mentioned by the Iraqi caller, as to who is the sleeper agent?"

"Sorry, ACE. We're still working on it. Haven't flushed it out yet. If we could find out what the word 'service' meant, we would have a place to start.

"Good news on the limousines though. They will be completed and put into service in two weeks. Won't have the construction on the escape tunnels completed until November. Union doesn't have all that many men who are cleared to work on top secret projects."

"Kevin inquired. "What's the latest on the Thiebold murders?" George became red in the face. "Sorry, got to report that the killer of Thaddeus Thiebold is dead of a knife wound at Riker's Island in New York City. We never got a thing out of this guy, and they killed him anyway. And still no word on who killed the mother. Detroit police won't give up searching, but we don't hold out much hope. Need a break on this one."

"We need a break on almost everything, if you ask me." Kevin forcefully asserted.

Peter Grace chimed in. "I have some interesting news. I'd like you all to review this surveillance tape taken at Naples Airport a week ago. Somebody interesting has appeared."

The picture was in black and white, and was somewhat grainy. A big man, wearing earrings, and almost bald, could be seen being detained at the gate. He fit a profile that the Italian's look out for.

"I was called when they checked and found that the visa issued to this man, supposedly by the American Embassy, was an excellent forgery. Apparently the passport is a fake too. His prints were run, and he turns out to be a low-level petty thief who was deported to Italy after spending the last five years giving grief to the Spanish authorities. Take a close look at him." The tape was rewound and then stopped.

"Unless I'm mistaken, that's Kevin's man, Rick. A few months earlier I received an alert to assist in getting his criminal history entered into the Interpol files. I thought you would like to know where he was. I received word from my agent in the Camorra that she had been in contact with Rick, or better known now as a hood named Ricky Blanco. He's been able to infiltrate the Camorra. I used my influence and had him released, in time to make his plane to Denver two days later. We just got lucky, now we know two of our people are undercover trying to head off this plot to kill the president."

* * * *

They met in Saila's room at the Brown palace. The three recently arriving in the country from Italy met with Dr. Wilhem Ahrens and his two henchmen. After introductions, the doctor got down to business.

"The man we're going to implant with post-hypnotic activity is the senior judge on the Supreme Court of the United States of America. His name is Abraham Benjamin. He's eighty-two years old and walks with a cane because of an injury received in the Korean War. Remember the cane; it's the most important reason we need him. Widowed now, he spends two weeks every year in complete solitude, except for a cook and a guide, while he trout fishes in the mountains outside Denver. He spends the first day at the Brown Place. This is where he hires his staff. He rented a log cabin about fifty miles west of here. My two men have been changing the inside of a cabin near the one he rents. They are making it look like a hospital room."

"How do we take him?" Queried Saila.

"Your men are going to rent an ambulance for two weeks. Don't steal one, we may need it for that long. Can't take a chance someone will be looking for it. The judge will eat something in the hotel restaurant that will make him violently ill. I'll tend to him when he collapses in the restaurant. You, the big guy, what's that name again, Ricky, right? You'll act as an Emergency Medical Technician; you Santanna will drive the ambulance. Be sure and take his cane with you when you pick him up. He will never see either of you two guys. You'll take him to the cabin that I've rented. Saila, you'll be his nurse.

"I'll keep him drugged and unconscious for the first three days. I'm concerned because of his age and I want to watch him carefully. After that it will be post hypnotic suggestion that will put him back under my control at exactly four each afternoon. But I'll need to give him a booster shot each day. I'll be showing him a film of the area where he'll be doing exactly what I'm programming him to do. Make sure he's back in his cabin by no later than three thirty. You shouldn't have a problem since he likes to nap before dinner."

"And what will these two guys be doing?" Asked Santanna, wanting them to do their share.

"While you're arranging for the ambulance, they will finalize work on fixing up the room at my cabin. Just worry about what you have to do. These men are technicians and they have another assignment. Once I've started the judge on hypnotic therapy they will have only ten days to transform the cane into a device hiding the many parts necessary to be able to assemble a weapon from it. The shank of the cane will hold three Teflon-coated bullets. After he's released he'll take his cane anywhere we want. You'll learn more about the plan later."

"That's a lot of trouble your going through to kill a guy." Blurted Santanna. "Who the hell is the target?"

"Let's just say it's for more than one person." Explained the doctor. "If you're in on it when it happens, you'll know who it is. For now, it's none of your business. And you were chosen for this job because you're supposed to keep your mouths shut. Stop asking questions I can't answer."

Both Ricky and Saila didn't miss the slip of the tongue when Doctor Ahrens indicated the weapon was for more than one person.

"How can you be sure that he will hire me as a fishing guide and Santanna as a cook?" Ricky pre-empted Santanna in choosing assignments.

"You'll be the only applicants. The hotel usually pre-screens and recommends experienced people to work for the judge. I've already made the payoff."

"It's a good thing I can cook." Griped Santanna. "Mostly Italian food, but I can make other stuff too. I guess I gotta' do the shopping for this old geyser. Ricky, you had betta' be able to fish and all that shit the man wants you to do?"

"Don't sweat it, Santanna. My uncle taught me to fish when I wuz a kid."

The judge arrived the afternoon of the next day. He had just checked into his room when Ricky and Santanna knocked at his door.

"We're the guide and the cook. We've been told that you want to see us before we start working for you." Ricky had spent the early morning and most of the afternoon checking out the fishing holes in the general vicinity of the cabin. He purchased some used poles and other fishing equipment. Santanna had shopped. He purchased all different foods, as he didn't know what the man usually ate.

"Which one's the cook?" Santanna stepped forward. "What kind of food is your specialty? I prefer Italian when I'm out in the woods. You can cook Italian, can't you?"

"You're in luck, Judge Benjamin. I'm the best Guinea cook there is."

"As for you, big fella', do you know how to put me into the right stream? You're an American Indian, aren't you? Can tell by the color of your skin. What's your tribe?"

Ricky winked at Santanna. "Yeah, I'm a Nez-Pierce; come from up in Idaho country. Don't worry about catching any fish, Judge. I've got all the right equipment and know all the spots around here."

"Well, I guess I'll see you two tomorrow at seven in the morning. I like to get an early start. You better know how to cook trout and not just variations of spaghetti. I was stuck with one of those guys last year. I'm expecting gourmet meals."

After they came out of the judge's room, Santanna remarked. "What the hell is a gourmey meal? And where did you come up with that stuff about being an Indian? You sounded almost believable."

"It means he wants to eat various Italian meals. You should be able to do that. Would you believe that I just read about that tribe in a magazine this afternoon?"

"Sure was lucky for you. I never woulda' thought about that."

That evening in the hotel restaurant, Saila and Doctor Ahrens were dining when Judge Abraham Benjamin was seated at a table across from them. As the appetizer was being served the judge, Saila went past his table on the way to the ladies room. She tripped on the carpet and almost fell into the judge's lap.

"Oh, how clumsy of me. I'm so sorry." The concoction prepared by the doctor was sprinkled onto his shrimp cocktail. She pulled herself to her feet.

"You can fall into my lap, young lady, anytime you want." Then he muttered. "What a way to start my vacation?"

Ten minutes later, the judge passed out. Doctor Wilhem Ahrens went immediately to where he was lying on the floor. "I'm a doctor. Does any one know this man?" Before any of the waiters could answer, the doctor took out a stethoscope and pulled open his shirt. After listening for only a moment, he began to check his pulse and shouted orders to his dinner associate. "Call for an ambulance. This man is having a heart attack. He must go to the hospital immediately."

Saila called the number on her cell phone. Ricky answered after the first ring. "I need an ambulance at the Brown Palace Hotel in the restaurant area. This is Nurse Saila Ewe. Doctor Ahrens is currently administering to him. Hurry, please."

Ricky and Santanna showed up with a rolling stretcher ten minutes later. They had to drive all of one city-street to get there.

They carefully lifted their merchandise onto the stretcher and rolled the judge out to the waiting ambulance. His cane was placed next to him. Ricky noticed it had quite a bit of ornamental brass on the handle, extending down the tapered shape of the walking stick. It was passed to one of the two men who were with the doctor when they first met.

Then they drove fifty miles to the doctor's cabin, undressed him and put him in a gown, placing him in a hospital bed. The doctor hooked him up with an IV, while Saila put oxygen breathers into his nostrils, and wired him up to the machine registering vital signs. About two hours later when she was checking his heartbeat he began to wake up. She immediately called for the doctor.

"Where in the hell am I? Do you know who I am?" The doctor was already administering his drug to the judge.

"He never should have been allowed to come back to consciousness that fast." He complained to Saila.

"Look Doc, you can't blame me for his waking up. You only trained me in the basics of nursing care; what did you expect? I don't know what to look for."

"Never mind. All it means is I'll have to erase this little episode from his conscious memory when we get ready to release him."

It was midnight when Doctor Aherns put the judge into a hypnotic state for the first time. Once he was under he started playing a tape, which repeated the same thing over and over. He also showed a movie that looked to start at the entrance to the House of Representatives, go into the chamber, and take a seat where directed by an usher. The words on the tape coincided with the areas on the picture screen where he was to walk.

'As scheduled you are to go to the chamber of congress in your limousine. Tell your driver that you want to arrive at eight fifteen exactly. When you leave the car, greet every person who addresses you. Be your usual self. Take your seat as soon as possible after arriving. At eight thirty-five excuse yourself, and head to the bathroom. Be sure and use your cane.'

The movie showed him where he was to walk and where he would find the bathroom. *'Use the first toilet on the left as you walk in. Place the cane in the corner on the inner wall inside of the stall. Leave the stall and take care of any personal business. Return to your seat. You no longer need your cane. You are fully capable of walking without it. If anyone questions you as to where it is, say that you don't remember.'*

'At four in the afternoon each day you are instructed to enter into a hypnotic state. When you're prompted to become alert you will feel completely refreshed as if awakening from a peaceful nap. You will feel right with the world, and will become hungry and ask for your evening meal to be served. Remember, you have not done anything wrong.'

This process was repeated for one hour. It would be the same routine for the next nine days.

As instructed, Saila called the management of the Brown Palace hotel at exactly eight AM. "This is the admissions nurse at Wellfield Hospital. Last evening we admitted Judge Abraham Benjamin for what was originally diagnosed as a heart attack."

"Oh yes. I was just about to call and find out how he was doing."

"That's very considerate of you. The doctor treating him on the way to the hospital was able to identify his problem as an adverse reaction to a new medicine he recently started taking. I'm happy to report he was administered an anti-histamine, which brought him back to consciousness almost immediately. He stayed in the hospital overnight for observation, and left this morning for his cabin in the mountains. He asked that we call and let you know it was not the food, and that he now feels well and he is sending someone to pick up his clothing. Please check him out and bill his credit card."

The judge stayed in the false hospital room where the doctor could monitor him. He was fed intravenously. Saila was forced to empty the bedpans. Two days later the judge awoke in the bedroom of his rented cabin. He found himself fully clothed, but with his shoes set at the side of his bed, as if he had just taken his nap. He didn't remember anything that had happened the last three days. After eating his first solid meal since he collapsed at the restaurant, he went to sleep.

The next day he dressed early and was ready for breakfast and some trout fishing, "Did I catch any yesterday, Ricky? I just can't seem to remember from day to day. It must be another of those senior moments. Been having them all too often lately."

"You caught eight fish, Judge. We all had our fill of trout last night for dinner. Santanna gave the leftovers to the people in the next cabin. Are you up to try for some large mouth bass today? I rented a boat, so you don't have to wear those heavy waders. They've been tiring you out too much. We'll do good today; I'm sure of it." Ricky hated lying to this old man, but it was his job.

For five days the judge and Ricky floated up and down the lake near the cabin. It was a relaxing way to spend the day. They caught enough fish to last a month, and they were big ones. Santanna would have to give most of them away. Ricky had him back to the cabin and ready for his nap each day at exactly three thirty. The judge appreciated just floating around and talking with Ricky most of the time. He leaped up from his seat in the boat as a bass hit his line. He wasn't too steady and he fell overboard. "Help, I can't swim!" Ricky went into the water in a flash, and pulled him back to the boat and helped him to get in.

"I never would have taken out a boat if I knew you couldn't swim. Why didn't you tell me? You're supposed to be a smart man." And then they both started laughing at their situation; out in the middle of the lake soaking-wet. "I really wanted to find out how to fish for bass.

But you're right, we better go back to trout fishing for the next four days."

"Hey, Judge. We only have two more days to go. Remember, you told me that you seem to have lost your memory for a few days."

He shook his head slowly from side to side. "I really am getting old. I can't even stand up in a boat without falling out. Good thing you were with me. And now I keep forgetting things that are important to me. I can't even remember where I left my cane. Sometimes I really need it to get around."

"Don't worry, Sir. We'll find your cane. I'm sure of it. Judge, when you get back home why don't you retire? You did your share all these years."

"Can't do that. The president asked me to hang in there until the next election. He expects his party will take control of the Senate. That way he can pick a replacement with my conservative leanings. I won't retire until my replacement has cleared the senate. Then I can fish all the time. I think I'm going to buy that cabin. I like it here. I may be looking you up for a full-time job next year. Think you may be interested? Pay will be good, and you can live in the cabin all year round, if you want." Then the judge paused for a moment, and had another idea.

"Why don't you come back to Washington, DC with me. I can hire you right now as my helper and all around handyman. There are many things you can do for me. I'm eighty-two now, I can't get around as well as I'd like, and I've got a lot of money I want to spend. I can't take it with me. My wife's gone and I don't have any children. Why, you can even start to put yourself through college back there; I'm sure you can get a scholarship because of your Indian heritage. There will be plenty of time for yourself in the townhouse where we'll be living."

"Judge, that's a generous offer. And I will think it over carefully." Ricky started rowing towards the dock. "Time to get back to the cabin so you can dry up and have your nap."

"I don't feel like eating fish tonight. I wonder what Santanna has for dinner this evening. He's quite a cook, isn't he?" Ricky didn't answer.

The judge went into the hypnotic state as the chime of the clock in the cabin hit four. The doctor and Saila immediately came into the room when he started to stare. Ricky pulled the judge's pants down and the doctor gave him the shot in the backside. Then he turned on the tape and started the movie. No body had to stay in the room with him. Besides, they had heard the message and saw the film many times before. They all went into the kitchen to have a cup of coffee.

"You had better start giving him that shot in his other cheek. He's been complaining that he's got a sore spot on his rump. He says it bothers him while he's sitting in the boat. Is this really going to work? It's such a…" Whoops! Ricky caught himself in time. He was about to mention the *'long time until the fourth week in January'*. That remark would have given away information he was not supposed to know about.

"What did you start to say?" Asked Ahrens.

"I was about to say it's such a boring thing having to watch that film over and over. Does this treatment really work? I find it hard to believe you can control what somebody will do in the future."

"Really. For your information, I have used this process six times already. The last time it was used I had someone blow up a dam. Different people were programmed to do different things, the result, boom. Believe me, it works."

"The old boy is about at the end of his hour." Said Saila. "Santanna had better start to get his meal ready."

It was Santanna's night to baby sit the judge while he slept. There was no phone that Ricky could use privately. He took a chance and drove the ambulance to the outskirts of town. Finding a pay phone in an all night liquor store he dialed. "This is CONSPIRATOR." While he waited for the return call he purchased some booze for Santanna and himself.

The callback occurred in only twelve minutes. "Jesus, Rick. I've been waiting for your call for almost three months. I trust you have information."

"It's nice to talk to you too, Kevin. I'm fine, in case you want to know. Make sure your tape is running. I'm only going to have time to say it once, and there's a lot to report. Here goes…"

"…I don't have the slightest idea where they will be sending any of us. Have you been able to find out who the sleeper agent is yet?"

"No luck. George Papadopilis is really unnerved about what's going on. The first chance you get I want you to return to being yourself. I need you on the trail of this sleeper agent. They were able to identify her as a woman. Let's end this conversation now. We've been on the phone for twenty-five minutes already. See if it's possible for you to attend the next meeting of the vice presidents task force that's scheduled for a week from Wednesday. Hopefully I'll see you then. And you can brief the group."

"Where the hell did you think you were going in that ambulance?" Queried Dr. Ahrens when he saw Ricky getting out of it." You stupid lout. You could have blown the whole thing."

"Me and Santanna ain't had a drink in over a week. I was careful. Nobody saw me but the guy who sold me the booze. Look, I bought a bottle of wine for you and Saila." The doctor stepped into the light of the moon and Ricky could see a dark shadow on his right eye. He also noticed that his lip was puffed. He didn't say anything to the doctor. Ricky could only surmise that he had made a move on Saila, and that she had protected her virtue. *Good for her,* he thought quietly.

"Look Doc, I got me an idea. In only a few more days we'll be releasing the judge, right. I think I've got a chance to stay with him, and be able to watch him for you. That is until you have him do his thing, of course. He's already asked me if I want to go back with him and become his manservant. I haven't got any other assignment lined up, and none of us can go back to Italy because of what we did to la Cosa Nostra."

"Let me think about it. I'll check with the powers that be. It's not a bad idea. Thanks for the wine. I'm not going to share it with that she-bitch." Ricky was sure he sized that up correctly.

The following afternoon the doctor's two henchmen joined them while the judge was being treated to his movie. They had the refurbished cane with them. "Show these three what you did to this cane." Ordered the doctor. One of the men quickly took it apart, and almost as fast, fashioned the brass parts of it into a handgun. The metal at the base of the walking stick became an elongated barrel. It looked a little unconventional, but the man assured everyone that it would shoot all three bullets rapidly, without jamming.

"Okay, put it back the way it was. Santanna, make sure the judge starts using it. Tell him he had it all the while; and that you found it in his closet. My two guys will return the ambulance. Then they have other hardware to work on. Tomorrow the judge goes back in the evening after I give him his last treatment. I have to make sure that he doesn't remember seeing Saila when he first woke up. Ricky, make arrangements to have a limousine pick him up at the cabin and take him directly to the airport. He's been ticketed for an overnighter to Washington; scheduled to arrive at six. I've got approval to let you go with him, that is, if he really wants you. If you live in the house with him I want you to call weekly at (202) 715-8570, and let them know how things are going. The judge is on a fully booked flight, so plan to fly out the next day.

"Saila, you're to go to Spain and meet with Alfredo Surtain for your next assignment. He'll pick you up at the airport. He's six foot-eight and has bushy black hair, just so you won't miss him. Santanna, you're going to Chicago. You're to report to Gunter Bendt. I understand that you've worked with him before. He specifically asked for you. Grab a cab when you get there and go to 564 Williams Street, in East Chicago. That's it; you all have your assignments.

"I'll drive you three into Denver after the judge has been picked up. Make your own arrangements from there. And show up where you're supposed to be, on time."

During the final day at the cabin Ricky took the judge fly fishing for trout. He used the opportunity to discuss the job offer made to him. "Did you really mean it? You know, me going to work for you in Washington? I've been thinking. This is one opportunity I can't pass up. If you still want me, I can get there a day after you arrive home. I still need a day here in Denver to close out my affairs."

"Here, Ricky, I've written down my home address and the phone number on the back." He passed him one of his business cards. "I'm looking forward to having you with me. We'll make a great team."

Once back at the hotel, the three schemers went to the bar to have a last drink together as a team. Dr. Ahrens had dropped them at the entrance of the Brown Palace and left immediately to catch his flight. To a person, they were glad to see him go.

"Gunter's a pretty good guy, but he likes to give me orders all the time. Boy, I'm gonna' miss you, Ricky." He waited for Saila to go to the ladies room. "I'm not gonna' be around to remind you. Remember now, you should bathe regularly, Ricky, like you did when we were in the cabin. Also, make sure that you brush your teeth every day. Don't let me down now." Santanna was sounding like a mother hen. He was dead serious. Ricky had all to do not to laugh in his face. "You know, I think Saila likes you. Why not bang her good tonight? Last chance to knock off that piece of ass."

"Santanna, do you realize that I don't even know your last name?" Ricky said, trying to seem choked with emotion.

"It's Santanna Santanna, stupid. Everybody has two names." Ricky continued the charade. He and Santanna embraced and wished each other good luck. Saila returned to the bar and Santanna excused himself, leaving them alone, at last. They went to Saila's room.

Before they made love Ricky called Sgt. Mario Amati at his home in Detroit. "Pinkie, there's a guy by the name of Santanna Santanna heading your way sometime tomorrow. He's hooking up with another hood called Gunter Bendt. Gunter's a bad one. I had a run-in with him once before, when he tried to kill me. I let him think he did. Do everybody a favor and put a 24/7 tail on Santanna. Never know what may turn up since he's going to be running with a wolf."

"Stay safe, Red. Thanks for the info."

After the lovemaking was over, Saila spoke. There was trepidation in her voice. It was a sign not missed by Ricky. "Ricky, I told you before that I think you're a great lover, and a pleasure to be with. Even though I feel we're growing closer every day some things were just not meant to be. Tomorrow we'll be going our separate ways. We don't even know if we will ever meet again. I want to let you know that I'm ever so grateful for the time we've had together. Could we part as friends? Let's make love one more time as our parting gift to each other."

Ricky filled her wishes, finding his spirit lowered by what he heard. After Ricky left her room, Saila broke into tears. She cried for awhile and tried to push thoughts of Ricky from her mind. She was in love with him, and she had sent him away because she felt that she had to. There just was no future that she could see for them together, not in this lifetime.

Ricky went to his room and had trouble sleeping. He had lost a love, not for the first time, nor for the last. It hurt.

Chapter 7

Santanna's plane landed at Chicago's O'Hare on schedule. It was four in the afternoon on a rainy, windy day. He followed instructions and grabbed a taxi, which dropped him at the address he had been given in the East Side of town. It looked seedy, and he was not impressed. All the houses on the street were attached. He walked up seven steps on a dilapidated wooden porch and rang the doorbell. Gunter opened the door almost immediately.

The two old friends and working partners embraced. "So how have you been, Santanna? It's been many months since we worked on a caper together. I'm sure you could use a cold one after that trip. Have you eaten yet?"

Santanna sized up Gunter. He looked the same; five foot eleven, weighing about 200 pounds. He had definitely grayed around the fringes and was bald on the top. It's funny, but Santanna only remembered seeing him when it was dark. "I'd like that brew you offered. I've been pretty good. Got picked up in Spain and dropped in the clink. Met a good guy there. I helped him over the rough spots. Both of us were deported to Italy. He had a rap waiting for him, but he beat it."

Santanna took a big gulp from the can of beer Gunter handed him. "Man, that's good. I cuddin' drink nuthing on the flight; makes me sick to my stomach while I'm up in the air. I know that's strange, but I gotta' grin-n-bear it. Well, we teamed up later; you know me and the guy I was telling you about, to pull off a kidnapping. Went off pretty clean; made some good extra money on the job. Problem was we hit the Cosa Nostra. The three of us on the job had to get outa' town in a hurry."

"Whoa. You're not hot now, are you?"

"Naw! They paid them back. Just picture it, the Camorra paying off the Cosa Nostra. I guess our boss didn't want to keep them pissed off. They just wanted us, thems that pulled the job, gone. Ricky, that's my partner, cut off the Vic's finger to force them to pay up, not once, but twice. We didn't know why the daddy didn't want to pay the ransom and get his boy back. Yes sir, Ricky's a real smooth dude."

"This guy, Ricky, sounds like my kind of guy."

"You bet he is. He's beholdin' to me too. Anyway, after we arrived in the United States we got a nice job for a cupula' weeks in Denver. Then they told me to head to Chicago to see you; tellin' me you'll fill me in on what's next. Oh, before you tell me anything, I gotta' tell you about the broad we worked for on the last two jobs. Tall, thin, nice tits, drop-dead gorgeous. Had pure white curly hair, this broad has. She musta' bleached it to get that color. I think my partner dicked her. I saw how he looked at her. She was a good lookin' piece of ass if I ever saw one."

"Come on, leave your bag here. I'll take you out for a great steak. Your gonna' like it here. Chicago's a famous town for steaks."

They left when they saw the cab that Gunter called pull around a utility van in order to get directly in front of the house for the pickup. Neither of them took note of it.

* * * *

Mario's detective, acting on Rick's information, had spotted Santanna the moment he walked off the plane and into the terminal. He followed him to the baggage claim and out the exit. The cop's partner picked him up in an unmarked car and they followed Santanna as his cab left the airport.

He immediately called Lieutenant Mario Amati. Mario moved fast. He went to a judge who owed him one, and received an open warrant for a wiretap, and approval to bug the place along with a search warrant. It was all more than a little illegal, because they didn't know where Santanna would be going. Chicago was a very large city. They needed to pinpoint his destination. The judge wrote all necessary documentation in block print, and signed and time stamped it without the address listed on the paperwork. Then he gave Mario his pen, and a nod of approval, telling him to fill in the blanks. "This makes us even now, right, Armiti?" The judge always liked to mispronounce his name

Mario headed out the door to his car, where he would await the call with the address from his detective. Once he received the street and house number he started his car and proceeded there with the papers essential to make his people, who were already on-site, legal. As soon as the technical team saw him arrive and waving papers, they immediately entered the house. They didn't know when the two hoods would be coming back. To the team of techies who were waiting at the house, time was of the essence. As soon as he stopped his car, Mario made the necessary additions to the documents he had been given.

It took them exactly one and one half-hours to set everything up. Time would tell if they were to get lucky. No one would know they were ever there.

* * * *

Kevin Winslow was waiting at the gate when Rick walked off the plane in Washington, DC. "Got your hair cut a little shorter than the last time I saw you?" It was a question that didn't have to be answered. "And what's with the earrings? Cute little crosses you got there."

This one he wanted an answer to.

"All part of my disguise. You should have seen me awhile back; had big hoop's back then. Somebody you told me about gave me these. Her code name is 'LambieDog'. You won't believe where I was when I found out who she was. On second thought, never mind."

"I want you at the meeting tomorrow. I hope you can make it. We hold these meetings now only on demand; i.e. when we get some new information and everybody in the task force has to be informed. What you told me about the Associate Justice Abraham Benjamin, now that's big news."

"I don't think I can make it tomorrow; I'm supposed to go over to the judge's house, and to live there with him. He knows me only as Ricky Blanco. But he's a cagey old fox; picked up on my Indian heritage the moment he saw me. I'm supposed to settle in and become his manservant. You know, drive him, and help out where ever I can around his house."

"Rick, you have to find a way to cut out for about two hours."

"I know what I'll do. I'll enroll myself in college. The judge said he wants me to continue my education. That ought to take me awhile, but I need some help from you, and fast. Remember I'm supposed to be an Italian, name's Riccardo Blanco, and I've got to have records made available to the college admissions office. Can you fix me up? I need you to create some false records under the name I just gave you to allow me to enter into a few graduate courses at George Washington University. I don't want to be wasting my time if I have to attend some classes in order to keep up my cover. You know what I need."

"You sure get yourself into the craziest situations, don't you? Sure, I'll get you covered. Make sure you don't slip up with the judge. Better make up some reason why a nice Indian kid like you, uses an Italian alias. Let me get on with what I have to do. I'll see you tomorrow at ten AM in the Watergate. It could be an interesting morning. You should be able to check in at the school by the afternoon."

Rick went directly from this meeting with Kevin to the home of Associate Justice Abraham Benjamin, where he received a hearty welcome. "Hey there, young fellow. Been waiting for you to arrive. Got your room all ready. Housekeeper comes in every day to clean up our mess and make the beds. We'll be eating out most of the time. That includes breakfast; unless you know how to cook?"

"I make the best cereal with milk you've ever tasted." He saw what he said bring a look of shocked disbelief come over the judge's face. "Only kidding, judge. I'll be happy to make breakfast. What do you prefer?"

The banter went on for quite awhile while the two got to know each other. Then the judge asked: "Ricky, where did an American Indian man come up with a name like, Riccardo Giovanni Blanco? Sorry, but I had your background researched. So, you're here on an Italian passport, and you have a Spanish name. Plus, you've got a police record a mile long, that reaches back more than ten years. You're a real bad guy."

Then the judge asked the question he was sure would shock Ricky. "You don't happen to be working for the CIA, do you?" He believed this to be a fact or he never would have brought a known felon into his home.

"No, judge. I don't work for the CIA. Sorry, I can't really tell you whom I work for. You have to trust me when I say, I'm really a good guy. If you want me to leave, Sir, I will?"

"Don't bother. Today before you arrived, I called a guy I know in the government named, Kevin Winslow. I was lucky; he had just arrived back at his office. Don't know exactly whom he works for, either, yet I know him a long time. All I have is his number to call if I need him. He says to trust you, so I will. But you should know that I'm still going to ask questions every time I think of one. How does that suit you?"

"Fine by me judge. By the way, I'm enrolling in the university tomorrow, as you suggested. I hope that suits you." Rick said with a broad smile across his face.

The Watergate meeting was called to order by the vice president. In attendance were, Kevin Winslow, his special agent, Rick, George Papadopilis, and both Peter Grace and Vince Green were there, providing double representation from the CIA. "I'd like to welcome Rick back to our group. Kevin tells me he's been real busy as of late. Would you please give us your report, Rick?"

Rick went on to spell out all pertinent details of what he had uncovered. When he came to explaining about what had been done to the associate justice's cane, he also offered a suggestion.

"Since I'm living with the judge now, I will have no problem in getting my hands on his cane. We need somebody on our side who will be able to adjust the gun, which is made by re-assembling parts of the cane. I'd like to see someone make sure that it explodes when it's fired. I'm assuming that we have people available with this kind of skill."

"You bet we do." Chimed Vince. "You get it to me and I'll see that it's fixed to blow."

"You understand, that even if we don't know the person who will be using the converted parts of the cane, we will know who that person is as soon as the gun explodes. Thus, the president will be safe; at least from this assassin. I still think Victor Salvetti has arranged for other attempts on the president's life that night."

"Are you going to tell the judge who you are and what you know about what happened to him in Denver?" Asked George.

"Not unless the old guy sees through my cover. I'm going to have to play this one close. He's one clever old geezer, that man. If absolutely necessary, I will brief him. I'd really like to keep him as only an actor as this thing plays out. After this is over we will have to provide him with protection. The Camorra likes to eliminate every person that they have used. It makes no difference to them that he's a Supreme Court Associate Justice. They don't leave any trails back to them, not if they can help it.

"One other thing to update. I received a call from Lieutenant Mario Amat of the Detroit police. They have established surveillance on a pair of hoods operating out of the East Side. They hope to get information on some of Salvetti's plans, but also a possible lead into the murder of Bill Thiebold's mother. Bill is about ready to graduate from the FBI Academy School later this month. That's all I have, at least for now."

Kevin asked. "Where do we stand on the president's armored limousine's?"

"They're going into service as we speak. There will be about three weeks of tests on the use of the escape hatch and the vehicle's remote operation. Unfortunately we have to simulate getting out of the vehicle through the trap door, as construction on the four identified escape tunnels won't be completed until November. That will give the president only six weeks to practice getting out of the damn thing." George coughed and he took a moment to clear his throat.

"Rick, you should know that we still don't have any idea who Saddam's sleeper agent is. Can you give us any help on this?"

"I'll try, George. Give me a little time to think this out. Where do we stand on the tracking of Salvetti in Europe?"

"You handle that, Peter." Replied Vince Green.

"My agent, the one with the code name *LambieDog,* is back in Europe." (Rick swallowed hard after hearing her mentioned. He really liked that woman, a lot.) "She was also assigned to work on the judge, along with Rick. She was reassigned to work for a creep in Spain named, Alfredo Surtain. He's been in the kidnap business for about a year now, which is a field where *LambieDog* has excelled in Italy. She is going to try to get close to Salvetti. I haven't any idea on how she will do that. I'm in contact with her. So I'll keep you posted if she comes up with anything. I'm heading back to Europe after this meeting."

ACE asked. "George, have you decided to tell the Speaker of the House, Thom Crowell, that we found out Victor Salvetti carries a grudge dating back to when he sent his older brother to prison, and that the brother was killed there?"

"No, I was not. We don't need any more people to know about this conspiracy."

"Well, the least you have to do is furnish him Secret Service protection, don't you think?"

"We already have two agents assigned to him. They work alternate twelve-hour day shifts. Christ, I can't put any more agents on him. Even now I'm short of trained agents. And remember, I still have to cover the president more so as long as this threat is present."

"I don't see that you have any choice. Can't you rehire some retired agents to fill the gap? How about trying to acquire some of the agents that have left the secret service for personal reasons. Maybe some of them may have solved their problems, and will be willing to return to active service?"

"I'll look into it. My goal will be to cover him twenty-four/seven. But I'm not going to tell the speaker that he's under extreme risk, not unless I have to. ACE, I'll need your authorization to hire more agents. It's going to put me way over budget."

Consider it covered. I'll get the president's approval for the overrun. Unless there is anything else, this meeting is closed. You will each be contacted when we plan to meet again. Thank you all."

After the meeting was over, ACE pulled Kevin aside. "What's with Rick? He seems to have changed his appearance. And those earrings, where did they come from?" She asked rhetorically.

"The man you know as Rick, is no more. What you see is a different person. Please accept that as necessary, ACE. Believe me, you don't want to know. It provides you with deniability."

She nodded her understanding.

* * * *

Santanna and Gunter left the restaurant. Each had their fill of food, as well as drink. They were both a bit tipsy. Exiting the cab in front of

Gunter's house, Santanna fell on his face. They both laughed. There was no idle talk to be captured by the surveillance team this evening.

But the next morning, as they sat having their breakfast, was another thing. "So what's the caper I'm here to assist you with?" Asked Santanna.

"First we're going out this morning and buying a car. It will help us to get around Chicago. You'll do the driving."

"What do you mean, me? I hate to drive. And this is a strange town to get around in."

"Okay, than I'll drive and you make the hit."

"You want me to make a hit on someone. I…I've…I've never killed anybody before. I'd be happy to be the driver and let you handle the important stuff. Besides, I don't know who you're going to kill."

"Back in early February, before I went to Spain, I was sent out here to get rid of an old lady who knew too much for her own good. I put her in her car and started it; then I closed the garage door. She was killed by asphyxiation. Everybody thought it was a suicide, because her old man had recently been killed. Everybody except the son, who just so happened to be a sergeant in the Detroit police force."

"Gee, Gunter, how'd you get her to sit in the car while she was being gassed?"

"That was the easy part. You see I just pinched this spot in her neck," Gunter grabbed Santanna's neck in that vital spot, taking his hand from him when he could tell he was ready to black out. "And she passed out."

A groggy-feeling Santanna fought his way back to consciousness. "What the fuck did you do that for? Scared the shit outa' me, ya did."

"Sorry Santanna, but you asked. I thought you would like to see how I did it. Let's get back to the caper. The son has still been calling and asking his police friends about what he calls his mother's murder. He's changed jobs since back then, and has been spending these last months attending school at the FBI academy. He 's coming back to town after he graduates. The word came down that we should snuff him, and put an end to all his rabble-rousing."

"Cheez, we're gonna' hit an FBI guy?"

"Makes no difference; a hit's a hit, is the way I see it. That's about it. He's attending a special award dinner sponsored by his father's union, before he goes on to his first assignment with the bureau. I'll nail him with a Teflon-coated bullet when he leaves the place after getting the award. You'll be driving the car. All you have to do is drive me to the union hall where the award meeting is to take placc, and pick me up when you hear the shots. Then we'll both drive to Washington, DC for our next assignment. That's all there is to it."

"I'm glad I'm the driver. I never killed anybody before." He said it once again, as he wanted Gunter to be sure he heard him.

The police heard every word. Lieutenant Mario Amati was notified, and he put in an immediate call to Bill Thiebold, who was in his final week at the academy. He gave him the details of what was recorded so he would be ready for the man who would try to shut him up, as they did his parents. It would be a chance for him to partially even the score, at least just a little.

Mario called Rick and told him they were about to capture the killer of Thiebold's mother. They were going to wait until he made his attack on Bill Thiebold, and only then arrest him. They couldn't use the wiretap information they had recorded, since the warrant used was fraudulent, and they didn't want to take a chance that it would be thrown out of court at a later date. Deep down, Mario wanted Bill to be given a chance at his mother's killer.

At the academy Bill Thiebold had recently been shown the new type of vest that was supposed to deflect any type of bullet. It was large enough to cover the full body, as well as the groin area. Best yet, it was lightweight, and not nearly as uncomfortable to wear as earlier models.

Bill was one of the first operatives to receive the new FBI issue of protection. It was exactly what he needed.

On the evening of the award he donned his protective vest and made sure his thirty-millimeter Glock handgun was cocked and fully loaded. He set the safety in the off position; he knew from his recent training that every second in an altercation would count.

The award presentation went off without a hitch. Bill could see many of his ex-buddies from the department stationed at various places in the hall. He spotted Mario amongst them, moving from place to place and checking on the placement of his men. As Bill shook hands with everyone who offered to do so, he looked around to see if he could spot his attacker. As he stepped out of the vestibule his eyes scanned 180 degrees in front of him, searching for movement. He spotted the shadow of a man emanating from the alley next to the building, simply because a light in the back of the building was just switched on.

He reacted by dropping to one knee while pulling his gun and reaching out pointing it towards a target, as he was taught to do at the academy. This stance limits the silhouette seen by an adversary. A volley of bullets whizzed over his head. He started sending return fire. Every one of his bullets hit their mark in the general area of the man's chest. Gunter dropped to the ground; he was dead.

Santanna heard the gunfire and approached the hall, driving at approximately thirty miles per hour. He could see Gunter's body, seemingly void of life, lying in a crumpled heap. He drove right past the pickup spot, and kept going all the way to Washington, DC.

When he arrived there he tried to find where Ricky was staying. He remembered hearing that he was supposed to stay at the home of Judge Benjamin He found the judge's name in the phone book.

The judge picked up after two rings. "This is a friend of Ricky's calling. He said I should look him up if I ever came to Washington. Is he there?"

"Ricky, someone for you. For Christ's sake, give him your cell phone number. I was just about to doze off." The judge heard him pick up, thought about listening, but then thought better of it. "Ricky, here."

"Ricky, it's me, Santanna. Bad things have happened. Can I see you? I don't know who I'm supposed to contact."

"Meet me at the all night place called *Greektown Diner,* located on the grand concourse. Do you think you can find it? I'll be there at eleven thirty. Trust me, few people will be around there."

"I'll find it. I'll be there; count on it."

Later that evening, they met at the diner. "Hello, Santanna. What the hell is going on?"

"It's Gunter, he's dead. Shot to death outside a union hall where he went to make a hit. I drove him. Heard it confirmed on the radio. They were waiting for him. He didn't have a chance. I don't know where to go; I was supposed to come to Washington with Gunter. Can you call your contact for me and tell them what happened? Then can you tell me where to go so I can get some sleep? I've been driving for a day and a half straight. I'm not being sought after as an accomplice. No one knows I wuz the driver."

"There's a small motel up the road from here. Sorry, Santanna. I can't bring you home with me. The judge will have my balls. Eat here before you leave. I'll call my contact the first thing in the morning. Then I'll come by and pick you up. The judge is home now that court's no longer in session. Stay safe, Buddy, I've got to get back now before I'm missed. We can catch up tomorrow, and get you a new assignment."

* * * *

They were having a heated argument. "I know that I was told to report to you, but I'm not the person who makes the snatch. I'm the one who plans it all. Supposed the guy we want to take overwhelms me because he's stronger than I am? Think about it; you're being unreasonable." Saila was giving her argument all she had.

Alfredo Surtain snarled. "Listen here, you she bitch. I'm the one running this show. If you don't like it we can both go see the boss, Victor Salvetti. I know that he's in town. He can make the call."

"That's fine with me. I'm sure he'll see it my way. I've been doing kidnappings for him for three years now; only one went wrong. Let's go see him, now. Place the call."

Victor was staying at the Hotel Esplanade. It was a high-class luxury hotel located in the heart of Madrid. Victor always went first class. He was at first annoyed with the call, and then he remembered he wanted to see this gal, Saila Ewe. He heard she was a knockout from the guy who recruited her into the Camorra.

Alfredo stated his case. Then it was Saila's turn. "Mister Salvetti, I don't know if I can work for this man and be as effective as I was in Italy for you. He wants me to do the physical work. I'm the brain who is used to planning everything out, not the brawn. He doesn't even want to discuss the matter. He just wants it his way. He's so damn aggravating."

"Do you have trouble following orders, Miss Ewe?"

"No sir, I don't. But what he wants me to do just doesn't make any sense. I'm a college graduate, with a doctorate no less. Can't you use me someplace else? I've got broad-based skills and I'm very adaptable. Don't you think I've earned a chance to move up in the organization? I think I've paid my dues."

Victor thought about what she had proposed for quite some time before he replied. "You know that you cost me a lot of money with that botched kidnapping, don't you?"

"The kidnapping wasn't botched. It went off as planned. No one told me to steer clear of the Cosa Nostra operation that was going on back in Naples. I don't think that my men and I blew it."

"Okay young lady. I'll give you a try at becoming my personal assistant. You can go now, Alfredo. Go hire someone else to help you. Make sure you check them out first, or you'll end up paying for the mistake."

After he left he asked Saila to have a seat opposite him. "You are as beautiful as they have told me, my dear. You also have quite a bit of spirit. I like that in a woman. I often have a need for a female escort to attend some affairs pertaining to business. You will make a nice addition to my presence on these occasions. Don't worry, I have no designs on your type of woman, preferring someone with less than a delicate taste for lovemaking; I need a dominate woman to fulfill my sexual fantasies. In addition to your other duties you, Saila, will be making these special arrangements for me in every location where we go. I'll provide you with a list to work from so you can make the necessary contacts."

"You're really making me your assistant?" She asked with a somewhat bewildered look on her face. Saila's plan had worked. She was delighted. "That's wonderful, Mr. Salvetti. You won't be disappointed. I'll do anything that you want, anything."

"Please, I want you to call me, Victor. Now let's review what your other duties will be…

After speaking to her for about an hour he brought the conversation abruptly to a close. Good, so far. Your first assignment is to get us two round trip tickets to the United States, first class of course. I don't like to do anything that's not considered the best. Understand I don't like flying on the Concord, so contact one of the other large airlines. My business cover, Victor Fine Italian Leather, Ltd., requires that I attend a meeting at my Maryland offices. Hurry, Saila, we have much to do to get ready."

* * * *

"I'm telling you, Santanna." Ricky was meeting with him once again in the diner. "The powers that be want you to get a permanent place to live near Washington. Get a job, so that you don't call attention to yourself. You'll be receiving your paycheck, which includes cost of living expenses, until your next assignment. And they tell me that's not going to happen until after the first of the year. I'm pretty much in the same boat, except that I have to nursemaid the judge. I don't know what they have in store for us."

"Ricky, what am I supposed to do all that time? I'll go crazy."

"I think you know how to mix drinks. Why not get yourself a job as a bartender? Also, get a girlfriend to help you while away the hours; a good looking guy like you shouldn't have any trouble."

"What about you? Will I see you a lot?"

"Not all the time, Santanna. The judge has me going to college no less, as part of my condition of employment. I'm in summer school now. It's eating up most of my free time. Don't worry, we'll keep in touch." Ricky gave him a paper with his cell phone number, and the number of his contact in Washington. "You give me your address and number as soon as you're settled."

"Oh, one other thing, and it's important. I was told we'd both be contacted shortly to go to a meeting with the big boss, Victor Salvetti. He wants to meet us and tell us what assignments are coming our way. Should be an exciting year."

* * * *

George called the vice president directly. "Yes, George, what is it?"

"Something has recently come up and I want your permission to proceed. It seems that my wife, Carma, who being an ex-agent, received a letter from the government personnel office. She was one of three thousand people contacted and asked to apply for either a full-time position, or a limited-time position with the secret service. It's what we talked about at the last meeting."

"So what do you want me to do? If she wants to come back until after January next year I don't believe that's a problem. You can assign her to work the speaker of the house detail. I don't think anyone will say that it's nepotism, especially if she only takes a short-term assignment. We're in a personnel crunch. Anything else I should know?"

"Good news to report, ACE. The murderer of Thaddeus Thiebold's wife was killed when he went to take out the son. It was the son who shot the man after he was attacked. I guess you can say that's exceptionally good news. Everybody on the team is being notified. We don't have to call a special meeting. There's nothing else new to report." He heard the click as she hung up. George was sure she was on her way to tell the president.

* * * *

"Hey there, Ricky, or whatever the hell your name is these days." Ricky was driving the judge to the restaurant for their evening meal. The judge sat next to him in the front seat where he liked to ride.

"You don't have to yell, judge. I'm sitting right next to you. My name is still Ricky. There is nothing happening at the moment on what you think is my assignment." He smiled."

"I still think you're in the CIA;" and then as an afterthought, "or something like it. Would you tell me what is going on if you thought I had a need to know? And where the hell is my brass-embellished cane? I don't like that plain one that you got me as a replacement. You are going to give it back, aren't you."

"That's a lot of questions; more than usual, judge. Let's take them in order. I am not, nor have I ever been in the CIA. As for 'something like it', I can't tell you anything more…at this time. I would love to tell you something that I think you have a need to know. Right now, that's not anything. As for your cane, the brass part of it needed to be polished, and there was a screw that holds the brass attached to it that's missing. I'm your valet, so I sent it out to have it fixed. I gave you only a temporary replacement. Give it another week. You'll get it back as good as new. You can place a bet on it. Let's change the subject. What are you going to have for supper? I'm having veal."

"All you give me is a lot of doublespeak, and then you start to talk about something else. I still think you're a *spook*."

* * * *

Saila had made the arrangements where they were to stay in Maryland. They took a suite of rooms, with two bedrooms and two baths, and a large living room with a built-in bar. It was at the best hotel available in Harve-de-Grace.

Ricky had received his call to attend the meeting scheduled with Victor Salvetti only an hour before it was to be held. He had to drive very fast to be able to arrive on time. He had thought about trying to smuggle in a tape recorder, but thought better. Victor would surely be able to detect the use of such a device. When he got to the hotel, Santanna was pulling up in the parking lot. They went to the suite together. Victor's men had swept the suite for bugs one half hour before any of the invitees arrived. He was always a cautious man. Saila had the bar stocked with only the finest liquor.

She had also made arrangements for Victor's pleasure to take place after the meeting. He told her:

"Go get yourself laid, and don't come back to the suite until tomorrow morning. Get another hotel room. I'll pick up the tab. Next time, set me up in another room where I can enjoy myself without any interruptions."

He could see a pained expression on her face. She thought she had done something wrong, and she had.

"Don't be so upset, you didn't know, but now you do."

Santanna was the first to enter after Victor called for them to come in. As Ricky entered, Saila exited her bedroom. It was a shock for both to see her; actually, Ricky was more than shocked. Victor introduced himself to those present and asked them to have a drink and to sit down and wait for the others scheduled to be at the meeting. Last to show up were Doctor Wilhem Ahrens, and his two ever-faithful goons who came along with him. Victor called the meeting to order.

"I like to meet all the people who work for me personally, especially when they are going to be working on a job that will bring a huge amount of money into the organization. I believe you all know my personal assistant, Saila Ewe. If she tells you anything, assume that it came directly from me. Now, the main reason why I've called you here today is to let you know that in your own small way you are all going to become part of history. You see, the Camorra has been hired to kill the President of the United States."

He paused for effect, and to let what he said sink in.

"There will be three separate prongs to the plan to assassinate him. At approximately the same time, confusion caused by an attempt on the president's life will be used as a diversion to also kill the Speaker of the House of Representatives. There is a blood debt to be paid. A sleeper agent, a person that has been supplied to us by a foreign power, will perform the latter assassination. You will not be involved in this attempt."

"When are we supposed to do this? I won't be able to finish construction on the device until August, and the explosives won't be available until October." Asked Ahrens.

Victor gave him a hard look. "I'm getting to that. The date of the attack is set for Thursday, January thirtieth next year; so as you can see we have plenty of time. Doctor Ahrens men are currently working on fitting a dumpster with explosives. Don't look so puzzled. The side of this dumpster will be made to house the charge. They are building a false wall to the unit to place the explosive device into. It is what they call a SHAPE charge, and when detonated by remote control, will discharge all of its destructive power in an outward direction. It will be of sufficient strength to topple a very heavy limousine on its side."

"It will absolutely be ready on time, Mr. Salvetti." Offered Ahrens, attempting to gain back grace with Victor.

"Once on its side, the top of the limo is vulnerable as the stanchions holding up the roof have been compromised. However, this is only the backup plan. Yet there are more details you must know in order to prepare. Approximately one week earlier, on the main road leading directly to the White House from Hall of Representatives, and directly opposite an adjoining side street, a construction project has been scheduled to begin.

"Santanna and Blanco are to search the area and identify the best place to mount this attack. I suggest that you two scout the area tomorrow, and call in to your contact with the street coordinates. The construction plans are to be performed by others, including placing a look-alike dumpster directly out in front. You will not be concerned about this part of the plan.

"During the morning hours on the day of the planned attack, Santanna will drive a special truck loader to the spot and pick up the dumpster, now filled with building debris. You will drive it to an identified location four blocks away, where Blanco will pick up the modified dumpster and return it to the pick-up point. Place it exactly in the same position where Santanna picked up the other one. There will be marks on the ground. Secret service agents can check it out all they want. The false wall in the new dumpster will hide the explosives. Dr. Ahrens will be standing one thousand feet from the dumpster, and will detonate it as soon as the limousine comes abreast.

"You, Santanna, will then be positioned down the adjacent side street in an SUV. Once you see the limousine lying on its side, start the car and aim your vehicle to hit the top of the limo. As soon as you are in a direct line with your target, push in the red lever on the dash and the wheels will lock and the speed will stay at twenty miles-per-hour. You should have no problem exiting the vehicle. There is another explosive device in the front of the SUV that will explode on contact. You will be far away when that happens."

"You're sure that I can get out of the SUV, Mr. Salvetti?"

Salvetti was annoyed at what seemed to be a dumb question. "Should be no problem, since the vehicle will be traveling slow. Now I said three prongs. This is only the final plan in the event the first two attacks are not effective. You all know about the brass cane that the Associate Justice will bring to the State-of-the-Union speech that evening. Once he leaves the cane in the bathroom stall as programmed to do, a janitor who works for me will take it into a secure area and assemble the brass parts into the gun. He will then shoot the president from a hidden perch that has been selected to provide him with the best angle for a shot. The Secret Service agents assigned to protect the president will kill the assailant. He expects to die, and his family will be rewarded for the remainder of their lives. Do not fret; the man has pancreatic cancer and has only been given a year to live. He told me that he was expendable for the good of the organization. I applaud his dedication."

"That's the second prong that you've told us about, Mr. Salvetti. What if the man fails?" Queried Ricky.

"Then I have someone else who will be standing near the president who will touch him with the tip of a needle, one that has been coated with a fast-acting poison. And if that fails, then we have the attack on his limousine as a fallback. Do not worry, the president will be dead that evening, and so will the speaker of the house. I guarantee it.

"This meeting is over. Make sure that you perform your assignments. Please leave now. I have other plans."

"Hold up a minute, Ricky. Would you like to buy me a drink in the bar?" Asked Saila.

"If he won't, then I will." Chimed Santanna. The three of them went to the bar.

After only two drinks, Santanna said. "I want you two to know I never killed anybody before. I hope they get him the first time. I gotta' go now. I got a lot to think about."

"Where are you staying?" Saila asked Ricky. "I'm supposed to get a room at this hotel. Would you like to join me?"

"What happened to change what you told me when we last met? You know that I won't refuse you, don't you? I thought I'd never see you again."

"I was wrong, Ricky. I can't get you out of my mind. Make love to me. I need you so much." They left the bar arm in arm. When they entered the hotel room, a shadowy figure stepped out from the darkness. He had been following them. It was one of the goons who worked for Dr. Ahrens. Mr. Salvetti wanted to know whom his assistant was sleeping with. There were no secrets to be kept from this man.

CHAPTER 8

Rick had spent the evening with Saila. After they had made love for the third time she asked.

"When do you think we can get together again?

He looked at her funny like with a frown on his face, as if to say he was not *Superman*.

"Don't be silly, I don't mean now. I mean when do you think we can meet again?"

"I'm not sure when that could be. We can't make a regular thing out of us meeting, at least until we are both finished with our assignment. Then we have to find a way of getting ourselves out of the Camorra. That will be no easy task. We can lay in some plans when we see the light at the end of this foray growing brighter. Until then, we are victims of chance."

CONSPIRATOR called his contact immediately after leaving the hotel room. She was asleep when he left the room at six AM. It was difficult to leave her side but he knew how important it was he forward the information they had been provided, by non-other than Victor Salvetti himself, to the task force.

While he waited for the routine call back to the pay phone, as per contact protocol, he thought about the latest tryst with Saila and the immense pleasure he had while he was with her. He allowed his mind to wander, and to even wonder what it would be like to spend the rest of his life with her. She had expressed her love for him and he too was falling in love with her; it was something he knew they had no right doing, given their current line of work. Unfortunately, the human sprit doesn't always follow the rules set out by other people in charge.

He understood she was under close scrutiny because she worked directly for Salvetti. "I'll see that the information we obtained last night gets to the right people," he had told her before they dosed.

The ringing phone broke into his deliberation of pleasurable thoughts as to what was possible and what was not. He reached for the handset. "This is CONSPIRATOR."

"Rick, its Kevin. You just caught me going out the door. What's up?"

"I'd like to meet with you now, Kevin. Could we meet somewhere for breakfast? I've got a lot of information to give to the task force, but first I'd like to discuss some strategy on tracking down that unknown undercover agent. Set up the meeting with the task force for two PM this afternoon. I don't want everyone in the room privy to what I'm planning to do, and I'd like to talk over some of the details. I need your input before I put myself into motion."

They met in a private dining room at a Japanese restaurant that was not open to the public for the day yet. The owner was a friend of Kevin's who let them in. His name was Johnny Yamoto. "Long time no see, Kevin. You two can talk to your hearts content back in my office, that is, after I get you some breakfast first. Then I have to head over to the market to pick up fresh produce. None of the help will be showing up until eleven. No one can hear you in the office as I have it rigged with white noise." In about fifteen minutes he served them hot coffee and ham and eggs with toast.

"Let yourselves out when you're finished talking. Just lock the door on the way. And don't bother saying anything. I owe you plenty, Kevin. This is only a small payback."

They spent a few minutes while devouring their meal during which they had a few light moments. Then Rick gave him the details about what had gone on in the meeting held by Salvetti.

"Okay, Ricky." Kevin smiled when he used his alias.

"This is great news for the task force. I'll want you to make the presentation to them. Do you have any more information on the CIA's plant, *LambieDog*? Peter Grace said that he wanted her to get close to Salvetti. She apparently arranged to do just that."

"Saila, that's her name, Saila Ewe. She told me that she pushed her luck with Salvetti, and that it held. Now she's his special personal assistant."

"So, what's this idea you have about uncovering the deep cover agent?"

"You're aware I speak Arabic, and I also understand Farsi, although I'm rusty on both. Summer school is drawing to a close in another week, so I have a whole week to talk with my Egyptian friend and have him sharpen me up. I'm planning on taking a couple of week's break from the judge. I have a few friends in the Iraqi National Congress; they're an underground group operating in Iraq; mostly in Baghdad. The can get me in and out of that country, where I'm going to find out the name of the person assigned to kill the president. As for a disguise all I have to do is wear a mustache, since almost everyone there does. My skin coloring will get me past any local scrutiny. I figure that from this side of the world were not going to find out anything. From the people in Baghdad I hope to find out whom that person is and what's being done to guarantee she will do Saddam's bidding."

"Jesus, Rick. That's a tall order you're setting yourself up to fill. What makes you so sure you can pull this off?"

"There's an old Indian saying: If you got balls, use them. I plan on doing just that. Remember I've already spent time in Iraq during the Gulf War. I'd tell you not to worry, but I know you will. First thing I've got to do is to tell my employer I'm leaving him for a vacation of sorts. He's a cagey old guy and will want to know what I'm doing for the CIA. He still is convinced I work for them. Tell me, Kevin. Do you see any holes in my plans?"

Kevin lowered his head as he spoke; he said it from the depth of his heart. Rick was like a son to him.

"No, I can't see any holes. It's just that what you're doing is so damn dangerous. May God speed you in your travels and keep you safe, Rick. I wish you luck and good fortune in this endeavor; you'll need it. If I can be of any help, let me know?"

"I'll see you at the meeting with the task force." Rick said as he walked out of the restaurant.

The vice president opened the meeting. Attendees were George, Kevin, Rick and Vince. Peter Grace was unavailable having only recently flown back to Europe.

"Why don't you lead off and tell us what you found out, Rick?"

"Thank you, Ma'am—I attended a meeting called by Victor Salvetti. I'm part of his in-group now since I've been able to penetrate the Camorra. Peter's agent also attended. I've actually got an assignment on the day they're going to try and kill the president. Here's what I found out…"

After he finished, it was George who broke the silence.

"I'll have them fix those limousines immediately. I find it hard to believe they obtained this information."

"Please, don't do anything." Rick chimed. "If you do you'll give me away. Victor has to believe that his plans are running in place and are fine-tuned. All he has to do is get word that we are re-welding roof supports and he'll know that we know. The only place anyone could find that information out was at the meeting. Neither Peter's agent or myself can withstand another run at our credibility. Besides, the president will have already exited the limo via the trap door."

It was obvious George was frustrated. He immediately fired back at Rick. "Have you got any leads on the sleeper agent?"

"Not yet, George, I'm still working on it. But you had better direct yourself to the other problem I've just pointed out during my briefing. Somebody who has access to the president as he leaves the hall will try to jab him with a needle coated with poison. The only persons who will be near the president at that time will be members of either the House or the Senate. Thus, you have another unknown to identify. I wouldn't worry too much about finding the janitor who will be using the exploding cane. That's covered. I'll be out of town for awhile trying to get a lead on who is the sleeper agent."

ACE spoke. "Let's end the meeting now. I have a lot to tell the president. Vince, you had better update Peter on what's going on. Perhaps his agent can get more information about Salvetti's plans." Neither Kevin nor Vince had said a word. However, they were intent listeners.

Rick was the first one out the door. As George left the meeting room he was subdued and deep in thought.

Back at the house during the next week the judge asked him many questions, all to no avail. Ricky wouldn't crack and tell him anything. In the end he wished his manservant well on what he called his big adventure. He didn't begrudge him the few weeks he was taking leave of his duties. The judge just knew Ricky was doing something important. He waved to him as he entered the waiting cab to take him to the airport.

"Stop off and pick up my associate at seventy-five South Worth Street. He should be waiting outside his apartment house." Rick welcomed his Egyptian friend, Saad Saada, into the cab. Saad had decided to go along with him, when he questioned why he wanted to upgrade his language skills. Rick had told him he was going into Iraq on an information-gathering mission.

Saad was in Iraq during the Gulf war for the same reason as Rick. They were members of an elite special-forces group brought directly from civilian life into the armed forces, after being sought out by the government because they knew the language and they needed people to operate behind enemy lines. He was not as fortunate as Rick. Saddam's Republican Guard captured him and his two associates, and they were tortured almost constantly for three days. The fast moving forces of the coalition rescued him from the hangman's noose in the nick of time. His two associates were already put to death as spies. He had a score to settle with the Iraqi's; the cigarette burn marks all over his body still hurt whenever the weather changed.

Rick was using his own passport and not the one he carried for his alter-identity, Ricky. His hair had grown back fully by now and he did not wear the earrings that Saila had given him. While waiting to board their plane to take them to Amman, Jordan, Rick for the first time provided Saad with some specific details of the plan. They discussed what they would do if they were caught while in Iraq.

"Suppose the police or that Republican Guard picks us up?" Asked Saad.

"We have to be prepared to do whatever it takes to get free. There's too much hanging on what we're going over there to do." Answered Rick.

"I just wanted to be sure if we had to take a life, that you would be up to the task. I have no qualms about what I may be called on to do. It sure as hell beats spending any amount of time as guests of Saddam's prison system."

Saad placed a lot on the promise of Rick that he could be trusted and that he could not tell Saad more than he had a need to know.

He explained that they would go by truck to the border crossing leading into Iraq. After entering Iraq at night by foot, only then would they don their mustaches and other clothing disguises, and pick up necessary forged papers Rick had arranged for them by phone and a wire transfer to a numbered Swiss account. Rick's name on the documents was Ibrahim Eddin, and he was alleged to be an Iraqi citizen. Saad Saada used his actual name and he was also listed on his papers as an Iraqi. It was easy to bribe the local tribesman, even by long distance, which wanted nothing to do with Saddam and his Baath' Party. They mounted camels in Jabal 'Unazah, Iraq, for the 450 kilometer trip to Baghdad, most of it through the vast desert making up more than half of the western portion of the country.

"If Kevin finds out that I've enlisted your help without first receiving his authorization he would throttle me. But I'm glad you talked me into taking you along. I'm not so stubborn that I don't think I can use your help. You said your cousin, Hafez abu Saada, has close ties with members of the Iraqi National Congress."

"Yes, he has already made arrangements with three men who are plotting the overthrow of the regime who had brought so much devastation to their homeland. We are meeting them at a place called The Oasis. It is a watering hole west of Baghdad on the outskirts of a town called Habbaniyah. They will wait there for us for only five more days, so we must make good time across the desert. They are prepared to answer any of your questions for which they have knowledge. They will of course request a donation for their cause, whether they help us or not. You do have the one thousand US dollars in five's and ten's; all worn bills?"

Three days later they met up with the three men; all were Kurds from the northern part of Iraq. To show good faith Rick gave them the money up front. They seemed very eager to help in any way they could. They sat around a campfire and Rick began his inquiry. He spoke in Arabic. Saad had to break in a few times as he mispronounced some of his words.

"Someone has been pledged by Saddam Hussein to perform an assassination in the United States. This person is believed to be an Iraqi citizen that has been an undercover sleeper agent residing in the USA. I need to know the name of this person. I already know it is a female we are looking to identify. I would also like to find out what kind of a hold Saddam has on this woman. Is he holding a family member hostage? Or possibly, is the woman a fanatic who feels she owes total allegiance to Saddam to perform this heinous task. I need all the details you can uncover. It's not much to go on, but please see what you can find out? Saad and I will only be able to remain in this general area for seven days. Any longer will put our lives in jeopardy. To arrange a meeting set these rocks as I am showing you. If we see them piled in this manner we will meet you at the same location later that night. Contact us with any information that you can come up with. Remember, time is of the essence."

They had to stay somewhere close in order to be able to check and see if a meeting was to be made. They decided they would go into Baghdad to find food and logging, as it seemed a better cover to be where there were many people. They would return each night to check the position of the rocks. Once in Baghdad, Saad sought out his cousin, Hafez abu Saada, who ran a small Egyptian restaurant located in the heart of the city. He had lived in Iraq for almost twenty years. His one claim to fame was that Saddam's son, Qusay, had come to his establishment once and stated that he liked the food. He said that he would tell his father to eat there. Hafez fed them and let them sleep in the back of his establishment.

Early the next afternoon they started their trek back to the place called The Oasis. They found the rocks stacked as Rick has shown them. They waited until it was dark when the three hired spies arrived. The men were excited with what they had found out. The non-bearded one spoke for them. They never did get his name. He spoke using Farsi.

"We have made much progress. Twelve years ago, an entire family of Italian nationality, consisting of a husband and wife, and two daughters were arrested by the Republican Guard and brought before Saddam. No one knows what the charges against the group were, but two days later they were deported back to Italy, all except the older daughter. She was reported to be a college graduate and spoke English fluently along with her native Italian. It is said that she was sent on an Iraqi approved student visa directly to the United States. Three members of Saddam's elite Republican Guard staff escorted the rest of the family back to Italy. That's all we have, so far. If we have additional information by tomorrow, we will set the stones. Stay safe, my friends."

On their way back to Baghdad, two policemen stopped them and their papers were examined. They never showed any identification. One policeman got right in Rick's face. "These papers are forged. Anybody can see that by looking at them. However, for a small fee we will let you go about your business."

There was no one around while this confrontation was taking place. They were currently standing at the edge of the desert. Rick reached under his outer garment as if searching into his pocket for his money, in order to pay the bribe. From a point below his waist the heel of his hand rose swiftly into the bridge of the nose of the policeman. The man dropped into a heap at his feet. Rick was sure he was dead before he hit the ground, because the bone in the man's nose was driven deep into his brain. The other alleged policeman charged at Rick when he saw his partner drop, but Saad moved with lightning speed, and grabbed the man from behind with an arm around his throat. With his other hand he twisted the man's neck and heard a snap. He had broken his neck.

Saad spoke. "Let's see whether these two really are the police. I have my doubts." All they found was money on the two of them; no official papers or badges, or whatever they used in Iraq to identify police, were found on either one. They kept the money these men had taken from other people they had robbed. Rick would use it to purchase transportation out of Iraq. They buried the two in the desert in the deepest graves they could manage using only their bare hands to dig with. Roaming around Iraq was certainly not a safe thing for two visiting strangers to the area. They made their way back to their lodging at Saad's cousin's place, believing that no one had seen them.

Checking the next day they found the rocks were not stacked by late afternoon. They used the free time to purchase a small powerboat with the money they had stolen from the two robbers. They planned to leave the country by taking the boat down the Tigress River from the heart of Baghdad into the Persian Gulf at the port of Al Faw. They would then head to Kuwait where they could catch a flight home, so they thought. This was a five hundred-kilometer trip. During the trip they would actually skirt Iran as they entered the gulf, and would have to be extremely careful.

The next late afternoon they found the rocks stacked. Rick was hoping against hope the men had more complete information to report, although he was grateful for what they had already told him. As the sun went down only two of the three men showed up at The Oasis. The one who had done all the talking for the group so far was not with them, and they were upset.

The tall one offered an explanation. "Our friend and fellow patriot has been taken by Saddam. I do not believe we will ever see him alive again. This is the price we must pay if we want to liberate our country. But this is not your worry. Besides, we have found out more about the Italian woman and her family. The men who accompanied them back to Italy are assigned to kill the family if and when this woman, the daughter living in the United States, fails to complete the assignment when it is given to her. Also, in the event Saddam is ever overthrown they have instructions to terminate all of them. The men assigned to this task have been living close to the family in Italy all these years."

"Did you happen to get her name?" Asked Rick.

"Not the name of the woman as she is now known in the United States. We hear that she is married to somebody high up in the government. But we do have the name of the family..." He hesitated for a moment as he tried to formulate the words he had heard into Farsi. "The family name is Cappiletti. They are supposed to be living in a place called Leuica. This town, *it is said to be positioned on the southernmost tip of the heel of Italy's boot.* Forgive me for not making any sense, but I am only repeating what I have been told. I have no idea what I am telling you."

"Thank you for the information you have been able to get for me. It's a shame that you were unable to learn the name of the woman, or what she now calls herself."

"No, I'm sorry that we could not get her married name, but I was able to find out her first name when she was taken by Saddam. It is Carmella. Is that any help?"

"It will have to be. Thank you again." Rick gave the two men most of the extra money taken from the bandits, that he did not have to spend on the boat. "I am sorry about the loss of your friend. Use this money for your cause."

"He was his brother, and he pointed to the other man who was with him." He said it in passing as the conversation ended.

Rick and Saad went back to Baghdad to stay the evening. Their plan was to pick up supplies that evening and head over to the boat they had purchased to allow them to make their escape down the Tigress. Hafez was sorry to see them planning to leave him. He thought quite awhile about joining them and leaving Iraq, but had decided he had too much invested in his restaurant.

The next morning, after saying their goodbye and offering Hafez their thanks for his assistance, they gathered their supplies and went to where the boat was moored. Two of Saddam's police arrested them before they could board the boat. The arresting officers allowed them to put their supplies on board the boat before taking them into custody. They were actually friendly and bantered with them on the ride into town. They were taken to headquarters for questioning in regards to the murder of two men who were found buried in shallow graves at the edge of the desert. It seems a dog digging in the area had led a curious nomad to discover the bodies. He had remembered seeing two men matching their descriptions leaving the area with damp sand in evidence on their knees.

While in custody they were questioned separately in small windowless rooms. There were bloodstains on the walls; no doubt from some unfortunate souls who had ran afoul of the Iraq police. It was found out through intensive questioning that they both denied emphatically having anything to do with anyone on the edge of the desert. Unfortunately the interrogation also brought out the fact that they had no one whom could vouch for where they were during the alleged time of the murders. They did not want to involve Hafez. They were questioned all day, and put into a holding cell without being fed. They were told to expect more of the same until they confessed to their crime.

Once in the cell Rick let Saad know that he still had his bone knife. It seemed that the arresting police were careless and had failed to search them thoroughly. After midnight there was a shift change. Only one guard replaced the daytime jailers. At one in the morning the prison occupants had settled down for the evening. Snores were loud and the smell of farts permeated the cellblock. Rick called the guard feigning sickness. He loudly complained that he had violent pains in his stomach. When the guard went to the cell he found Rick rolling on the floor in pain. The guard opened the cell and attempted to get the prisoner on his feet. The next thing he knew there was a large white knife at his throat and he was warned not to sound an alarm.

Saad tried some reasoning with the man. He spoke in Farsi. "Look here. We have a few options. We can kill you and make our escape. Or you can let us go and if anyone asks about us you can say that we were probably already gone when you came on duty. Claim that you never saw us in the cell and that it was empty. We know that no one checked out the cell when your tour began. Now if you do as we're telling you we will give you all this money. Remember, nobody escaped from your control because as far as you knew nobody was here."

The man was eager to accept the offer. He knew that if someone escaped from the cellblock he would be in serious trouble. Besides he needed the money. Rick made up his mind for him. He drew a trickle of blood at the nape of the man's neck, and said. "If you alert the authorities to our being missing and we are returned to this prison, I will personally cut off your head." He had made his point and Saad gave the man some money.

Once out of the prison they headed to where the boat was moored and found it was not guarded. Saad took a copy of a map of the area and drew a route taking them north up the Tigress to Dahuk near the border of Turkey. He marked the name of the boat at the bottom of the map. Since there was no one in the harbormaster's shack located at the end of the pier, Saad forced the map into the space under the door of the shack. "Rick, I'm hoping this will buy us some time. At the very least it should show that we are not avoiding the police and have nothing to hide by leaving them with our planned route. It's what I hope they think."

They set off at three in the morning with a semi-bright moon and clouds moving west and obscuring the moon as they passed down the Tigress at slow speed. If they attempted to move too fast they would use up their petrol supply rapidly and be forced to stop on their journey to obtain more. It was their desire to make the entire trip without putting in to shore.

They were able to travel 200 kilometers during the next fifteen hours, averaging a little more than thirteen kilometers per hour. Traffic grew heavy during the day and this allowed them not to stand out. By mid afternoon a helicopter warship could be seen flying up and down the length of the Tigress. That they were looking for someone was obvious. It was almost dark when the gun ship made a low swooping pass directly overhead. Rick and Saad went below deck after locking the steering straight ahead. Other boats in the vicinity were warned by loud speaker to pull to shore. The Iraqi's had apparently found who they were looking for. With the next pass overhead the gun ship raked the boat from stem to stern with machine gun fire. One bullet that penetrated the boat's cabin hit Saad in the forearm, while another bullet creased Rick across his cheek. It did not look good for them as the gun ship readied for another pass. Rick was in the process of putting a tourniquet on Saad's arm when they heard the loud roar of a jet engine. It was close. Rick stuck his head outside the cabin in time to see a missile from an F-16 American fighter jet leaving the plane and heading toward the helicopter. Moments later he saw the explosion as the helicopter was blown to bits.

Rick steered towards shore while he wiped the blood from his face with the back of his hand. He nudged the bow of the boat into the shoreline. Checking the map he found they had made it as far as approximately ten kilometers further downstream of the town of Al 'Amarah.

"How's the arm doing, Saad? It looks like it went clean through."

"You stopped the bleeding with the tourniquet. I'm going to sprinkle some sulfur powder that I found in the first-aid kit on both wounds. It should help to control any infection. But the arm hurts like hell. The bullet went through muscle tissue. I'm not going to be much help to you if you need me to use it. Here, will you tie this bandage around my arm and make a sling for me out of my shirt? Do you know what the hell just happened?"

"I'm pretty sure we got lucky enough to get beyond the southern no-fly zone that America and Great Britain had been enforcing in Iraq ever since the Gulf War. With the threat of further attack from the air eliminated we still will have to change our plans. They'll surely send some fast watercraft after us now that they know approximately where we are. Sorry, old buddy, but we're going to have to travel the rest of the way on foot to be able to get out of this fuckin' country. I think that our best bet is to head by the most direct route towards Kuwait."

Rick packed a backpack with provisions, having no idea how long it would take them to clear the country. He checked their cash on hand. All they had left from the money they found on the two desert robbers was a banded pack of 25 piastres notes of Egyptian currency. There were three hundred of them totaling 7,500 piastres. Unfortunately he didn't have the slightest idea as to what it was worth relative to the dollar, or what they were worth in Iraq. More important was how much transportation that much could buy them. Saad had lost a lot of blood and Rick knew that additional stress would wear heavily on his body.

They abandoned the boat after Rick rinsed his face clean of the dried blood in the water of the Tigress. He applied some triple-antibiotic cream and used three Band-Aids he found in the first-aid kit. The final leg of their journey was about to begin. They started the trek on foot while staying as close to the river by walking south along the river road. They came to a small store located on the riverbank where they were able to purchase some dried beef and pastry pancakes that were stale. It was time to test their luck. Rick spoke to the owner in Arabic. The man didn't understand, so he spoke in Farsi.

"All we have is Egyptian money. How much do you want for what you've given us?"

To his pleasant surprise the man smiled and said: "I'll have to charge you more because you have foreign currency. It will cost you fifty piastres for the food and another twenty five for my trouble."

When the man saw the size of the stack of bills that Rick possessed, he wanted more. He seized the moment. Rick could read it in the man's eyes. "What else do you have that we could use?" He asked.

"I have a small gun that I can let you have for only one thousand piastres. Your friend looks like he will need protection."

"Not interested in a weapon. Can you sell us a boat with a motor and enough petrol to take us down to Kuwait?"

"It so happens that I do have a boat with a motor. It will cost you five thousand piastres."

"Throw in the gun and the petrol and we have a deal."

Rick counted out the money and handed it to the merchant. He knew he was being taken, but he had no other choice. He asked, "How many kilometers do we have to go to get to Kuwait?"

"It's 125 kilometers on the Tigress and then you'll have to beach the boat at Al Basrah where it veers off into Iran. After that you must go the remainder of the way directly south on foot, for another twelve kilometers. You should have no problem crossing into Kuwait, as nomads cross the border there, both back and forth, all the time."

Rick peeled off another five hundred piastres and gave it to the merchant. "Swear on the love of Allah that this extra money buys us your silence."

"I swear to Allah. You don't mind if I take back the boat after you have made your trip, do you? I'm sure you won't need it once you leave Iraq."

The engine on the rear of the boat chugged for seventeen hours, but never quit. They arrived in Al Basrah at seven the next evening where they rested and ate their meager rations. The next morning they set out for Kuwait. It was fifteen kilometers, not twelve that they had to travel. The sun was extremely hot and depleted them of all moisture. Saad collapsed in sight of the Kuwait border. Rick carried him the last two kilometers across the border, where they were given water, food and shelter until the evening. At a hospital in Kuwait City Saad's wound was tended to by a doctor who had been trained in the United States and spoke fluid English. It was indeed a small world. Saad opted for a trip to Egypt to recuperate while staying at his family's home.

"You may as well visit your folks while you're in this part of the world. I've received a voucher from my Great Britain office so I'll be leaving you with enough cash to get back home in style when you're ready. Thanks a lot for all your help. I couldn't have done it without you. Get well soon. I'm heading directly back to Washington to plan a strategy to identify that sleeper agent. The information we obtained was worth the trip."

They had been gone for thirteen days.

* * * *

"So, what did you find out when you watched the meeting of the group calling themselves the CLIQUE?" Salvetti asked his agent.

"The meeting bogged down and focused only on a single subject; discussion on the status of the assassination attempt on the president. Since you didn't tell Tobias Whitman anything to pass on to them he made up things to tell them. He said that the plan has been set and that principals involved have all been given their instructions. He also stated that multiple backup plans are in place already." Victor mused quietly. *That idiot has actually guessed where I stand on the attempt.*

"All six of the attendees advised Whitman they were sure they had spotted men who had been following them since that night in January when the contract was set. Two of them asked if they could get their money back and wanted to withdraw their participation. They were scared. No one has seen or heard from Harry Hansen; not even a phone call had been made to any of them. They're all sure that he is so scared that he has left the country and is in hiding. Whitman did a pretty good job on calming their fears and reassuring them that they had done the correct thing for their country. That guy really is a bullshit salesman."

"Do you think any of them are going to spill their guts to the FBI? It's obvious that they're the ones who are following them."

"I don't put trust in any of them. The meeting ended with four of them having a second meeting at the bar in the hotel where they were staying. I listened in on their conversation. There scared shitless. I wouldn't be surprised if they all capitulated to the government and tried to turn *States Evidence* on Whitman and blame him for everything."

"I think you're right. Take the four of them out. Be sure to make it look like an accident."

The headlines of the next week's newspaper read as follows:

> AP October 26 **PRIVATE LEAR JET CARRYING FOUR EXECUTIVES EXPLODES. THE FOUR MEN ON-BOARD WERE RETURING HOME AFTER ATTENDING A BUSINESS MEETING FOLLOWED BY A GOLF OUTING. THE**

JET BECAME ENGULFED IN FLAMES SHORTLY AFTER TAKEOFF. BUSINESS WORLD ROCKED.

Larry Gelbhart, Abhend Ibsen, Bear Crowell and Justin Active, each owner of their own business, along with the plane's pilot and copilot were killed by an explosion after the pilot of the private jet reported to the Control Tower that they had smoke in the cabin following takeoff. The pilot was attempting a hard bank, in order to be able to land immediately, when the plane exploded.

FAA initial investigation indicates a fuel leak ignited when a spark, created by a piece of loose luggage rimmed with metal edging scraped the baggage compartment wall, caused the explosion by igniting fumes that had flooded the area.

Owner of the aircraft, Larry Gelbhart, and his three associates had attended an all night strategy meeting designed to improve the economy, thus enchancing profit margins for their businesses.

* * * *

Rick picked up the newspaper after spotting the headline soon after landing at Washington National Airport. He immediately called Kevin using proper protocol. The return call was fast. He advised him as to what he found out in Iraq, and asked when the next task force meeting was scheduled. After finishing his conversation with Kevin he put in a call to Aldo Frondzi at his Italy office. He was surprised by who answered the call.

"Frondzi Investigations, Vito speaking."

"Vito, this is Rick Banyan. What the hell are you doing answering the phone at the office? You're supposed to be in Bosnia with the Italian army and guarding Maria Tamari while you're on a peacekeeping mission. I've got a big assignment for Aldo and I sure as hell don't want to worry about Kevin's niece."

"Sorry, Rick. The United Nations didn't need the Italian troops anymore. Then we received word the Italian Army didn't want any of us on active service either, so the entire contingent was cashiered out of uniform with Honorable Discharges. Marta, err, I mean Lieutenant Maria Tamari, even received a medal from the United Nations for work she did with the refugees. She's with me at the office now. We're living together; we're planning on getting married when you give us the all clear. I hope that's soon, Rick. She's seven weeks pregnant. I put a call in to your New Jersey office and left a message that I had to talk to you a month ago. We weren't trying to hide anything from you. I've already told Aldo everything. He's going to be our *Best Man*."

"Where's Aldo? I've got to speak to him in a hurry." Rick was already resigned to the facts of life. He would have to rely on the Frondzi brothers to protect Marta. He quickly mulled over the situation, thinking *Chances are the Camorra believed she was dead as a result of what they had staged back in Spain.*

"He's coming in the door as we speak. Don't be pissed at us, Rick. We really love each other. We would have been married already if she wasn't hiding in the army."

"Don't worry, Vito. I'll be attending your wedding around February, next year; that is if everything works out as I've planned. Put Aldo on the phone."

"Pronto, Aldo here."

"I need you to take a contingent of people down to a town called Leuica and make contact with a family named Cappiletti. Family consists of a father, mother and a young daughter who's got to be about twenty or twenty-one by now. Be extremely careful, as they are being watched by three of Saddam's goons. They've been doing that for the past eight years since the family returned from Iraq. Once you size up the situation they're in, I'll be over and we'll lay in plans to take out the goons."

He went on to provide Aldo with all the background details of the situation. "Also, these people must be free of this death squad before Saddam is brought down. I hear that he could go any time now and that will spell immediate trouble. If that is to happen, don't wait for me. Stop them from killing the family as they close out on their assignment."

"I'm just coming off a case, so I can leave for that part of Italy today. What do you want me to do with Marta? I'm going to need Vito to help me with this operation. I can't leave her here on her own."

"Well, you've got the responsibility to watch after her. Tell you what; hire her to work for you. Take her with you out to Leuica. She can be used as cover when you make contact with the family. I guess that by now she speaks pretty good Italian. She can make first contact with the daughter. I don't suppose that she looks pregnant yet? At least I hope not."

"That's good. It will keep Vito all but attached to her. I'll let you know what we find out."

No sooner had he put the phone back in the cradle than it began to ring. Rick surmised that it had to be Kevin calling again. "This is Conspirator."

"Christ, I thought you'd never get off the phone. The task force meeting is scheduled for three this afternoon. We can expect updates from the FBI and the CIA's agent in Europe. You'll be on the docket to make your report last for a change. Unless you have anything else for me, I'll be seeing you at the Watergate."

"Don't hang up, Kevin. Unfortunately, I do have more to report."

Rick filled him in on the unexpected turn of events with his niece, Marta. He also told him what he had set in motion to protect the Cappiletti family. It sounded to Rick like Kevin was shaking it off, and had accepted what had happened. He was heard muttering to himself while he was hanging up the phone. *Damn over sexed* youth…

Chapter 9

Rick stopped off at the judge's house to drop off his bags. He was glad the judge was in session at the Supreme Court, as he didn't want to have to lie to him any more than was absolutely necessary. He had hardly slept on the plane, his mind racing in many directions seeking the best solution. He had arrived early that morning. Thinking he had at least two hours to crash before attending the task force meeting he headed to his bedroom. There was a note prominently displayed on his bed.

Ricky,

Your friend, Santanna, was unable to get in touch with you so he keeps coming around the house asking for you. He's been making a pest of himself. I didn't tell him anything because I don't know anything. He wouldn't tell me what he wanted you for. You had better call him ASAP.

Your employer,

The Judge

PS
Welcome home. I hope you're going to tell me what you were doing for the CIA during the two weeks you were away.

"No rest for the weary." Ricky said out loud, as he dialed Santanna's number and slipped back into his alter ego. It was picked up after the first ring. "Whadda' ya need, Santanna? I told you not to bug the judge. You keep doing that and you're gonna' get me in trouble,"

"Where have ya been? I've got myself a problem. There's this here woman wants me to marry her. I've been stalling until you can tell me what to do. She thinks I love her. I guess that's because I told her I did while I wuz screwing her. Now she wants us to get married. I've never been so scared in my life. You can help me, can't you?"

"Meet me in the restaurant in fifteen minutes. We'll talk about this over breakfast. I ain't ate in more than twelve hours."

Ricky was into a plate of bacon and eggs when Santanna arrived and spotted him at their usual table. "Gee, it's good to see you again, Ricky. Boy, you got one hell of a gash on your face. Where the hell were you?"

"I got a call and had to go somewhere on business. You know, the kind I can't talk to anybody about." He winked at Santanna when he said it

"Sure, Ricky, I understand. Well, here's my situation. I sure hope you can help me. I told you that Anna Mary wants me to marry her."

"Just tell her you're not interested in getting married; tell her you're not the marrying type. If she don't take that for an answer then go find yourself another broad."

"That's the problem. I can't. You know I work tending bar from six at night to two in the morning. I'm working six days a week and I'm making pretty good bucks what with tips and all. But it gets so lonely in that small apartment. One morning Anna Mary comes home with me for a little fun and games. She's really got a great figure; she's great in the sack. She came home with me and..."

"And what?"

"She never left. I guess it's because I asked her to stay. She moved in with all her clothes two weeks ago. Now I don't know how to get rid of her. And you already know that I told her I loved her during a weak moment. But it gets worse."

"What the hell do you mean, it gets worse?"

"Well, you see, I don't really want her to leave. I really like her."

"So you're falling in love with her and you don't know what to do and you expect me to help you. Christ, Santanna, I can't live your life for you. You're no different than anybody else. You're afraid of a commitment. Tell you what. Take her out to dinner on your day off and tell her that while you really like her you're gonna' need some time before you can even think of marriage. Buy her a ring; nuttin' too flashy now. That oughta' get her off your back, at least for awhile anyway.

"Don't get into any knock down drag out breakup with her. It will call attention to you. Remember you and me got a job to do in January. After that we'll have to leave town; maybe go back to Italy. That will end it for you and her in a hurry. So enjoy yourself while you can."

"I knew you could help me, Ricky. You always know what to do. You're right. That's exactly what I'm gonna' do. Thanks, buddy. You really are my best friend, you know. I knew that you would come up with the right thing for me."

They each went their separate ways. Ricky was feeling like a heel, setting up Anna Mary that way, but he had to help Santanna get over a rough emotional moment. Besides, that little talk got him thinking again about how Saila and he would get out of the Camorra when all this clandestine work was put in the past. He had to put it out of his mind and get back to the business at hand.

Stopping off back home he cleaned and put some medicinal makeup on his face to cover his wound. Then he went directly to the Watergate, hoping to have a chance to meet first with Kevin before the task force met.

ACE called the meeting to order. It was a full house. Besides Rick Banyan, Kevin Winslow, George Papadopilis, Peter Grace and Vince Green, there was a new face in the group. "I'd like to introduce the Director of the Federal Bureau of Investigation, Audrey Pidgen. As you all know the FBI has been working on investigating all the members of this group calling themselves the CLIQUE. In light of the recent news making the headlines I've asked her to make today's initial briefing, and to attend all subsequent meetings of this task force."

"Before I comment on the plane explosion, I'd like to tell you what we've uncovered about each of the men in the CLIQUE. Let's start with their leader, Tobias Whitman. At age 58, and being the same age as the president we looked for some personal reasons why he hated him so much. We found out that they knew each other back in high school, and both went on to the same college. It was there that the president started dating a girl by the name of Betsy Speigel. He was a star on the football team and she left Tobias for the dashing and popular football hero. The fling only lasted three months and the future president broke it off, but she was smitten with him and had already become pregnant. She opted to have an abortion performed by some butcher calling himself a doctor. Tobias paid for it to happen, as he was still in love with her. As near as we can tell, he's the one who talked her into having the abortion. Unfortunately, the girl became quite ill and had to leave college. She became despondent after a long illness caused by an infection. Her family put her into a sanitarium for the mentally ill where Tobias visited her frequently. She remained there until her death in 1990."

Kevin asked. "What did Germond Faller do back then when this was taking place?"

"He never knew about the pregnancy nor anything that happened after she left school. He was simply not interested in the girl when he broke up with her. And Tobias Whitman made sure that he would never know. This is the reason why he hates the president so much, even though he was culpable in what happened to her. He's got a lot of money that he inherited from his family, and he's using that money to settle his grudge. Unfortunately he was able to talk the rest of the simpletons in the group into thinking they were going to save their country by having him assassinated."

ACE prodded: "What's going to happen to him when this plot is dealt with and the truth comes out about his involvement?"

"He'll be arrested and charged with conspiracy to commit murder along with an assortment of other charges stemming out of this plot. He's being kept under tight surveillance and will not be allowed to leave the country."

ACE again. "Audrey, I don't feel you have to report on the details of the lives of the four who recently died."

"All I wanted to say about them is that they were really afraid and had been heard talking about backing out of the agreement. I'm sure that agents of the Camorra murdered them. The account of the blast put forth by the NSA and the FAA is basically correct. What was left out of the report was that a catalyst explosion initially penetrated the fuel tank and allowed fumes to fill the fuselage. We know the men who did this and they are about to be taken into custody unless this group wants me to wait until the entire plot is exposed. As for the four dead CLIQUE members, I'm officially closing the file on them. They have already paid the ultimate price for their treachery and treason."

"I think you are wise to sit on this information." Offered Kevin. All the other members of the task force agreed with this course of action.

"Harry Hansen is still under witness protection. He will eventually be granted immunity when he testifies. After he completes his testimony, he will have to live with himself knowing what he has done. That was the agreement."

"There's a few more bad apples in the cart. What's going on with Anton William's and Joseph Polking?" Rick was reading from the confidential transcripts available to all the attendees.

"They're both hiding in their homes under self-imposed captivity. They've spoken to Tobias and he told them to stay cool and not to talk to anyone. We have them under surveillance. We don't need their help to make the case.

"On a lighter note, our new agent, Bill Theibold is on assignment in Texas, He seems to have what it takes to be a fine agent. He told me to send his personal thanks to Rick Banyan for all his help in tracking down the killers of his parents.

"Got one more thing to tell you all. We've identified a number of agents of the Camorra who are active in the United States. As per directions from this task force we have not been arresting these suspects. We've got people following them wherever they go and we know what they're doing at all times. That is, all except one. There is this fellow, Ricky Blanco, who's an Italian petty crook. He's altered his appearance, and is now sprouting a full head of black hair. When he received his Italian passport he was shaven bald. He recently slipped by my men and went out of country and was gone for two weeks, but he's back now and we are unable to confirm the final destination on his trip. We believe he has used a passport under a different name.

"I don't know how he managed it but the only name on the flight manifest was Ricky Blanco. That certainly was not the name on the passport he used. My men thought he was at the airport only to see a friend off and didn't pay enough attention to him. That's how he got by them. They took the plane to Jordan. My people now suspect that they went from there into Iraq to get some information from Saddam. The guy he left the country with has not returned to date. All we know is that he is an Egyptian student by the name of Saad Saada. That's all I have."

The revelation about Rick's undercover personality would call for some modification in his report. Apparently not all members of the group were putting together the pieces of what he had been doing. And now he knew that he too was being followed.

"Next we will hear a report from Peter Grace." Said ACE. "His undercover agent, *LambieDog*, who's working directly for Victor Salvetti, has reported what she heard from a telephone conversation her boss had with someone in congress."

Peter Grace was on center stage, and all eyes and ears were focused on what he had to say. "Saila, that's my agent's name, for the benefit of any of you who didn't know. She recently overheard a conversation Victor was having with someone he called Art. He was talking about this man's ability to get very close to the president on the night after he gives his State of the Union speech. At great personal risk to herself she deemed it necessary to call me immediately to forward this information to us. I think she may have identified the person who is to attack the president with a fast acting poison stick."

ACE spoke up, "Audrey, it looks like this is in the bailiwick of the FBI. I still find it hard to believe that anyone in congress could do such a thing. You'll have to check out every member of the house and senate. Having the name Art should help to cull the list in a hurry, although no one comes to mind with that name. Plan on reporting back to the group on who this person is a week from today. That should be enough time."

Rick's comment was made directly to Audrey. "Ma'am, I suggest that you spread your search to look for anybody with either a second or middle name of Arthur, or Art, or possibly it's even a nickname you have to look for."

"Thanks, Rick. That's a good suggestion."

"George is on next." ACE said. "What do you have for us, George?"

"I'm still upset that I can't reinforce the roof stanchions of the new presidential limousines. But they passed all the other tests of their armament and driving capability. I can also report that the escape tunnels are complete and the president has gone through the routine exiting the trap door on three separate occasions. He's bitching about it but he's doing it as scheduled. He's got to be able to do it without a hitch at least seven more times."

"What about the protection for the speaker of the house?" Asked Vince.

"I'm coming to that. I've been able to re-hire, on a temporary basis until this emergency is over, ex-agents who are fully experienced. In fact, my wife has come out of her self-imposed retirement to be one of them. Nobody is going to get the speaker; the man is being covered 24/7. He's well protected at all times. Now if Audrey can just pin down who that third prong of the attacking force is?"

"I believe that you're up next, Rick." Chimed ACE. She broke into George's wandering diatribe in order to focus attention away from his area of responsibility.

"I've had only limited success in pining down who she is. For starters, Saddam is having the family of the woman who is the sleeper agent watched for more than eight years now. She is not doing this because she has any allegiance to him. There are three agents with orders to kill her family if the sleeper agent fails to act when activated, or even if Saddam is overthrown. This family, named Cappiletti, consisting of a husband, wife and daughter, live in Italy. I have my people over there working on a plan to remove the threat to them."

"Are you saying that she's doing this under duress?" Asked ACE.

"Yes, Ma'am. The sleeper has been here in the USA since they latched on to her family, and she's remained in deep cover since then. Her first name is, or I should say was, Carmella, when the family was taken by Saddam's police while they were visiting Iraq. They were there to assess the effects of the embargo on the children of Iraq for the United Nations. I've learned she is now married to a high-level government employee and no one knows her married name. I still don't know who she is, but I expect to have more information on the family by next week."

"Where did you get this information from, Rick? And what happened to your face? That's an ugly gash you're sporting."

"Sorry, ACE, err Ma'am, but you know I can't reveal any of that kind of information."

"I'm sorry for even asking, Rick. I should know better by now." Kevin smiled when she remembered what he had told her. "Let's break this meeting and plan to meet back here in a week."

Now all Rick had to do was face the judge and tell him that he needed another week off.

* * * *

"What do you mean you will be leaving town next week? You should know by now that I hate living here alone."

"Judge, I'm really not trying to hold out on you. There's a reason why I can't discuss any of my actions with you. I'll tell you this though. I am definitely not a member of the CIA. I've told you this before. I do work for a US government organization, and I do get called away from time to time in order to do certain things. This is another of these times."

"But you're missing so much of you're school work. How can you hope to make it up and graduate on time?"

"Okay judge. You got me. So I'll let you in on one of my secrets. I already have a law degree; in fact I have a few of them. I'm only taking some advanced courses at George Washington University, primarily because you insisted, but I also needed the cover. Now I've told you more than I should. I don't want to leave this house unless you want me to."

The judge's eyes lit up when Ricky told him that he was a lawyer. "Hurry back, Ricky, if that is your name. I told you I'm lonely being here all by myself. I can read just so many law briefs. I've already told the president that I plan to retire early next year. That will give him time to create a short list of replacements. In the meantime, go do your thing."

Ricky retired to his room and dug out his satellite phone. It was dead, having not been in use for too long a time. He put it in the charger, set the alarm on his digital clock, and laid his head on his pillow. He awoke hearing the beeping sound at three AM and called Aldo. It was already nine in Italy.

"Aldo here."

"Where are you now?"

"We're in the town of Leuica. It's a seaport town located at the heel of Italy and sticks out into the Ionian Sea. Aldo and Maria are at the door of the Cappiletti house as we speak. These folk live a quiet life from what I've seen so far. The daughter is supposed to be a part-time real estate agent. They are going to tell the Cappiletti's that they are recently married and are looking for a place to live in Leuica. They heard that their daughter could help them. Good, they've just been invited into the house."

"Aldo, tell them later that if they get a chance to speak in a casual way with her at some point, to try and have them find out what she knows about her sister, the sleeper agent, who lives in America. Get me a name that she goes by and how they contact her."

"From where I'm positioned I can see a man with dark hair and light colored skin observing them from a parked car about seventy-five meters away. We're right behind him in my own car. I've got my other brother, Salvador, with me. It's up to us to find out where the watchers live. I'll call you back in eight hours. I should know a lot more by then. Chow."

A short while later the front door opened and a young attractive woman led Maria and Aldo down the front steps. She was pointing and gesturing in different directions while they walked to their rented car.

Aldo called Rick back at five PM Italy time. "We picked up a lot of information on this family and their watchers today. The younger daughter attends the local college when she's not selling real estate. She has a boyfriend. Hold on to the seat of you pants—he's an Iraqi, one of the three men who have been located here to make sure the sister in America known as Carmella, does what she's supposed to do when she's asked to do it. He lives with the other two approximately four kilometers from the Cappiletti house. As near as we can tell the family is unaware that these three are permanently assigned to cash out the family if found necessary."

"Whoa! She dates one of the Iraqi agents."

"It's worse than that, Rick. She's engaged to marry him next year. There's more. The other two, both light-skinned so they fit in with the Italian neighborhood, are supposed to be his brothers. They all live together and the young engaged one is also attending college. That's where he met Tamara. The other two own the Raquif Florist Shop in town, as a cover for their observation of the family. The Raquif brothers are well-liked merchants. It's going to be hard to take them out without disrupting the whole town."

Rick didn't answer for a moment; he was thinking. "Rick, are you still there?"

"Aldo, I want you to make an offer to the two men for their florist shop. Pester them about selling the place to you. Make sure that many of the town folk know that you're interested in buying the shop. Tell them that you own a string of florist shops across Italy. Offer to hire two or three of the locals to work the shop when you take it over. Actually plan to run the business for the next year at least. The exit of those two from the town has to have the look of being seamless to everyone once they're gone."

"What about the younger brother? How are we going to get rid of him?"

"You're going to dig up his wife. Bring that old girlfriend of Vito's, named Valerie, down from Rome. She's supposed to be an actress. Offer to pay her a bonus if she can pull this off and be convincing. I don't think that the young love exhibited by Tamara for her Iraqi stallion can stand an ex-love that's still attached to him as a wife. Look, Aldo, I've just given you a pile of work to do while I'm in transit to Italy. It's going to take me at least two days to get there as the FBI has a tail on my alter-personality, Ricky Blanco. I'll see you as soon as I can. Then we'll decide how we're going to take them out."

After hanging up Rick called a friend of his who had a small plane.

"Joe, I need to rent your two-seater with you acting as my pilot. Lay in a flight plan that takes us from Washington to that small airport in Wilkes-Barre/Scranton, Pennsylvania. Then on the next day head to that small private airport located in northern New Jersey, Teteaboro. I want you to lay in at least three more stops and end up back in Washington. Do this over a six day period, staying overnight every place you land. Book separate hotel rooms for both of us each night. I go by the name of Ricky Blanco now, for a while anyway. I'll be leaving you once we get to Scranton. Make it look like I'm with you all the time your traveling. Can you handle this little charade for me? I have a need to go out of town for awhile."

"You bet I can. Seems like old times, Rick err Ricky. Bring along some extra bread. This trip is going to be more than just a little expensive, you know."

"Say no more. All your expenses will be covered from start to finish. Thanks, Joe."

Rick flew into the Pennsylvania airport and actually checked into the first hotel with Joe, after which he went directly back to the airport by taxi after slipping out a back door. Thirty-six hours later he arrived in the town of Leuica and was met by all his operatives.

"Anything new happen while I was traveling, Aldo?"

"Just a minor complication. The family had the three Iraqi brothers over for an Italian feast last night. Maria and Vito were invited as well. I'll let them tell you. Also, I've got Valerie due in town later tonight. I've made the offer to purchase the business. They turned me down as we expected. So I upped the ante. They're still not interested. It's going as we discussed."

It was Vito's turn to speak. He found it hard to look Rick directly in the eye. "These three have completely fooled the Cappiletti family into thinking they are their friends. After eight years these men have convinced them that they are not there for any reason other than they like living and working in Italy. You can tell that the two alleged older brothers are university trained and are smooth characters. I believe they would kill the family in a minute if they were ordered to do so. They mentioned that someone from up north was trying to buy the florist. Maria talked to Tamara in depth while she was showing them houses."

Maria was left to talk next. "Tamara is madly in love with Josuf, the younger brother, and he in love with her. They are both twenty-two years old and are already sleeping together." Rick frowned when she said that. She caught that look. "What can I say, they're young people living in the twenty-first century. Get with the times, Rick." It sounded a bit nasty when it came out. "I'm really sorry for that remark, Rick. I'm just trying to tell it as it is. Well, she told me all about her sister who she called, Carmella. All she knows is that she's married now to some high-level government worker and that her parents get letters from her every two months. She says she's happy in America. She doesn't know her married name. But she said that her mother may know."

"I'm betting that this character, Josuf, is just playing Tamara for a fool. Men are like that, you know. Not all men, but some men." Rick immediately started to think about Santanna and what he was doing to Anna Mary. He focused back to the present situation.

"These people from Iraq are all trained agents. I'm sure that he's a lot older than twenty-two. He had to be that old when he was given the assignment. Probably is at least thirty by now. Have you given Valerie her marching orders?"

"I've only briefed her. I think that you have to spell it all out for her, chapter and verse, as to how this act is to play out. We'll set the confrontation meeting to happen tomorrow morning at the college before classes for the day begin. In the meantime, Aldo, you and Salvador are to press the two owners of the florist with another offer. Keep them busy. Meanwhile, we have a show to put on."

Valerie was dressed to kill. She wore a leather mini-skirt and a silk blouse, which exhibited her ample bosom, and accentuated her cleavage. She waited under the balustrade entrance to the college for the man that was pointed out to her by Rick, even though he never saw Josuf before he knew who he was. To him, he could tell an Iraqi anywhere. Before he made it to the entrance, Tamara called for him to wait for her. It couldn't be better. The couple brushed a kiss at each other and walked toward the entrance.

Valerie came up to the two of them and they just walked past her. She grabbed Josuf by the arm and turned him around to face her, and she began to yell, loudly. She wanted to attract attention.

"You lousy bastard. You're so engrossed with your new little whore that you forgot you already have a wife and a child starving in Rome. I've had to plead with the authorities to provide us with a monthly stipend in order for us to live. I spent the last money that I had tracking you down and you act like you don't even know me. You Iraqi son-of-a-bitches are all alike. I should have listened to my sister when she warned me about marrying a foreigner."

"What the hell are you talking about, lady? I never saw the likes of you before."

"I'm going to have you arrested for desertion. Don't you care what happens to your child? He was asking where his Papa was just before I left Rome."

"I mean this, lady. I never saw your face before today." He was looking at Tamara when he made his claim of innocence. She was already in shock and had turned and started to run away. A crowd formed and watched the real life drama being played out before their eyes. He tried to run after her, but Valerie tugged at his jacket. She yelled, actually pleaded to the crowd that someone should get a policeman and have the wife beater and deserter arrested. She started to hit him with her purse as she shouted select obscenities at him.

He finally lost his temper, and threw a roundhouse punch to the head of the woman claiming to be his wife. Valerie went down and her head could be heard hitting the ground. She had used the device Rick had given her to make the sickening sound of her head hitting cement.

She was lying there as still as she could be. Rick came to the woman's defense. He belted Josuf with a two-punch volley that dropped the man to the ground. Someone from the crowd that had gathered planted a kick to Josuf's mid-section as he tried to get to his knees. He collapsed in a heap and Rick went over to assist Valerie to her feet.

"You earned your bonus, Valerie. That was a superb performance. Rick slipped a wad of high numbered euros into her purse. Grab a cab and head back to the airport and return to Rome. I'd like to see him try to explain this to Tamara and her parents."

Then Rick did a strange thing. He helped Josuf to his feet and steered him behind the registration building. Then he worked him over. When Josuf awoke for the second time he found the point of Rick's knife at his throat.

"I want you to tell me what you're doing here in Italy? If you don't come clean, you will feel great pain."

He cursed at Rick in Farsi. Rick broke his arm and took a nick out of the skin in his neck. He asked again. "What are you and your so called brothers doing in Italy?" The man was a pro and had been trained to take great amounts of pain. Rick cut a ligament in his leg. He would never walk again with full use of his leg, but he continued none-the-less to resist interrogation. After receiving much more physical abuse from Rick, he finally gave into his pain and incapacitation and told him everything about their assignment. They were not brothers, but the three of them were a team put together by Saddam eight years ago, and were sent to Italy to keep tabs on the Cappiletti's. He was thirty-two years old now but looked much younger. His assignment was to kill the young girl if the sister failed to do what she was assigned, or in the unlikely event that Saddam was overthrown. Information was flowing out of him faster now. He spilled everything. Rick had heard enough.

"I'm going to give you some money. Take a cab as far as it will take you. Return to Iraq or wherever else you want to go, but get out of Italy or you will be killed, and it will be a painful death. There will be no second chance. Do you understand what I am telling you? You are never to even come close to the Cappiletti family again. I have friends who will be watching you." Rick left the man who was crawling in the gutter. He was sure that he would heed the warning. The other two would not be as lucky.

Maria and Vito caught up with a sobbing Tamara Cappiletti before she went into her home. They took her to a restaurant where they let her spill out her story of how she was betrayed by the man she loved. Maria helped her to collect herself and simmered her down. Then they told her of the plot to use her sister as a sleeper agent, and that her boyfriend and the other two brothers were waiting assassins of her entire family in the event the sister didn't do her assignment to kill someone. She started to breakdown all over again.

Meanwhile, Aldo entered the florist and went to the back of the store. He had drawn his weapon. Salvador locked the front door. He would open it only when Rick knocked. By the time Rick arrived he found the two men tied to chairs. They both had missing teeth and were battered around their heads. Aldo was explaining to them their options. Then Rick took over.

"Your associate has told me everything about your assignment here in Italy for the last eight years. He has decided to forfeit his monthly stipend from Saddam in favor of his life with an opportunity to heal from his wounds." Rick went on to explain the problems their associate was now facing for his lifetime.

"We would like to give you the same opportunity to release yourselves from your charge and spend the rest of your days in relative good health. What do you say?"

"Will you let us talk alone and discuss this. After all, you are asking us to break a sacred trust."

"You have fifteen minutes to get your acts straight. Cabbish?"

Rick, Aldo and Salvador waited in the front of the florist. They were hoping that Saddam's henchman did not take their generous offer. When Salvador reentered the back of the store he found that the two men had somehow gotten loose and had taken off. One of the men had a hidden knife concealed in his ring and had been able to cut their bonds.

Aldo shouted. "They're headed over to the Cappiletti's. Let's go."

The house was locked as Maria and Vito went up the front steps of the Cappiletti's, ushering their daughter home. A car screeched to the curb and the two Iraqi men pointed their weapons at the three of them. Tamara unlocked the door and they all went inside and re-locked the door. Mr. Cappiletti came into the entrance hall and asked what they were doing. He was greeted with the handle of a gun cracked across his forehead. He fell to the floor in a state of semi-consciousness.

Rick and his guys had arrived at the back of the Cappiletti house and had entered through the basement. They moved quietly up the cellar stairway with their weapons drawn. They could hear orders being given to their captors by one of the Iraqi's. They were to lie face down and put their hands behind their backs. Vito refused and was hit on the head for his trouble. He started to bleed from the cut on the back of his head. The second Iraqi had gone upstairs and was dragging the mother downstairs pulling on her hair. She was shouting. "Is this the same man who only a few days ago was sitting at my dining room table and eating our food. I find this hard to believe."

"Shut up you stupid woman. We're in charge now."

One of them had found some duct tape and was tying the captives' hands behind their back. Once this was done they would each receive a bullet in the back of their head as the agents had been taught to do while they were in training back in Baghdad.

Before the first bullet was put into the skull of Mr. Cappiletti, Rick's gun fired. The bullet pierced the man's head between the eyes. A second bullet fired by Aldo hit the other Iraqi in the back of his shoulder spinning him around. Another bullet he fired unerringly found the man's heart.

Vito's wound was patched, as was Mr. Cappiletti's. Rick was giving orders. "We'll wait until it's dark before moving the body's out of the house. Salvador will dispose of them someplace out of town. Make sure that they're never found. We don't need any police investigation. Aldo, get those people who you hired to run the florist shop to start working there in the morning. Just tell them that the brother's Raquif couldn't refuse your last bid and that they sold you their house as well. They have left town and are returning to their homeland as wealthy men. In the meantime, I'd like to explain to Mr. & Mrs. Cappiletti just what these men have been doing in Italy these past eight years. Then I'd like to ask them some specific questions about their daughter who is living in the United States."

After explaining what had been going on to them, Rick had to ask the question he had come to Italy to find out. "What is the first and last name that your daughter goes by today? I'm aware that she is married."

"I don't know her by any other name than Carmella." Said the mother. "She sends us a letter and a package every third month mailed from a different place either in the town of Washington or from a place called Virginia. She always signs it with her given name, Carmella. I'm sorry, but that's all I can tell you."

"Don't you ever write to her?"

"Yes, we do. She sends us a return mailer. I think I remember that it is to a Postal Box number 752 at the Falls Church Station in Virginia. I hope that it helps. I only sent one back to her two weeks ago. I'm not expecting any more mail for awhile now."

"Well, you actually helped more than you know, Ma'am. If I can get to her I can let her know that you are safe and she no longer has to fulfill her sleeper task for Saddam Hussein. It will relieve a great deal of pressure on her. In the meantime, use the next mailer she sends you and let her know that all three of you are safe from the Iraqi killers."

* * * *

Rick was back at the judge's house twelve hours later. All he had to do was find out where the sleeper agent was. Nothing had changed. When he arrived home he went first to the Falls Church Post Office and checked to see if there was a mailer in box number 752. The postal clerk told him that a young woman had picked the letter up only the day before. When asked to describe the woman all he could remember was that she had black hair and seemed nervous.

He would be meeting with the task force the next day. The following week was Thanksgiving, and they still had much to learn about the attempt to be made on the president's life. Time was running out on them. They needed a break.

Chapter 10

All the same members of the task force who attended the last time were present. Audrey was asked by ACE to present her report first.

"Here's what we turned up based on information provided by Peter Grace's undercover agent. The man we identified as the possible assassin is a long time personal friend of the president. In fact they play golf together with regularity when the weather is better. He's in the House of Representatives, and has been there for thirty-five years now. He represents the State of Alabama, and has been heard to say that he's ready to retire rather than run for reelection again. He's a maverick. Was originally elected as a Democrat. After eleven years he switched to being a Republican. Eight years later he changes his mind again and declares himself to be an Independent. Surprisingly all that switching around with his party affiliation hasn't hurt him at the ballot box one bit.

"His name is Rafter Grosky. Thanks to Rick's input that we check for nicknames, we found out that he is called 'Art' because of his physical similarity to the actor/comedian called Art Carney, who achieved fame on a show named 'The Honeymooners'. Either the agent heard wrong or there is the possibility he really is our man. No one has approached him on this subject yet, leaving that to this task force to decide. However, he is contained and will not be allowed anywhere near the president, especially on the night he makes his speech. He's not going to like it when my men restrain him that night when he will be prevented from being one of the dignitaries who escort the president from the hall. I personally don't think we have identified the right man. It makes us ask is it possible that she heard incorrectly when Victor Salvetti was on the phone? Also, this man does not carry a cane. How would he manage a poison stick? In my mind, what we found out doesn't make him out to be our potential assassin. We need a different lead to follow."

"Where does that leave us?" Asked ACE. She looked frantic. Audrey did not have an answer.

Kevin then asked. "Have you checked out all members of congress? It's obvious that someone in congress is going to make the attempt on his life."

Audrey replied. "We routinely check the backgrounds and even go deep into the private lives of the members of congress. All I need is a written order from the head of the Secret Service and authorized by the president. George, will you please make that request in writing? Give it to ACE to get the additional counter-signed signature. I'll need that to make it legal. I'll have my people start the investigation immediately, as soon as I receive it. We'll be looking deeply into people's private lives. Unless we turn up anything that is deemed damaging to our country, what we find out about them will automatically become sealed data."

"What you're doing is all well and good, but I think that we're missing the obvious." Rick stated. "Is it possible that Victor Salvetti has let himself be overheard and is testing his new assistant's loyalty to him? I think Peter has to warn her immediately. When can you get an alert to her, Peter?"

"Not until she contacts me. And I'm not scheduled back in Europe until after Thanksgiving. I suggest that we keep this information she provided low key. We certainly shouldn't talk to this congressman Grozsky. If, as Rick suggests, Salvetti's testing her, then we have to keep what she gave us under wraps. He's bound to be watching."

"Where is she now? Can we send someone to warn her, in the event you can't make telephone contact?"

"Really, I don't know where she is or where she's going to be. She travels anywhere at the whim of Victor Salvetti. That's the way the game is played."

It bothered Rick knowing Saila was at more risk now than even she knew.

"Rick, why don't you tell us what you have found out about the family of the sleeper agent?" Suggested ACE.

"I've got a bag of mixed results to report. First I'm pleased to tell you the family is safe in their home in Italy. The three agents dispatched by Saddam over eight years ago are no longer a threat to them."

"Where are these men now?" ACE persisted, searching for positive results.

"They're completely out of the picture. They have been dealt with. You have to believe what I say about this, and I'm not at liberty to reveal how this was accomplished."

"Rick, have you found out who the sleeper is?" Asked Kevin.

"We know now she contacts her family every three month. They in turn write back to her and send it to a post office in Falls Church, Virginia, in a special mailer that she supply's whenever she writes. I checked and found out she recently picked up her mail, so unfortunately I missed her. At my urging her mother is going to try and send a letter directly to her post office box, but she probably won't be looking for any mail, because the last mailer she sent her folks has already been used.

"This is a well-thought out scheme, and it creates a dilemma that so far defies all attempts to find out who she is. I have someone watching the postal box, with the remote possibility the sleeper breaks her regimen when the new mail arrives. If she does see a non-recognizable piece of mail, she may bolt. It's so close to the date the president is to give his speech I thought it worth that risk. There is probably not enough time for the complete letter cycle to repeat."

"What's your next step? Where do you go from here?" Kevin kept searching for the next path for the group to follow.

"We have one thing working in our favor. We know for a fact she has been specifically assigned to shoot the house speaker on the night of the speech. If we can't alert her that her family is safe and thus call her off, we'll have to increase our protection for him. He will be her target, her only target. I still am of the belief that hasn't changed one iota."

"This has not been a productive meeting." Boomed ACE. There was a tone of frustration in her voice; it was something she was not prone to show to anyone. I think that we should meet again next Wednesday before Thanksgiving. Maybe we'll pick up some additional information by then. We need a break. It's getting too close to the date. See you all then."

Rick was beginning to get frantic as well as he left the meeting, but for a different reason. He kept thinking, *how am I going to warn Saila that her boss suspects her?* His cell phone rang and broke his train of somber thought.

"It's me, Saila. I'm in town at the Stafford Inn with Victor. He's off tonight getting his jollies wagged by his favorite dominatrix, and I've got the night free. We're here for a meeting of his stateside company heads. He told me that he likes being in the United States over Thanksgiving."

"Look Saila, something's come up. Don't trust anything your boss says. We believe that the information you passed on to Peter Grace was planted for your benefit in order to test your loyalty. He still doesn't trust you." And then a pause in his voice as he thought about what he had just said. "Have you noticed that you're being watched? Are you being followed?"

"I don't think so, but after your warning I'll be extra careful. I haven't been checking for that possibility, now that I started to work for the Camorra headman. Rick, does this mean that we can't meet and have a little tête-à-tête? I've missed you so much. I dream of you every night. I have a need to make love with you. Where can we meet? I'll be sure that I'm not followed." There was a pleading sound in her voice; he was fully aware she was under tremendous pressure.

"I've got a better idea. Tell me where you are now and I'll be watching you as you break free from any tail that Victor's put on you. When I arrive at where you are and you spot me don't acknowledge I'm there. By then I will have already slipped my FBI tail. Oh yes, I recently found out that I'm under surveillance as well. It complicates our meeting, but I won't let it deter me.

"Once you're clear and on the move head to the Watergate Hotel where I'll have a room reserved under the name of Mr. & Mrs. Angelo Spado. If I see that you haven't been able to shake your tail, then I'll remove the tail physically. Don't worry. My being with you will make all this necessary fooling around worthwhile. Pack an overnight bag. We'll be playing house."

Rick started the process of losing the man following him by first taking multiple taxis. Then he switched to a bus heading to the airport, and once there moved around the terminal fast in the midst of all the travelers. He went through a bathroom and exited through another door he found on the other side immediately. Then he caught another taxi and after observing that he was finally in the clear he was free to move on to part two. One man, even if there were two, assigned to follow Rick, would not be able to stay on his trail. He instructed the driver to go to the Stafford Inn.

Saila was waiting in her hotel's lobby when she received a page to pick up a courtesy phone.

"It's Rick. I'm on my cell phone directly outside of the front entrance revolving doors. Your tail is one of Dr. Ahrens goons. He's standing behind a rack at the magazine stand. Don't even look in that direction for him. Go out the revolving doors and catch a cab. Tell the driver to take you to fifteen E. Rocker Street. That's across town."

"Won't he be following me?"

"You bet he will. Here's what you do. Once the driver gets three blocks away from the hotel, change your mind and tell him you forgot something. Ask him to return to the rear of the hotel and let you out there. Give the driver twenty dollars for his trouble. Go through the back door entrance and come out the front door again. You'll find a rented green Mustang out front with the keys in and running. Go directly to the driver's side and drive off. Make a right at the corner and go completely around the block. I will watch to see if you lost him. If you see me out front when you pass the hotel, then head directly to the Watergate. I'll be there shortly, once I'm able to verify with certainty you've lost him. I'll see you in the room, Mrs. Spado."

Rick had rented the bridal suite and had a bottle of chilled champagne awaiting them. She was checked in and already under the satin sheets when he arrived fifteen minutes after her.

"What took you so long, Rick?"

"It seems that tail Victor has on you is, or I should say, was very qualified at following someone. I don't know how he managed it but he traced you back to the rear door of the hotel. I had to take him out in the side alley. Don't worry, he never saw who hit him. I took his wallet to make it look like a mugging, and then I crippled him by dislocating his ankle. You can be sure he won't be following you anytime soon. It's not a permanent injury; he should be hopping around on crutches for the next two months. I gave the cash to the mission down the block, and put his wallet in a dumpster."

They made long passionate love. As they lay there side by side they both knew that it was now time for talking and planning a new strategy.

"Rick, why are you so deep in thought? Why not take a moment and savor what we just had?"

"I've been thinking about us, Saila. Victor is certainly not stupid. I believe he already knows we've been together. He must have had us under surveillance since the last meeting he called. So, here's a strategy for you to follow. If he questions what you've been doing during your free time tell him about us. Don't hold anything back. This will assure him that you're completely honest with him. You'll only be confirming what he already knows. From here on, always play into his hand. He's got to feel he can trust you. Don't be so quick to pass on any information that you may overhear, unless you can confirm it by some other means."

"You're right. Victor's always looking into having his own sexual pleasures, the pervert. He can't deny me mine. He has me make arrangements for his encounters with his dominating type women. I think your suggestion is a good approach to take. Now, where do we stand on finding that sleeper agent? Peter told me the last time we spoke that you took on that challenge."

He told her everything that had taken place and what had been reported at subsequent task force meetings…

"Does Peter Grace still want me to try and find out who will be the president's attacker?"

"I believe he does. We're sure that it is someone in congress who's carrying a grudge and is willing to do Victor's dirty work, even if it cost him his, or possibly her, life. But you must be extremely careful, my darling. I don't want to lose you now that I've found you."

"I'm going to be in town until after Thanksgiving. Victor has told me I have the day off. He's been asked to dinner at one of his CEO's homes. He's a single man and will be sure to arrange some weird type of entertainment for them both. I'm not invited, thank goodness. Do you think we can meet again and have dinner together? I hear this is a time of the year when people gather and eat large turkeys, and a lot of other food too. It will be the last chance we have this year to be together."

"I have a slight problem. I've already agreed to have dinner with the judge at his favorite restaurant. I've been living at his house since I came to Washington. It's been a good cover for me. Say, did he see you when you were attending him back in Colorado?"

"Don't you remember? I was sitting in a restaurant at a table with Dr. Ahrens when he gave the judge the sedative. Then he saw me once again in a nurse's uniform when he started to awake prematurely in his phony hospital bed. I really think he will remember me."

"It may be time to let the judge in on a little more of what I've been up to. I'm not going to miss what could be the last time I have to spend with you before this whole thing comes to a head. I'll pick you up at your hotel at two PM on Thursday. I'll handle the judge. I bet he does recognize you. You certainly are striking to look at."

"Judge, I'm going to bring someone with me when we have Thanksgiving dinner."

"You're not going to tell me your bringing that Santanna person with you. I won't stand for that ingrate sharing anything with us. You know I don't like that man."

"It's not him judge, It's a woman whom I've been seeing whenever she comes to town, which is not often enough to suit me. She's someone who I believe you have met before when you were in Colorado. After you meet her, I promise that I'll answer more of your probing questions. I'm sure you'll have some."

"With all the running around you've been doing for that organization you work for, I can't imagine where you found the time to meet someone. Are you sleeping with her? All you young folk don't think that they have to be married before they hop in the sack with someone."

"I'm not going to dignify that remark with an answer. Suffice to say I'm in love with this woman, and some day we're going to be married. Now let's talk about Thanksgiving. I'll be driving you to the restaurant but I'll only be dropping you off. I have to take your car and go pick her up at her hotel, which happens to be close by. Have a drink at the bar in the meantime. I think you're going to like her."

"Humph! I hope she's not some frizzed out blonde. I hate that type of woman."

"No, she's not. You'll just have to judge her after you've had a chance to meet and get to know her."

Sailia was back at work the next morning. Victor was uncharacteristically in a good mood. He handed her a cup of coffee and it was obvious to Saila that he wanted to chat.

"You look ravishing this morning, Saila. What did you do on your night off? Your radiance tells me that you had a great evening."

"You are correct on that account, Mr. Salvetti. You remember Ricky Blanco. He's the man I hired back in Italy to help with the kidnappings. Well, for the second time now we have shared an evening together. When you held the last meeting you must have noticed that we were attracted to each other. I spent the night with him. He is one of the greatest lovers that I have ever had. Your suggestion the last time that I go out and get myself laid was one of the best things that has ever happened to me. I originally thought that while I was working for you that you would not look kindly on me for any female transgression. You made my day when you released me from that immature notion. Thank you."

Saila cringed when she had to tell this hated man, things about her love life, which were very personal. But it had to be done. "He's going to take me out for Thanksgiving dinner. We understand that it is a tradition here in America. They have so many other foolish customs, and then to top it off they give thanks for the material things they have in life. I'm looking forward to a great meal and then finishing it off with a nightcap, my style." She changed the subject away from her.

"You're in a good mood, as well. I assume that you had an enjoyable evening too." She didn't give him time to reply; deciding that she would feed him more useless banter.

"I trust that you're going to enjoy the American holiday also. You said something about meeting at the home of one of your CEO's. Do you need me to line up any entertainment for you that evening?"

"Actually, that won't be necessary. My man has taken care of everything, thank you. I just found out that two American congressman will be bringing their wives to his home for the dinner feast. I may have to take some time out of the evening to discuss business affairs with them. Once they leave the house though, the fun and games will begin. I hope that you have as much fun after as I usually do. It's a shame that you're so straight. You don't know what you're missing."

Saila had just received information. Now she knew that she had to find a way to confirm who the congressmen were. That would be no small task. She would discuss what she found out with Rick. Salvetti never mentioned that one of his men had been mugged.

* * * *

It was Wednesday as ACE convened the task force meeting that she had hastily called because the last one had not produced much positive news. Audrey was asked to provide an update on investigating all the members of congress in an attempt to find one of them involved in the presidential assassination attempt.

"This is turning out to be a monumental assignment. I've called all FBI personnel back from leave in order to focus on checking them out. To start, I've already put tails on each of them now because of tomorrow's holiday. We're barely able to cover them for surveillance and I've had to hire additional private investigators to take up the slack. It will be Monday morning before we can launch into extensive background checks of these people. I expect it will absorb all of the bureau's time, meaning we'll be providing only short shrift to our other duties. Sorry I don't have any more positive information to report."

"Okay, Rick. You're on next." ACE announced.

"I was contacted by Peter's agent who has recently arrived in town with Salvetti for business meetings. She was advised of the dangers presented by Salvetti feeding her bad information in an attempt to check her loyalty to him. I'm sure she will not be susceptible to fall for this type of treachery again. She advises that she will remain extra vigilant. That's all I have to report. I'm attempting to plan a new approach to find the sleeper agent."

"Does any one have any additional information to report?"

There were no replies, and ACE ended the short meeting without setting the next date for them to meet. A somber feeling was emanating from all attendees as they left the room to enjoy the holiday.

* * * *

Rick had dropped the judge off at the restaurant as they planned, and promptly went to pick up Saila at the Stafford Inn. The judge noticed that he was not wearing any earring, and he commented on it. Ricky didn't respond. Then he mentioned that he was pleased with the way he had dressed. He was dressed in a suit and wearing a tie matching the color of his pastel shirt. She was dressed conservatively because she was about to be formally introduced to the judge. Her dress was slightly below her knees, and with her slim figure it had the effect of making her look even taller than she was. Her white hair was set in an upsweep and she was wearing an imitation diamond tiara on her head.

"You look beautiful, Saila. As if you don't always look that way."

"Are we going back to the Watergate again tonight after dinner, Mr. Spado? Did you book the room?"

"You bet we are, and I did just that. Did you tell Victor about us?"

"Does a cow give milk?" She smiled as she put her arm under his.

"I haven't told the judge anything about you yet. I'm going to play it by ear and see what he remembers. Don't worry. I won't leave you stuck in any embarrassing situation."

The judge was sitting at the table he had reserved, rather than wait at the bar as Ricky had suggested. He had ordered a bottle of Dom Perrigon and already had it decanted and chilled. When Saila and Ricky entered the restaurant and were being seated many heads turned to look at them. They made an extremely attractive couple.

"Judge Benjamin, I'd like to introduce you to my lady, Saila Ewe."

The judge rose and offered his hand, which she took in both of hers as a warm gesture. As they sat he began to stare at her.

"Judge, stop staring at her. You're going to make her feel uncomfortable."

"If you're thinking that you met me someplace before, you're correct. I was in a hotel dining room in Denver when you passed out. I am a part-time nurse. It was I who called for the ambulance as Dr. Ahrens advised me to do. I am so glad that it only turned out to be food poisoning and that you were back on your feet shortly."

"You're right, I do remember that incident. But then I think I met you again. Could it have been in the hospital where they took me? I don't remember too much of what happened to me. It's all a fog in my memory. You certainly are a beautiful woman, Saila."

"Why thank you, judge. That's a very nice compliment. And to answer your question, I do believe that you saw me at least one more time at the hospital. I told you that I was a nurse."

"So you did, so you did." He was staring at her again and she started to blush. "Are you aware, Miss Ewe, that your first name spells alias backwards?"

"Would you like to call me Alias, instead of Saila? Take your choice."

"Forgive me for my impertinence, Saila. It's a beautiful name. It was just an observation. Now let's have a drink." He raised his glass in a toast. They picked up their glasses.

"To my Indian valet, and to all the secrets he keeps from me. And to the beautiful woman who shares this moment in life with us both on this joyful day. May the future bring you both many things to be thankful for, now let's eat."

Later that evening back in their room at the Watergate Saila told Ricky what Victor had said in an offhand manner to her

"He may still be feeding you information that he wants you to use and become trapped by it. By no means can you tell Peter Grace what he said about the congressman. Remember what I said about getting secondary verification. Maybe he will slip up and provide you with the names of these men. If you happen to get both of their names, then I'm sure he's setting a trap. Also, watch and see if he's still following you. There is a tail on us tonight. He's got Ahrens other goon taking up where his partner left off. It's no matter. He knows about us anyway, right?

"Something else you should know. I just found out that the FBI has started surveillance on all members of congress. They may have picked up the names of the congressmen who will be meeting with Salvetti. It could provide us a new lead."

The next day they parted. There would be no tomorrow's together for them until they had thwarted the Camorra's attack on the President of the United States. And after that, they would have to devise a way to break both of them out of the Camorra organization. The task ahead was as large as a mountain. They both approached the future thinking first things first.

* * * *

The month of December moved toward a close. No additional valuable information had developed and been presented to members of the task force. The FBI reported that they were pressing on with their research into backgrounds of members of congress. Rick's own investigation into finding the sleeper agent had dried up, Aldo had been in touch with the parents. Their daughter had made no contact since she had last corresponded with them.

Rick took the opportunity presented by the slow activity to touch base with all the managers of his worldwide detective organization. His manager, Cameron Taylor, from New Jersey reported a twenty percent increase in revenues for the last six months, most of it in the last month.

"We were contacted by the FBI and asked to provide agents for background checks on members of congress. I put on six extra personnel, all retired detectives, to meet the requirement. They tell me they picked us out to perform this job because we were recommended by the CIA as a reliable detective agency. I suspect that you had something to do with that, since you alerted me before you left that the CIA may contact me. I personally, and each agent assigned to research background information, were required to sign a confidentiality waiver; one that requires huge penalties if ever violated."

"I hope that you contacted the insurance company and had them add a rider to the standard liability office insurance policy, Cameron."

"Done, boss. I've been told that this is a hush-hush and rush assignment, Rick. We've been assigned one hundred and thirty-two people to collect any information about them that we can. We're working as far south as Rhode Island all the way up trough Maine, and all the states in between. Looks like we've got the entire eastern side of the U.S. assigned to us. The people who we are checking on are all home now for the holiday season, with congress currently being in recess."

"You've done good, Cameron. I told you when I hired you that you will be busy. I'll be dropping around to see you early next year. Call the other managers if you need any help with closing the year-end books."

Rick touched base with each of the others; all was well. Manuela wanted to know if he was still in character as Ricky Blanco. He told her he was splitting between himself and the Ricky character. After finishing that task, he could get back to the business at hand.

"What are you doing on New Years Eve?" Asked the judge as soon as Ricky arrived home. He was working out at the gym, since school was closed for the holidays.

"Don't have any plans, judge. Saila went back to Europe and I don't know when she'll be back in the states."

"I'd like you to drive me to the home of the head of the secret service. His wife decided to ask many of the people who stay in and around Washington, DC for the holidays to come to a party. Starts to gather around ten PM. Do you think you can drive me, both ways? I don't expect to be leaving until at least one AM. I have to make a good show of it, you know."

"Not a problem, judge. Got any suggestions as to what I should do while you're at the party?"

"I've got an invitation that says I should bring someone. Why don't you be my date for the evening? Don't worry, I won't tell anybody that you're my manservant. I'll tell them that you're being interviewed for a clerking position with me. Who knows? You may meet some important people who can help your career. You've got to do something once you're finished with your current assignment as a *Spook*. Why don't you wear that suit you wore for thanksgiving dinner? By the way, did I ever tell you that I approve of that young lady, Saila? She sure is a looker. Don't let her go; she's a keeper if I ever saw one."

True to his promise the judge introduced him as someone he was considering for a potential clerking position. He didn't fool anyone. They all knew that he was retiring shortly and would not have any reason to hire a new clerk. Ricky was introduced to a couple who immediately came over to them. They were dressed in formal attire. He wore a tuxedo. She was short, only about five-foot three, and wore a low-cut open back lavender evening gown. She wore her jet-black hair closely cropped. Her only jewelry was a single strand of ultra-white pearls, highlighting her Mediterranean skin coloring. She was actually stunning to look at.

"Riccardo Giovanni Blanco, I'd like to introduce you to the host and hostess for this gathering, Mr. & Mrs. George Papadopoilis. George is the Director of the Secret Service." George winced when he heard the name Rick was being introduced as, but thinking better of it he let it pass. He would talk to Rick privately later that evening.

"I'm pleased to meet you, Sir, and Ma'am."

"Please don't Ma'am me? My name is Carma, Mr. Blanco."

"I'd be happy if you called me, Ricky, Ma'am, err I mean, Carma. That's an interesting name. Is it of Greek origin?"

"No, I happen to be Italian by birth. Your name indicates that you're an Italian too." She took him by the arm and walked away from her husband and the judge. Ricky couldn't understand why she did this.

"I like to speak to new people while my husband is not standing next to me. Gives me a chance to get to know people better. George is a bit overbearing at times."

"I speak Italian, as well as Arabic and Spanish, and I happen to have an Italian name, but I received my name quite by accident. You see, my mother was a language teacher and my father was a diplomat." Ricky had successfully parried that question with the truth, twisted just a little.

Carma replied. "Well, I became naturalized as soon as I could after I entered the country. I couldn't wait to become a citizen. I entered into an accelerated plan because of my education. I met George when I later became an agent in the secret service. I retired when we married so that there was no chance for a nepotism charge. Shortly afterward he received his current posting. I'm back on special duty now by presidential fiat, but it's only for a short time. What did you do, that is before you decided to try your hand as a clerk for a Supreme Court Justice? You seem to be much older than most clerk applicants."

"After graduating from law school, the Army had a call for people who were linguistic and I fit the bill. That's more than ten years ago. Since then I've worked as a private detective, but I wanted to get some experience under my belt before I take the Bar Exam. I recognize I'm pretty rusty at law. The judge was being kind to provide me with this opportunity."

"Do you have family back in Italy?" Carma's face reddened before she answered.

"Not any more. Err. I think that we had both better start mingling with the other guests, don't you? I'll see you later this evening. Please, enjoy yourself?"

"Thank you, Carma. I'll make sure that I'll see you next year before I leave." Ricky answered

George grabbed Rick by the arm and dragged him off into a corner. "Where did you get the name Ricky Blanco from? You've got a nerve coming here into my house."

"George, I live with the judge in his town house. I work for him. It's part of my cover while I'm in Washington. He asked me to drive him and then he tells me to come along as his guest. Actually, you're the one who invited me."

"Don't go making any fuss here tonight. Just do you're job and stay out of my personal life. What did you tell my wife?"

"Why don't you ask her?" Rick walked away and looked for the judge. He was standing in a group with Kevin Winslow, Vince Green and Audrey Pigeon.

"This looks like a safe harbor for me. George dressed me down for being here. I can't help that the judge wanted me to drive him and stay around to take him home. Anything important happening?"

Kevin answered. "Everything has dried up. Have you come up with any leads?"

"Yeah, one slim chance that I don't want to comment on until I can confirm. I've got a plan to do just that. OOP's. Here comes George. Better lighten up the banter, or he'll get pissed off at me again. I'm going to find his wife. She a much better hostess, and I might add, a pleasure to talk to."

Everybody raised their glass and in unison counted down the seconds until the New Year, 2002. True to his word the judge sought out Ricky to tell him he was ready to leave at five minutes after one.

"Let me say goodbye to our host and hostess first, judge. I'll meet you at the door. This will only take a minute."

Rick singled out George to say his farewell and offer his thanks for inviting him. He knew how to rub it in, but by now George was not as hostile. "Don't forget to say goodbye to my wife. She seemed to have some sort of fascination with you. She's just coming out of the ladies room. There she is."

Rick headed toward the woman. He knew exactly what he wanted to say.

"Carma, thank you for your graciousness in allowing me to attend the festivities."

"It's been my pleasure, Ricky Blanco. I've still got some questions about that name. Perhaps we can discuss it at another time?"

"Certainly. But could I offer you a suggestion?" Not waiting for an answer he continued. "Why don't you check for your mail in Falls Church? You might find out some information that is vital to you."

Rick saw an alarmed look on her face as he turned and walked toward the door, where he met the judge who already was wearing his overcoat and hat. She never said anything more.

On the ride back to the town house Rick told the judge. "I'm going to drop you off at the house and I'd like to borrow the car for awhile. I'm hungry and I'll be going someplace to get breakfast. That is unless you want to join me? I plan to sleep late in the morning."

"No thanks, I'm too tired. Take me home and then do whatever you want."

Rick headed to his favorite diner. It was about two fifteen. He saw Santanna sitting in a back booth with a woman, and went over to greet them.

"Ricky, this is my fiancée Anna Mary. I'm glad you came in to hear the good news. We've decided to get married later today. We have to find someone to marry us. I got the license yesterday before everything closed for the holiday. I was going to call you. Do you think that the judge could do that for us?"

"If I call him now and wake him he'll have a shit-fit. Let me work on him during the day and I'll try and have him do the nuptials later this evening. Are you sure this is what you want to do? You don't know each other that long."

"I'm sure, Ricky."

"I'm positive." Claimed Anna Mary. "We really love each other."

"I'll call you about three PM and let you know if he'll do it. I can't promise anything."

Santanna Santanna and Anna Mary Petre were married in the Supreme Court Chapel at seven that evening. Rick was the best man and a female security guard became the maid of honor. Stranger things had happened.

Chapter 11

On January 2nd Rick received an urgent call from Aldo Frondzi. It was four in the morning.

"I've got news, boss. I know it's not going to make you happy. That third Iraqi soldier, Josuf, the one that you busted up and then let walk didn't heed your warning. He was in a wheelchair and on New Year's Eve he approached his former fiancee, Tamara Cappiletti, at a town dance."

"Christ, did anyone get hurt?"

"The man had a gun hidden under the blanket that covered him. He pulled out the gun and started yelling a tirade of hate against her. It was then that her father jumped in front of Tamara in an attempt to shield her. It seemed that Josuf had trouble holding and aiming the gun. As a result of his bold intervention her dad took a bullet to his arm."

"Didn't we have anybody in the area to protect the family?"

"Fortunately Aldo and Maria were attending the same dance in the town center. I had asked them to stay after we cleaned up there. When he saw the gun pointed at Tamara, Aldo threw his body at the wheelchair hitting it broadside, and knocked it over on its side. Unfortunately, that was immediately after the man had already fired a first shot. The would-be assassin died later in the hospital from an injury he received when his head hit the cobblestone flooring in the Town Square. We were fortunate. It all ended well. The father was treated at the hospital and was allowed to go home. The bullet went through the fleshy part of his arm."

"We literally dodged a bullet, didn't we, Aldo?" It was rhetorical and didn't require an answer.

"How are you doing on the identification of the sleeper agent, Rick?"

"I think I may have run into her on New Years Eve, by pure accident. Boy, I've got a lot of explaining to do. I think I led her to believe her family was out of harm's way as a ploy to get her to reveal herself. I'm glad that you called me early. I've got to get down to the post office to see if she retrieves the letter her mother sent her. Be seeing you, Aldo. I'll keep you posted."

Rick arrived at the Falls Church Post Office in Virginia as it was opening for business that morning at eight sharp. He spoke to his man working there who had been alerted to keep his eyes pealed for anyone who attempted to pick up mail from the box number Rick had identified.

"I'm going to take up a position where I can't be spotted. However, if she gets by me I'd like you to make a fuss if anyone comes up and asks for the mail in that box. There's an extra fifty in it for you."

"What do you mean make a fuss? You don't want me to give her the mail?"

"Of course, give her the mail in the box, but make some sort of a noise or disturbance in order to alert me."

At ten-fifteen that morning a woman with bright red hair showed up to wait on one of the long lines forming at the post office service windows. Because there was a note left in the box to alert Rick's man, the gal attending her went to him and whispered something in his ear. He switched positions with his coworker and then said loudly.

"Yes, you do have a letter in your box, but first there is a matter of payment for the box."

"What do you mean? I've had this box for almost eight years now, and I've always paid in advance. I last made my annual payment in November."

"I'm sorry, ma'am, but the record shows that you are one year in arrears. I can't give you the contents of the box until you make a payment to the U.S. Postmaster of forty-eight dollars. You can make the payment in cash or check."

"What's taking so long? Come on, lady. Pay the man and get this line moving. I've got to get to work. I haven't got all day."

The frustrated woman paid with a fifty-dollar bill, and received her two dollars change, and a letter postmarked from Leuica, Italy. She left the post office and headed to the public ladies room of the library next door. Rick followed and waited outside of the rest room for her to emerge. A bleary-looking red-eyed Carma Papadopoilis exited after about ten minutes. There was a clump of a red wig sticking out of her purse. Rick put his arm under hers and ushered her to a bench on the side. Her first instinct was to reach for her gun; Secret Service Agents are required to carry them on their person whenever under assignment. After seeing whom it was, she allowed him to move her out of the hearing range of others.

"I've read the letter. It would seem that you are correct, Mr. Blanco. That letter is vital to me, more than you'll ever know. My mother tells me that my family is safe in their home."

"That would be a little premature, since the letter is more than a month old. Only the other night, one of Saddam's agents, one who was severely incapacitated personally by yours truly, made a last ditch attempt on your sister's life. My man was there to take him down, but unfortunately not before he put a bullet into your father's arm."

"My God! Is he hurt badly? Are my mother and my sister safe from harm? Are they still in danger?" She started to cry.

"Your father is doing well. The bullet passed through the fleshy part of his arm. They are all safe, now. The final member of the threesome assigned to watch them is now dead. I think that he was out for revenge against your sister because she jilted him, rather than any dedication he had for Saddam. I'm sorry my man wasn't able to react sooner to the threat. I had a chance to permanently take out this guy when I first encountered him. But your sister had a schoolgirl crush on him, so I gave him a break and warned him off; at least I thought so."

"Are you going to tell my husband, George, what I was supposed to do whenever I was activated? It will tear him apart, and I know that he will want to resign his directorship. I assure you, Ricky, err, Mr. Blanco, I had no intention of ever taking the life of Thom Crowell, no matter what price I had to pay personally. I never was a viable sleeper agent for Saddam. I was hoping to learn more information from the man who contacted me, Victor Salvetti. He is supposed to call me again, on the day before the president gives his speech, to give me last minute instructions."

"First things first, Carma. Use my satellite phone to call your mother now and confirm what I've just told you. It's after four in the afternoon over there. Then we'll talk about what to do next."

The phone call took twenty minutes. They spoke in Italian. Rick was able to understand most of what he heard from listening to only this side of the conversation.

"So, my mother tells me that your name is really Rick Banyan, and that you work for someone high up in our government? My father is feeling much better. I'm not going to delve into how you found out who I was; it's all moot now anyway. And here we are. What exactly do you plan to do; about me, that is?"

"You're aware that this Salvetti character is putting on a full scale push in an attempt to kill the president on the night of his speech?"

"Yes, he told me that when he first contacted me."

"Do you know that the man you are supposed to take out during the confusion created by attempts on the president's life is someone who he, Salvetti, feels he has a personal score to settle with? If he plans to contact you as you say, then you're our best chance to uncover who is going to attempt to kill the president with a poison stick, or something like that. It has to be someone who is in congress."

"He didn't tell me why he wants the speaker of the house killed. I guess he didn't think it necessary. Am I reading that you believe me now?"

"Not completely yet, Carma. Although I think I may have to take a chance on you. You know some pretty important people's lives are at stake here? But with you knowing your family is out of danger now I believe you can help us. Don't worry, I won't be the one to tell your husband. I'll let you do that in your own good time after this is all over. Just get the information on who is the potential assassin and pass it on to anyone who can do something about it. Tell your husband if you can't find anyone else to alert. The important thing is for us to get that person and put them out of commission before they can complete their vile act."

"That's it? You're letting me go, just like that?"

"I'm trusting you to save the life of the President of the United States, that's how much I'm believing you. Don't let me down; don't let any of us involved down. You're our last chance to catch the culprit. Perhaps you can also salvage your career before this starts to go down."

"I'll keep you in the information loop, Rick. Will you be at the speech that night? I'm pulling a twelve-hour shift starting at eight that evening. Will I be able to contact you there?"

"I have every intention of being there, so I'll be keeping my eyes on you." Said Rick, even though he didn't have the slightest idea on how he would get in past all the security. If he was able to get into the great hall of congress he knew that he would not be allowed to carry a gun; that was the prerogative of only members of the secret service. He would talk to Kevin that very day to make arrangements. Thus it looked as if the entire plot would come down to the very end. There was so much at stake.

* * * *

Saila picked up the phone at Victor's French office. The man at the other end of the line sounded frantic. Victor was not in the office at this time. She was unaware that he was getting off the elevator when the call first came in.

"Mr. Salvetti is not back from lunch yet. Can I take a message and I'll have him call you back when he gets in?"

"I'm calling from the U S of A. Tell that son-of-a-bitch that if I don't get my weekly supply of high-nourishment product then I won't be doing that job for him later this month. He owes me big-time. I'm not about to be shit on."

Victor had just entered his office. Saila motioned him to the phone and, with a shrug of her shoulders and a questioning look, she hung hers up. She strained her ears to hear what Victor was saying to the man. He talked very softly, maintaining control and composure as he always did. Saila went through the motion of filing away some papers.

"Don't be upset. It will be delivered later today. I guarantee it. You know I'm counting on you to do as we arranged when the time comes. Simmer down now. Haven't I kept you in happiness the past three months? Remember that I came forth and contacted you."

"Wait a minute, there's someone ringing the doorbell for me downstairs." A pause ensued. Then he picked up the telephone again.

"I think I'm getting my delivery now."

"That's good. So some deliveryman is at your door now and you just buzzed him in? I told you that it would arrive soon. Go get your stuff. We'll talk tomorrow."

Now came a dilemma facing Saila. *Should she contact Peter Grace with the information she had just learned? Or should she do as Rick had instructed her i.e. wait until she was able to confirm what she had learned from another source. But what if she couldn't confirm it. Time was running out. There was only three weeks to go before the president was to give his speech. She decided to keep her eyes and ears open looking for confirmation, but if she were unable to get any she would notify Peter Grace at least a few days before the speech. In the meantime she would put Peter on alert that she was near to finding out something important.*

* * * *

It was the second week in January and the task force met for the first time in 2002. Peter Grace was not present, but all the others were. Ace called upon Rick to start off the reporting of where they stood. Rick had already conferred with Kevin. They had agreed that under the circumstances, trusting Carma was their only option. Rick was also assured that he would receive an invitation to the great hall of congress where the House of Representatives met to hear the speech.

Rick carefully spelled out what had happened to the Cappiletti family on New Years Eve. "Be assured, all three of the people assigned by Saddam Hussein to watch the family in Italy are dead. More important, I am confident that I will be able to identify the sleeper agent before that night, and that she will be called off from her task. I've got all the bases covered."

Audrey Pigeon let them all know that she was not happy with Rick's reporting on the sleeper agent. "I don't feel that you're being completely open with us. If you're that close to her, then you must know more than you're telling us."

Kevin came to the rescue. "Audrey, You weren't here from the beginning, so you're unaware that Rick works in a somewhat unorthodox manner. So far his contributions to this task force have been right on. I suggest that you take what he told you as the truth."

"He's right." George chimed in. "I don't know where we would be without Rick's input. I say, give him a break and trust what he says."

"I agree as well." Said ACE. "Why don't you tell us where you stand with the investigation of the members of congress, Audrey?"

She was in a snit because of the rebuke but none-the-less started her presentation. "We've picked up quite a bit of information on these guys and gals. Fortunately, I'm not going to tell you what they are all up to in their private lives, except to say that they're a wild bunch. None of them are paying ransom, I'm happy to say. Lot's of marital problems uncovered, and a lot of fooling around outside the bedroom. Here's what we turned up that we think is pertinent to what we're looking for. Seven of them have drug problems. Two of them had overdosed last year, which required their hospitalization. Two others were hooked on painkillers because of for a painful knee-joint ordeal. They're both receiving treatments. We're sure that it's not any of those four. That leaves three men who could be in Salvetti's pocket. We're working on gathering more information on them now. We feel that it's one of them. But for obvious reasons we have to be very cautious before approaching any of them. That's all I have. There will be more next week."

"I've got a small amount of news to announce." Vince Green voiced. "I heard from my European agent, Peter Grace. His undercover agent, the one who's working for Victor Salvetti, has contacted him. She told him that she's heard some of his telephone conversations, but that she must verify the information from another source before reporting any details. She suspects that he could be laying in another trap for her. She will tell us anything she knows when she speaks to Peter, regardless of receiving confirmation or not. I'll let you know what she comes up with."

Rick was happy to hear that Saila had taken his warning to heart. He tried not to think about her passing unverified information to her control, but then, he knew it was a calculated risk because time was running out.

ACE told them that they would be meeting every week from this point on.

A week quickly passed and the task force met again. Rick passed making an expanded presentation and said he had no additional information to report. He could feel the icy stare of Audrey emanating from behind her glasses. George was on next.

"I'd like to report that the president had passed the tenth and final test of evacuating from the limousine into the tunnel below. He has tested all four escape tunnels. On the last three tests the limousine was driven by remote control. His usual driver was at the wheel in the operations center. The president remarked that he felt weird not being able to converse with the person driving him around. So we made a modification and added a microphone and a speaker. He now is able to speak to his driver. That's all I have to report. The secret service has done all it can to insure the safety of the president and the speaker of the house."

Vince was up next. "I've not heard anything more from Peter. He said he would call me as soon as his agent checked in. I'll get the word out regardless of the time of day."

Kevin Winslow was his usual somber self and had nothing to report. Everyone focused on Audrey.

"I said last week that there were three congressmen that bore more scrutiny. One is a recently appointed congressman who received a political appointment to finish out the term of a member who died. He is a confirmed cocaine user and has just been reported as having a stroke and is in the hospital. My man spoke directly to his doctor. He's said to be in very bad shape. He obviously will not be attending that evening so we took him off our list.

"Are you sure that he won't make a recovery and plan to attend after all?" Asked Kevin.

"Not a chance. My agent says that he's out of it, especially since he can't get any cocaine in the hospital. He is reported to be in withdrawal and is suffering greatly. Moving on now, we have identified another congressman who is addicted to morphine. This man was badly wounded during the Gulf War and is a war hero with a Congressional

Medal of Honor to his credit. His doctors believe he has his addiction under control. For the sake of being ultra-cautious he will not be allowed to come within 100 feet of the president.

"The next man has a heroin as well as an alcohol problem. He went downhill after his wife left him just before Christmas. He was one of those who attended Thanksgiving dinner with Victor Salvetti. I have two men assigned to be literally and physically at his side every minute. We think he is our man, but we can't pick him up until we're sure. He also won't be allowed to get within a 100 feet of the president. With that said, I believe we've pinned down the last prong of Victor's attempts. Are there any questions?"

"What is this Congressman's name?" Asked George.

"I'm not going to release any names until we're ready to arrest. I'll provide the names to the Secret Service on the morning of the speech."

"Suppose you have not identified the right man? What are your contingency plans?" Asked Kevin.

"You're a hard man to please, Kevin. The contingency is that the Secret Service will have men positioned very close to the president. No unauthorized personnel will ever get near him. Am I not correct, George?"

"Yes, you're correct, Audrey. But for safety's sake I think that you should take this man that you've identified into custody right now. Sweat the truth out of him."

"And how do you think the press will take to my arresting a congressman, just because he uses cocaine. It will never fly. I need solid proof before I proceed. He'll have to be arrested long before he attempts to make his attack. All we need to do is to find the fast acting poison on his person. Then we'll nail him. It's the way it has to be."

"See you all a week from today. Let me remind you that's Tuesday the 29th of January, only two days before the president gives his speech." There was an ominous sound of somberness in ACE's voice as she closed the meeting.

Another week passed. Peter Grace received a call from his agent, LambieDog, alias Saila Ewe. It was eleven thirty in France. It was also Monday, January 28th.

"I've got to make this quick, Peter. Last week I overheard someone who called Victor from the United States. He was upset, using foul language and even threatening Victor because he didn't deliver him his 'high-nourishment product' on time. I'm sure he was talking about his drug delivery. He also sounded like he was drunk. He made mention of a job that he was going to do for Victor later this month. That's all I got. Victor arrived in the office and I had to get off the phone and let him talk to the man. Victor was able to calm this guy down and he spoke so softly I was unable to hear what he said."

"Were you able to verify this information from another source since you first gave me this alert that you had picked up something?"

"No, I was not. It is the reason I waited so long. However, I think it important enough that you have this information before any more time slips by. At least you can have it checked out."

"I hope that you didn't put yourself at risk with Victor. I'll forward this information to Vince Green right away. Thank you, Saila. Watch your back and stay safe."

Immediately after receiving this message Vince called Audrey, and then the vice president. Audrey called George, and ACE called the president and then Kevin, who called Rick. It was early morning now in the United States. Rick was not at home, so Kevin left a message for him to call him back. He was not about to leave any sensitive data on an answering system. He wondered where Rick was at this time of the morning.

Rick had brought the judge to the hospital late Saturday night. The judge had developed a bad case of the flu earlier that week. By Saturday morning he was running a high fever and had become badly dehydrated. Rick had spent the next three days and nights at the hospital by his bedside. On Tuesday morning the judge was feeling much better. Rick rushed home that morning to get a shower and dress in order to attend the task force meeting. He failed to pick up the message Kevin had left for him, and was unaware that Saila had forwarded any information for use by the task force.

Rick entered the meeting a little late. Vince Green's update to the task force had been given by telephone relays in the early morning hours.

Audrey was already expounding on her team's ability to identify their man for sure. She had made this decision based on recent details she had received about the congressman identified at the previous meeting.

"With the latest information we have received this man fits the bill of being our assassin. He has both an alcohol and drug problem and it matches the description provided us to a 'T'. And while it's only hearsay, we believe he recently spoke to Victor Salvetti. He is a four-term congressman from the state of Indiana, and there have been separate deposits of nine thousand dollars to his checking account for each of the last twenty-five weeks. The only thing missing is that we have been unable to connect him directly with Salvetti other than when he dined with him at Thanksgiving and other people were present. His phone has now been tapped and we feel it will only be a short time before Victor calls to give him his final instructions. I really believe that we have our man."

"What if he's been taking some sort of bribe to push some special interest legislation? It was Kevin who asked the hard question. He continued with more food-for-thought. "That only makes him a crook, not an assassin. I'm sure a good lawyer can explain away the booze and the dope, since he's upset because his wife has recently left him. However, if you're that sure it's him, then pick him up now. You can do it quietly and no one will be the wiser. That is, if you're sure." He emphasized.

"I think I'll keep him under close surveillance. I hope that satisfies all of you." Answered Audrey.

"You're on next, Rick. Do you have any additional information to tell us about who the sleeper agent is?"

"Sorry, ACE. I can't reveal the name of the alleged sleeper agent. Suffice to say the woman is not now, or ever was, capable of killing anyone in cold blood, regardless of any duress she was under. Her family's safety was a serious concern all along, but she was working behind the scenes to identify the person who will attempt to take the president's life. She is still working toward that goal. After the night of the speech she will come forward and identify herself. But for now it is important that she keep her identity secret."

"You didn't hear what I said while I was speaking." An emotionally charged Audrey shouted.

"I said that we have already all but identified the man. Why do you keep pursuing this woman's innocence? Why, she's the one who is supposed to kill the speaker of the house."

"I'm sorry, Audrey. You can believe what you want, but I don't think, in fact I'm sure, that you are on the trail of the wrong man. In any event I'm telling you that the woman who was the sleeper agent will show herself after the speech."

ACE jumped into what had now developed into a voice raising argument. "Everybody in this room has been under tremendous pressure for almost a year. We have to continue to conduct these meetings in a serious vein, and not let emotions enter into our discussions. Too much is riding on the outcome. Does anyone else wish to comment on this divergence of opinions?"

Vince Green decided it was time to take a stand. He stood to make his point.

"I think that each of the viewpoints do not interfere with the other. If, as Audrey believes, she has already identified the potential assassin, then we're home free. And if on the other hand Rick's mystery woman is able to disclose who it is, then we have it covered two ways against the middle. That is as long as Rick is sure there is no danger to the speaker."

"Believe me, I'm right about the woman. Even more so since the three thugs that Saddam sent to harm her family are dead, and there is nothing hanging over her head." Rick offered.

It was time for George to put in his two cents.

"I'm a cautious person by nature. I must agree with Vince that having two distinct ways to trap this vile creature makes sense."

"I'm thinking along those lines as well." Kevin volunteered. "Let me change the subject for a minute. Rick, I hear that Associate Justice Abraham Benjamin is in the hospital. If he is not at the speech, then his cane won't be there either. Vince has gone through a great deal of trouble to set up the cane to explode. It looks like that may not happen."

"I'm taking him out of the hospital after I leave here. He's much stronger now. I'll either get him to bring his cane into the building, or I'll make arrangements to have someone bring it in and I'll plant it in the bathroom stall myself."

"That's risky. Who would you use that can get past all the security?" Questioned Kevin. "Let me suggest that if the judge can't make it tomorrow night give the cane to Vince and let him bring it into the building. You can tell him where it has to be placed. We can set this up by having Vince pretend to sprain his ankle and go to the hospital this afternoon. Once we get the word out into the newspapers that Vince has injured himself we have a back up plan in place. If the judge does make it after all, then Vince has been put out a little."

Vince agreed to fake an accident to his ankle as soon as the meeting ended.

"It's a plan. But if I know the judge, he will be there."

ACE saw that a consensus had been formed and jumped at the chance to end this last meeting in a state of harmony.

"It would seem that we have an agreement on a number of vital points. It is a fitting way to end our task force meetings. The president has asked me to tell all of you how much he appreciates your efforts this past year. God willing, we'll all be smiling in a few days."

With the meeting over, Rick spoke to Kevin. "I'm going to get the judge. Are there any last-minute instructions you want to give me?"

"I left a message for you to call me at your home. With what you heard here today I don't have anything else to say. Here's your security pass. The president himself has signed it. You're attending his speech as one of his personal guests."

Rick never did hear that Saila had provided the information to the group, and that it was this information that Audrey had based her conclusions on.

As Rick entered the hospital he spotted Dr. Ahrens getting on an elevator. He watched to see the floor where the elevator stopped. He asked a nurse what was located on the third floor, and she said Intensive Care Unit, better known as simply ICU.

"Anybody important in there now?"

"The usual heart attack and stroke victims. They also have patients recently out of surgery in there. Are you looking for anyone in particular?"

"I'm here to pick up Judge Benjamin." *Rick didn't pursue asking about what Ahrens was doing there any further. He rationalized he was a doctor and had a right to be in a hospital to treat someone.*

"That one, he's been ready to go since yesterday. He never shuts up. Always has a wise comment to make to a nurse. He's up on the fourth floor. Better take a wheel chair with you or you won't be able to have him released and you'll have to wait for one to free up. Here, take this one."

"Hey, judge. How are you feeling today?"

"Ready to go home. I've been signed out for three hours now. Where the hell have you been?"

"I had some very important things to attend to. I'm here now, so don't make such a fuss."

Rick helped him into his car that was parked near the hospital entrance. The ride home was short, only about twenty-five minutes. It provided Rick with a chance to see how he really was feeling.

"Am I going to be driving you to hear the president's speech tomorrow night? The doctor tells me that you're almost back to full recovery right now. No fever spikes and you're no longer dehydrated. If you stay in bed with me pampering you for the rest of today and most of tomorrow, I think you'll be fine."

"I know the doctor thinks I'm better, but I'm feeling mighty poorly. You know what will return my vigor?"

"I can only guess."

"You got that right, Sonny. I gather that you want me to attend that speech. There's got to be a reason, so let's trade. I'll be attending, only if you come clean and tell me what I've got a right to know. You've been keeping secrets from me too long, Ricky Blanco. I'm sure that's not your name. You're an Indian, not an Italian."

By the time they arrived home Rick had told him everything. When he finally got the judge into his bed he was looking like the-cat-that-ate-the-canary.

"You just go about your business today, Rick. I'll be able to take care of myself, and I'll call out for dinner. I'm sure that you have many things to do in the next two days. Don't you worry. I'll be there; you can count on it, and I'll have my cane with me."

Rick called Santanna. It was time to cross the 'T's' and dot the 'I's'. Anna Mary picked up.

"Is he home? This is Ricky.

"He's working an early shift tonight and tomorrow. That's funny. You're the second person who called asking to see him tonight. He told me he's going to be taking Thursday off. Won't tell me what he's going to do. Do you know what he's got planned? He's really got me pissed."

"You'll have to talk to him about it. I'll drop over to the bar where he works and catch him there. If he calls you in the meantime, please tell him to stay where he is so I can speak to him."

It was a slow night and Santanna waved him to the end of the bar and poured him a cold one. He asked the other bartender to cover for him.

"What's up, Ricky? Why do you feel you have to see me tonight?"

"I'm just checking that you're ready for the day after tomorrow. You have a couple of things lined up to do."

"I've been thinking; I'm not going to show. I told you that I've never killed anyone before. For sure I'm not ready to kill anybody, especially the President of the Unites States. He's never done anything to me. Why should I want to kill him?"

Just then one of Ahrens goons showed up at the bar and headed back to where the two of them were talking.

"I'm glad I caught the two of you together. Saves me a trip over to see you separately, Ricky."

"Let's get down to the business at hand. Santanna, at precisely ten Thursday morning you're going to drive the first dumpster loading vehicle and pick up the one loaded with debris at the construction site. Take it to Jefferson Street, four streets away, and park it. There will be at least ten other loaders parked at this location; one more won't be noticed. Take a cab and go home and relax until eleven this evening."

He tossed a set of keys to Santanna. "You're going to need these for your evening assignment. They're to be used in the Lincoln Navigator SUV parked on Southwest Street. You're going to drive it straight into the top of the limousine when it's on its side at the bottom of the intersection adjacent to the construction site. Just drive at a speed of twenty miles an hour, aim the front of the SUV at the roof, and don't forget to push the red lever, which will lock the handle in place. Then get the hell out. Walk away at least three streets north and then grab a cab. Mr. Salvetti has a plane waiting for all of his agents. It's scheduled to leave from the Farmingdale Private Airport located just outside of

Washington. Go to Lane Freight Airways gate. Plan to get there by one AM. Any local cab will take you out there. Be on time and travel light. The flight leaves at one forty-five sharp."

"Can I bring my wife? I only recently got married."

Without even batting an eye, he said: "Sure, why not? The more the merrier, I suppose. There's plenty of room on the plane. Oh, yeah. Make sure that she brings along her passport."

Then he turned his attention to Ricky. "You'll be following Santanna by five minutes. You know where you're supposed to pick up the dumpster loading vehicle, don't you?"

Ricky nodded in the affirmative. "The keys will be in it. To recap, you're to drive over and pick up the empty dumpster with the explosives. Take it to the construction site and put it in the exact same spot that Santanna has taken the debris filled one from. You will find chalk marks on the ground so you'll know where to position it. Be sure that the side with the name of the Construction Company printed on it is facing the road."

"Won't the Fed.'s be checking anything parked on the street, since it is known to be a route the president's vehicle travels?"

"Of course they will, dummy. Don't worry, they won't detect anything. I'm a professional."

"Then drive the loading vehicle to the same place on Jefferson Street and leave it. The next thing on your agenda is to drive the judge to the Hall of Congress later that night. Make sure that he has his cane with him. Go back home and pick up your belongings and head to the airport, same as Santanna."

"Before I forget, Mr. Salvetti wants you both to have some extra cash to pay for cab expenses. He told me to give you each three hundred dollars in small bills. He doesn't want receipts. Any questions? If not, then I'll see you both at the airport."

He walked away slowly, an air of arrogance surrounding his gait.

Santanna said to Ricky. "I guess that settles it. If we don't follow instructions, I think they'll kill us both. I gotta' face all of Anna Mary's questions when I get home. She's mad at me now. How am I gonna' get her to take a plane ride with me in the middle of the night? I can't leave her, I love her too much."

"I can't help you with that, Santanna. I don't suggest that you tell her anything about what you're going to be doing on Thursday. And the fact of the matter is that I don't see that we have any other options. Be seeing you at the airport after it's all over. Did you ever think that maybe one of the other guys will get the president first. Then we won't have anything to do. Cheer up, we'll come out of this okay."

Rick had become attached to Santanna over the months, and he couldn't help but think of him as a friend, although only God knew why. It just happened, even though Santanna was a hood, albeit not a very good one. He knew how Santanna felt about him. He was sure that when it was all over he would be able to get him deported back to Italy and not spend any jail time. He could take Anna Mary back with him.

Rick was thinking as he walked out of the bar. *Well, this is the last time I'll have to be Ricky Blanco for anybody.* He was wrong. Rick silently left and headed for home to check on the judge. Once again he was thinking *tomorrow would be a big day.* He was right on that count.

Upon returning to the judge's town home he saw a car parked out front. A distinguished looking man was just leaving.

"Oh, Ricky, I mean Rick. I'd like to introduce you to my lawyer, Richard Raffelle."

"Pleased to meet you, Rick. I was just leaving."

"You take care of yourself now. Stay in bed as much as you can. I'll have those papers ready for you to sign the day after tomorrow, Judge Benjamin. You can count on it." With that said, he left.

"What's that all about, judge? More important, how are you feeling?"

"To answer the first question, it's none of your business. To the second, I'll be fit and ready to go to the speech if that's what you're asking."

"Sorry I asked. No, not really. I do hope that you're feeling better. Can I get you anything before I go to bed?"

"Nothing, Rick. Don't get so touchy, I'm just an old man pulling on your chain. Thanks for asking."

Chapter 12

Carma Papadopilis received a call at one in the afternoon on January 31st from Victor Salvetti. I'm calling from my office in Great Britain. Don't be concerned about a wiretap as this message is being scrambled by the best electronics money can buy. The NSA doesn't have a chance of deciphering it. It's really a great day, isn't it? The reason for this call should be obvious. Today is the day I've been waiting for for so many years. I want to review your part in this unfolding drama.

"I know what I'm supposed to do. Is this really necessary? Suppose you couldn't get in touch with me today?"

"I feel that it is necessary. I always have ways of keeping in close contact with those who work for me."

"I don't work for you. I'm only a hired gun who has been loaned out to you." She sounded testy.

"Whatever. That's only a technicality. Let's get down to the business at hand if you don't mind. Leave that attitude out of this and we'll get along just fine. I'm assuming that you have been able to be assigned to guard the Speaker of the House this evening?"

"Yes, I have. My shift starts at seven this evening. I am planning on shooting the speaker after the speech, while he escorts the president out of the hall of congress. I will not even be able to draw my gun until your man makes his attempt to inject the president with a fast acting poison. I need the confusion of the attempt to work for me. Who is the congressman who you've lined up?" There was a long pause.

"Why do you have to know his name?"

"Because when I see him making his move I will react accordingly. I can't take out my gun and shoot before he acts first, or one of the other secret service agents guarding the president could possibly shoot me when I aim my piece in that direction. I have to be sure that I don't hit your man before I get mine. I have a need to know who he is."

"I'll consider it. Give me some more reasons for me to tell you."

"It has to look like a stray bullet from my gun has shot him. I've been purposely doing poorly on the firing range lately, in order for me to be able to claim plausibility for my errant shot. I'm hoping to walk away from all this when it's all over."

"You're lucky that I'm in a generous mood today. I don't suppose that it will hurt to give you his name and some background. His name is Roger Speigel. He's only been in congress for a few months, having recently been appointed to fill an elected vacancy. I paid a great deal of money to the party leaders to have this happen."

"How in the world did you find a congressman who would do such a thing?"

"This man happens to be the younger brother of a woman named Betsy Speigel. She died after a botched abortion led to her developing an emotional problem, which eventually caused her death years later while she was in a sanitarium. This man really hates the president with a passion because he was the one who had made her pregnant while they were in college."

"How in the world did you obtain this kind of detailed information?"

"There's a very wealthy man who was in love with the woman while Germond Faller was courting her. This man was devastated when he abandoned her while she was pregnant. He fired up the anger in the woman's younger brother, and kept the flames fanned over the years.

The congressman is a drug addict. Thus, it was a simple matter for me to supply him with all of the cocaine he can possibly use."

"I assure you that I'm as ready as I can be. Read tomorrow's papers. You'll be satisfied."

"My dear, Carmella." He had called her by her given name and it gave her a start. "I want you to know that I have someone watching you, so I'm sure that you won't contact anyone with what I've told you. Remember that Saddam can have your family killed with just a phone call. I don't mind if you attempt to squirm out of this and try to maintain your reputation. As a matter of fact, I don't mind if you kill the man who has injected the president after you've taken out the speaker. I think that's a great idea. It will also enhance your plausibility claim. Have a real nice, and I might add, successful evening."

Carma's husband was not at home so she was unable to alert him. She couldn't phone Rick Banyan from her home either. In fact, she couldn't call anybody. She was sure Victor had both her home phone and her cell phone tapped. She thought that perhaps she would be able to pass her information on to Rick in the great hall before the president spoke. Her mind raced in all directions looking for a solution to her dilemma. She decided then and there that her best chance to thwart the assassination attempt would be for her to bring down the assassin herself, before he injects the president. Now that she had his name, she would have to find out what he looks like.

Victor heard the sound of a click on the phone, as he was about to hang up. He knew that someone had been listening in on the extension. He went into the outer office where Saila had just dialed out in an attempt to reach Peter Grace. Her back was to the door in which Victor came in and she failed to hear him enter. She had just been connected and identified herself to Peter. Victor reached around her and depressed the switch-hook. He backhanded her and she was knocked off her chair and rendered unconscious. He called one of his henchmen into the office.

"Take her to the holding area. Bind her carefully and put a twenty-four hour guard on her. We shall see how much damage she has caused before I decide what penalty she will pay for her treachery."

Peter knew instinctively that the connection with Saila had been broken because Victor had found her out. He put his head in his hands. He was devastated. There was nothing that he could do to save her now.

* * * *

Rick awoke the morning of the thirty-first with a start. Something had been bugging him all night and he did not get in much REM sleep. He checked the judge who was still sleeping and left the house at six, but not before leaving him a note. Driving the empty streets he arrived at the hospital seventeen minutes later. He went directly to admissions.

"I'm with the Department of Defense." He lied. "I'm a special assistant to the president." He was wearing the pass he'd been given to get him into the congressional hall later that evening. It was the only identification he had to show. He was lucky. It had the presidential seal on it and was official looking.

"How can we help you, Mr. Banyan?" The woman was reading his name in bold print on his pass.

"I was here yesterday and learned that you had a VIP in the ICU. I saw a Doctor Ahrens heading to that floor. Could you please provide me with the names of the people who were in that unit yesterday, and advise me if they're still in the hospital?"

"We've had two people released yesterday, one went home and the other was released to go into the hospital proper. The guy that checked out was a noisy and rude person. I guess that's because he is a congressman and wanted to push his weight around."

"That's the guy I'm looking for. Never mind the list. Could I have his name, please?"

"His name is listed as Congressman Roger Speigel. I saw him when he left the building. He looked like he was higher than a kite, you know, like he was on something. They don't give drugs that make a person behave like that in this hospital."

"Was he attended by Dr. Ahrens?"

"Yes, he was in to see him every day. Yesterday before he released him he gave him a package that looked like a pen set. My girlfriend was in ICU at the time and mentioned to me that she thought it strange."

"Please look up his record while he was here."

"He came into the hospital a few nights ago. Dr. Ahrens admitted him to be treated for a stroke. I'm looking at the medicine he was given. That's strange. They never gave him the clot busting injection. Also, nobody who has ever had a stroke leaves the hospital in less than ten days."

"Can you describe him to me? It will help my investigation a lot."

"I thought you said that he was a friend of yours."

"Looks like you caught me. I've been known to tell a fib now and then in my line of work."

"Let's see if I can remember. Oh yes, he's short, only about five-foot five, has a mustache and dark curly hair. Looks sort of like a short Afro."

"Thanks. I really appreciate it."

Rick went back to the house to give the judge his breakfast. He was looking bright, and he was in good spirits. After that he excused himself again.

"I've got to pick up a truck and make a delivery."

"What ever keeps you government spooks happy is okay with me." Replied the judge. Just be back here in time to drive me tonight."

While on the way to get the truck he put a direct call to Kevin's cell. He was breaking protocol. He felt that he did not have the time or opportunity to make the call as CONSPIRATOR. He got a busy signal and was switched to a call-messaging area.

"Kevin, this is Rick. I've got vital information on the person we're looking for. If we can't connect by a secure phone then I'll tell you all I know when I see you this evening. Right now I've got to do my job for my other boss."

Rick didn't notice, but his cell phone was below normal power level and required charging.

Rick saw Santanna pulling away with the filled dumpster as he turned the corner. He pulled into the space vacated and placed his recently altered dumpster directly into the area that was outlined on the ground with chalk marks. He had taken his first step in a conspiracy to kill the president.

His job for that morning completed, he drove the truck to the drop off point and grabbed a cab. He didn't seek out Santanna, not wanting to face him again until after this was all over. He returned home to await the call back from Kevin.

His lawyer was at the house with the papers the judge had him draw up. He had two people with him to act as witnesses. Rick was sure the judge had made changes to his will. This guy wanted to be assured that he got the changes made and filed correctly to make them legal. Rick couldn't understand the need for the rush.

It was none of his business, so he said hello to Richard Raffelle and excused himself. Then he headed up to his room. He laid his head on his pillow. The phone call never came, and his fatigue finally caught up with him. The judge knocked on his door at six thirty. He jumped up and for one of the few times in his life he had trouble getting his bearings.

"I'm going to grab a quick shower and start dressing. I'll be ready in about fifteen minutes. Thanks for waking me. I didn't get much sleep last night. We'll leave for the hall at seven sharp. It's only a fifteen-minute drive. That should give us plenty of time. I've got a few things to do and people to see once I get there. Do you mind being early?"

"Not a problem, Rick." Rick dropped the judge off in the front of the building and pulled around the back to park. Security was extremely tight. The judge's cane had to be hand inspected before they returned it to him. After all, he was an Associate Justice of the Supreme Court.

A little later as Rick went through the second of two full body sensing machines, called a magnetron, he asked the guard: "Has Congressman Roger Speigel come through the gate yet? He's a friend of mine." The guard checked the roster and replied.

"He's in the building since seven. Must be an early bird. Sorry I can't page him for you. Better look over in the congressional galley if you want to find him."

So much for Audrey's theory that the man would never be able to leave the hospital. He thought quietly to himself.

By the time he cleared security he saw the judge sitting in the place reserved for Supreme Court Justices. All nine were sitting in place and talking; and that's after being in conference all day. He watched as the judge excused himself and started to leave. Rick's heart skipped a beat.

Then he watched as the judge quickly returned to his seat and grabbed his cane. He was moving now in an autonomic fashion as he had been programmed to do. He passed right by Rick on his way to the men's room. He continued watching and saw the judge come out of the toilet…without his cane. Things were going as scheduled. The judge winked at him as he passed by heading back to his seat.

Rick searched the vast room for Kevin. He wondered why he hadn't returned his call. Then he looked for Carma. She was on station and positioned near the speaker who was already sitting in his seat behind the podium. When she saw Rick looking at her she waved her head from side to side. He observed that George was also standing on the podium talking to some of his people. The only person he could find to speak to was Vince Green. He was walking with a cane and limping badly. *At least he was doing what he was supposed to do,* thought Rick.

"The judge was able to make it here tonight under his own steam. You don't have to keep up the act, the cane has been planted as arranged."

Vince started walking away still limping. Rick didn't get it. Vince also didn't want to tell Rick about the bad news he had just received from Peter Grace, and was unaware how much Saila meant to him. He would tell him and the other members of the task force after thc president was deemed safe.

Before Rick had a chance to say anything else and ask Vince if he knew whom congressman Roger Speigel was, everybody rose and watched as the president entered into the congressional chamber to a resounding round of applause, which lasted for three minutes.

Rick started searching for the man. All he had was a thumbnail visual of what he looked like from the description the hospital admission's clerk provided. His eyes scanned the room, which was now filled completely. No luck, the president started his State of the Union speech at ten minutes after eight. It was scheduled to last ninety minutes, but with interruptions for applause it would take at least two hours. Rick was waiting at the back end of an isle when Roger came up to stand beside him. It would be disrespectful if the two of them began a conversation while the president was speaking. So they stood silently waiting for it to end.

* * * *

In the boardroom of Whitman Oil in New York City, four remaining members of the CLIQUE sat in silence as the man they all hated started to speak. One was missing from their group, secreted away in witness protection. They thought of him as a friend who was missing, perhaps even dead. He was ready to turn states evidence and rat them out in order to save himself. There were no catcalls or loud boisterous shouting as there had been only a short year ago. The FBI had the place wired for sight and sound to see if they would say or do even more to incriminate themselves. Only Tobias Whitman was ebullient. He was about to see the man he hated meet his maker.

The other three were scared shitless. The common thought amongst them was w*hat have we done? Are we crazy?*

One of Salvetti's soldiers was assigned to watch the CLIQUE's meeting in progress. He was already in custody; having been picked up in the small anteroom on a conspiracy warrant before any of them arrived.

* * * *

As the time neared ten PM one of Ahrens goons pulled up on the specified side street in Washington with a black Navigator SUV that had the front of it loaded with impact explosives. The man casually locked the doors and walked away; unaware he had put the final part of Victor's plan into place. He was only following orders. Nothing was being left to chance. Santanna would find it parked exactly where he had been told it would be.

* * * *

Back in the congressional hall the janitor Victor had hired picked up the brass encrusted cane that the judge had left in a bathroom stall. He quickly dismantled the brass from the wood and reassembled it into a pistol with a long barrel and a sight. Next he unscrewed the brass base of the cane and three bullets fell into his hand. He broke the remains of the wooden cane in half and stuffed it into the refuse can. It would be found later, but who cared. The man didn't expect to live much beyond the first shot. He had been assured that his family would be taken care of for life.

The president was approximately half an hour into his speech when the man took up the position he had selected. He had somehow eluded the secret service agents and climbed up into the rafters and hidden himself behind a large speaker. It was a tight squeeze but he finally maneuvered his way into his selected cubbyhole. From here he would be able to make a shot at the head of the president. He did have an unobstructed view of the podium. He was prepared to fire rapidly three times.

A loud sound interrupted the president while he started speaking again after pausing and waiting for the applause to die down. Two secret service agents immediately threw their bodies on top of the president after they pushed him to the floor. George and ACE had warned him earlier that this would happen. As a result he was not surprised. George grabbed the microphone and told everyone in the room to keep their seats, everything was under control. He further stated the president was unharmed and would shortly resume his speech. Then he breathed a long sigh of relief. The first attempt had been successfully thwarted.

It took a minute before secret service agents were able to reach the man who had fired the shot. His hand was hanging on by only a small piece of skin, he was bleeding profusely and his eye had been blown out of its socket. Fifteen minutes later they removed his body, and the man was pronounced dead at the scene. Once the body had been removed, the president returned to the podium. The CIA had done their job in sabotaging the makeshift gun only too well. The president seemed unflappable as the crowd roared with even more applause, this time lasting five minutes. Finally, he was allowed to speak.

"The poor misguided soul who attempted to kill me was a victim too. I understand that the man who hired him had lied to him as well. May God have mercy on his soul?

"...Now let me see, where was I?"

Applause boomed once again at the casual way he was handling himself. He continued his speech until the end without further interruption, except when applause was warranted. The speech ended at ten-fifty to another round of thunderous applause. He started moving towards the exit, shaking everybody's hand that was offered, despite the specific warning ACE had given him to be wary of strange and unknown faces.

Rick tried to head the president off at the doorway. He spotted the would-be assassin now known to be Congressman Roger Speigel. Rick could only watch, as the man seemed to be fumbling in his breast pocket trying to get at his fountain pen. He was too far away to do anything but yell.

He raised his voice in the great hall. "Watch out for the man with a fountain pen. It's been dipped in poison." He yelled it as loud as he could, but the noise generated from everyone in the room talking at once absorbed the sound. It was as if he were talking to someone next to him.

It was then that he saw Carma in the corner of his eye. She raised her gun, and aimed it in the direction of the house speaker, who was walking along the side of the president as he was leaving the hall.

"Oh my God." Rick stomach cringed, as he was immediately racked with pangs of regret. He had made the mistake of trusting her, and it was to be a fatal mistake, one he would never be able to make right.

A single shot rang out loudly in the slowly emptying congressional hall…Rick held his breath. He had no gun. Then he looked down and saw Roger Spiegel's body splayed across the floor. The poison fountain pen lay at his side. He was about to stab the president's hand when he abruptly died. Carma had been a deadly shot, not as she had been showing at the firing range. Her bullet hit its target square between the eyes.

George ran to the side of the president and then stared at his wife. She had saved the life of the President of the United States. He took another deeply drawn breath of air, and let it out ever so slowly as it brought relief to his racing heart. They had dodged the second prong of Victor Salvetti's best-laid plan. He made the sign of the cross and said a silent prayer, and he had his wife to thank for it.

The president's limousine had arrived and was waiting out front. The secret service wanted him to exit the building immediately. Two attempts on his life in less than two hours really stressed the team of agents who guarded him. The door was held open and he entered and sat stoically, as the door to the limo was slammed shut. One of the agents was already in the car waiting for him; a last minute change made by George. It made the president feel more comfortable. The car sped away heading to his living quarters in the White House.

After it turned the corner the car braked to an abrupt stop over what looked like a manhole cover, where he first and then the agent exited the vehicle into the underground passageway. Another agent was waiting for them in the tunnel, and the three of them made their way to the exit recently constructed. The limousine then resumed a normal speed and headed towards the White House via the streets usually followed. The agents would guide him back to his quarters. His wife and children had already gone back to the living quarters.

As the limousine passed a construction site an explosion occurred. Dr. Ahrens had depressed the button on the remote control as the limousine came abreast of the dumpster. Because of the armor reinforcement protecting the vehicle nothing penetrated its exterior. However, the limousine did flip over on its side.

Santanna saw what had happened. He started the SUV and began driving down the middle of the street keeping the speed at exactly twenty miles per hour. There were no other cars on the street. Once he judged that he was a half street away from impact he pressed the red button and pushed in the lever as instructed. He watched as the door locks snapped shut.

He tried to open a door so he could jump out; he reached across and tried the door on the passenger side to no avail. He was locked in. He thought quickly and crawled into the rear of the SUV and started kicking at the rear window glass. The SUV was almost at the point of impact, which was the roof of the limousine. The glass popped out and he threw himself out the back. The impact occurred only three seconds after he got out. The ensuing explosion demolished the SUV, and threw Santanna twenty-five feet in the air.

When he landed the whole side of his body scraped along the macadam giving him a burn. He staggered away and somehow was able to walk four streets away from the explosion. He caught a cab and instructed the driver to take him to where Ricky lived. The house was dark, so he waited in an alley at the side of the house. He was feeling a great deal of pain. He muttered out loud. "Son-of-a-bitch, they tried to kill me." He said it over and over, until the pain became severe and he passed out.

Rick dropped the judge off at the front of the house and then drove around the back to put his car into the garage. The judge let himself in and put on the front lights. Rick came around to the front of the house juggling the keys in his hand.

Ahrens goon was waiting there with a gun. Rick turned to face him.

"When you didn't react to Santanna telling you that he wanted to take his wife with him I knew that there was no plane waiting to take us out of the country. If that's how Victor rewards his employees, you can only guess your payoff."

"It's not going to give you any satisfaction because you guessed that little fact of life. Your friend, Santanna, has already had it. Nobody could have walked away from that explosion. It drove the roof of the limousine into the internal part of the car. The president couldn't survive that. Don't be worried. I'll make it quick and painless."

He started to squeeze the trigger and Rick tensed. He was going to take the shot as best he could and then he was going to leap at the man. The judge looked out the side window and saw the man holding a gun on Rick. His hand reached for the light switch and he flicked it twice. The effect of the lights blinded the man momentarily. Rick had quickly moved into a crouched position and pulled his bone knife out of its scabbard. The thug pulled on the trigger in reflex action. **Pfft.** It was a silenced shot and made only a small amount of noise. The thug had only gotten off a single shot.

Moments before he discharged his weapon, Santanna had leaped in front of his friend, Ricky. He took the shot in his side and fell to the ground.

In a flash Rick leaped at his attacker and had pressed his knife into the hood's side. He could see the blood spill from his mouth and his eye's roll back as the man he stabbed lapsed into unconsciousness. He had hit a vital organ. Meantime the judge had called 911 for an ambulance and the police. Rick could hear multiple sirens blaring out their erie-sounding signals. It was just another set of siren noises added to the many in Washington that night.

He went over and lifted Santanna's fallen body as he cradled him in his arms. Santanna looked into his eyes and spoke ever so softly.

"They tried to kill me, Ricky. They locked me in that car that exploded. I wuz lucky to get out alive. I knew that they would try and get you too. I cudn't let them kill you. Us guys gotta' stick together. I came right over here to warn you. If I don't make it, take care of Anna Mary for me, will you? Tell her I really love her."

Santanna slipped into unconsciousness as an ambulance and a police car pulled up to the curb. As it turned out only one person would need transportation to the hospital. Rick accompanied him in the ambulance.

At the hospital Rick watched the television in the waiting room while he waited for word on Santanna's condition. News about two separate attempts to kill the president was filling the airwaves. It was surprising how many different ways the news services were able to say the same thing over and over. Then there was an interruption for a Special Bulletin. A somber-faced broadcaster made the announcement.

"A third attempt has been made on the life of our president, Germond Faller. After successfully avoiding the first two attacks on his person, his armored limousine was knocked over on to its side. Another vehicle, one loaded with an explosive charge, rammed into the roof of the limousine. This collapsed the roof into the passenger compartment. They have not been able to remove the president's body from the limousine yet. However, the compression seems to be complete. It will be a miracle if he is still alive in all that wreckage."

No sooner had he said that statement and a picture of the limousine and the remains of the other vehicle that rammed it were shown live. A hovering helicopter was supplying pictures.

In the Boardroom of Whitman Oil, Tobias Whitman clapped loudly. The other members of the group sat in complete silence. The silence was broken when FBI Agents broke in and arrested them all for conspiracy to commit treason and attempted murder. One of the last things Tobias Whitman saw on television was another Special Bulletin. It quickly brought a frown to his smiling face.

"I'm pleased to announce that the president was currently safely sitting in his living quarters and will go on national television from the Oval Office at midnight. By some manner the secret service had apparently not allowed him to enter the limousine and had spirited him to an alternate vehicle to make the trip to his living quarters. Stay tuned to this station for…"

Rick smiled and thought quietly that: *The only important thing to report was that the president was unharmed. The details just didn't matter, not one single iota.*

He spotted Anna Mary coming into the waiting room. There was a policewoman accompanying her.

"Ricky, what in heaven's name has happened to my Santanna. All they told me is that he was shot and that he has some other body damage. He's in emergency surgery now. I don't even know if he's going to live. Do you know what happened? You have to tell me something?"

He didn't know how to answer her. Fortunately a doctor dressed in bloody scrubs had exited the operating room and was moving towards her.

"Are you Mrs. Santanna?" She nodded yes and clung to Rick's arm. "Your husband is a very lucky man. The bullet penetrated his lung, broke a rib, and exited out his side without hitting any other vital areas. We have been able to repair all the damage caused by the shooting. However, we must move him up to the burn unit. Do you have any idea where he received that burn across the side of his body and his arm? I don't know how he could have walked anywhere with that type of injury. But rest assured, he will recover."

Rick saw Kevin come into the waiting room and motioned him over. Rick saw Anna Mary to a seat and excused himself.

"What happened, Rick? Is Santanna in here being treated?"

"He was badly wounded in an explosion and made his way over to the house to warn me that Victor's hoods had a hit out on the both of us. He took a bullet for me, Kevin. I owe him my life. Do me a favor and keep the Fed.'s away from him. He's not going anywhere for awhile. He told me he wanted to back out of this operation completely, and I talked him into staying in this so we could keep the plan in tact. That's his wife over there."

"I'll see what I can do about him. Meanwhile you should know that ACE has called a meeting to post-mortem this operation at ten-tomorrow morning. As we speak, Audrey's people are in the process of rounding up all of Victor's people in the United States, and remaining members of the CLIQUE are already in custody. We have word that Victor Salvetti is currently in the United Kingdom. He's about to have a shit-fit when the information that all his plans were thwarted reaches him, that is if he doesn't already know."

* * * *

Victor Salvetti listened carefully to the short wave radio. He went through his own agony when he heard that the first two prongs of his plan had failed. He was really riled when he heard no mention of and shooting of the Speaker of the House during all of the confusion that followed. Then he was heartened by the news that his backup plan had worked. Moments later his elation was brought down to earth when he heard that the president was not in his limousine at all. He charged down the hall into the special room where his thug had taken Saila.

She was tied spread-eagled to the four posts on the bed.

"You she-bitch. Somehow you have been able to foil my plans. Now you will pay for that treachery."

With that said he pulled out a .038 mm revolver. He shot Saila three times in the stomach. The third shot went through her body and nicked her spinal column. She was not dead yet, but close to it.

"Let her lie there and die a slow death. It is the least that she deserves. Clear out of this place. It won't be long before they come looking for me. I'm heading back to Italy where they can't get me."

It took Peter Grace three hours to find out where Saila had called from when she made that desperate attempt to contact him. When he arrived, he found Saila alive, but only barely. She was taken by ambulance to an emergency care center. During the ride she grasped Peter's hand tightly for only a moment when she became conscious. She was as lucid as he had ever seen her.

"Tell Rick that I'm dead. I don't want to live in a vegetative state. I want to die, now. Do not do any unnatural things to keep me alive. Please grant me my dying wish? I've earned that much."

The wa-wa sound of the ambulance racing through the streets of London faded as she lapsed into unconsciousness.

* * * *

"Were you sent here as a sleeper agent for Saddam Hussein?"

George had begun an interrogation of his wife as soon as he took her home that night. She had received all sorts of compliments on her ability to save the president's life earlier that evening. Now was the time for her to 'Pay the Piper' for her years of subterfuge. She burst into tears. It was a natural release for the built up emotion that she had carried close to her heart for so long.

She told him the whole story. He sat back, unbelieving what he was hearing.

"Didn't you think that you could have taken me into your confidence? Never mind. It's obvious that you didn't."

"Don't you think that there were many times that I wanted to tell you? It was no fun for me knowing that my family would be killed at the whim of that madman, Saddam; I never knew when I would get the call to kill someone for him. I had long since made my peace with the fact that I would never kill anyone. I had hoped, actually I prayed, that something would happen to change the horrible situation surrounding my mother, father and sister. Then finally, Rick Banyan found out who I was. I still don't know how he managed that. But thank God that he did. Then I had to convince him of my loyalty to this country. He trusted me, and I delivered for this country that I have grown to love."

"Darling, you should have let me know. I am so proud of you, of what you have endured, and of what you have been able to do. I will talk to the vice president tomorrow morning before we have a wrap up meeting of the task force that I've been on. There were so many things going on that I was unable to tell you about. I will tell her everything. I'll resign if she talks to the president and he wants me to leave the government. The only thing that matters is that we have each other, and that I have your family alive and living in Italy. I wish to welcome them into our home."

The task force met at ten in the morning sharp. Only Peter Grace was unable to attend. He had sent his summary of the situation in Europe for Vince Green to give his report to the group. He was limping badly, and using the cane Rick had seen him with last night. Rick asked him what happened.

"I tried so hard to fake an ankle sprain in the event that I had to be the one to place the judge's cane in the toilet, that I actually twisted my ankle. I have to use this cane for the next three weeks."

His statement brought a chuckle to the group. It was good to have a little comic relief after the intense pressure they had been under.

"Stay up and give your report, Vince." ACE offered.

"I don't have much to report for myself. I'm happy to say that the work we did on the gun fashioned out of the judge's cane worked as planned. On a somber not, I just heard from Peter Grace. He was contacted yesterday by Saila Ewe, his undercover agent."

Rick's stomach tightened and he grabbed the arms of his chair at the mention of her name.

"While he was on the phone with her Victor Salvetti broke the connection. She never did get a chance to tell him anything. He was able to trace where the call was made from in England. He immediately took a chopper across the channel and arrived at the location in three hours. He found that Victor had shot her in the stomach three times. One of the bullets cut across her spine. She died on the way to the hospital. Per her last request her body is being shipped back to her home in Kuala Lumpur, Malaysia. She is to be cremated and her ashes spread in the Strait of Malacca. I'm sorry, Rick. Peter tells me that she mentioned you in her last words. I assume that you two became close during your assignment. That's all I have. I'd like to recommend her to receive the President's Medal of Valor, posthumously."

A profound sadness permeated the entire group. One of their own had been lost in the line of duty. Rick was asked to make his report next. He was not at his best.

"I suppose that we could say that all's well that ends well. There is a man who works for the Camorra and was involved in last night's attack on the president's car. He was used as a pawn in Victor's game, and since he recognized it for what it was and tried to get out of it. I talked him into doing the job as planned. Later that evening, despite a painful injury he incurred, he jumped in front of a bullet meant for me. I owe him my life. I am asking that consideration be given to releasing this man under his own recognizance now, and then returning him to Italy after he gets out of the hospital. He is an illegal alien and has married an American citizen under false pretenses."

ACE spoke. "I'll speak to the president on his behalf. I can't promise anything. Do you have any more that you have to report?"

"I think George wants to tell you all about the sleeper agent that I've been shielding from you."

"Thanks, Rick. I spoke to ACE before we met this morning and I have offered my resignation. You see, my wife was the sleeper agent. We know now, that she never would have acted to do anything Saddam Hussein had told her to do, despite the possible death threat to her family in Italy by his agents. She certainly vindicated herself when she shot the mad congressman who had attempted to kill the president. He was in Victor's pocket, and kept there with a steady supply of cocaine. My sincere thanks to Rick, whose organization in Italy liberated my wife's family. The details will be made available to all of you in my written report on protecting the life of the president."

Audrey finally got her chance to report. She made no apology for homing in on the wrong congressman.

"We have picked up every member of the Camorra assigned a role in the assassination attempts, with the exception of Santanna Santanna, and this other illegal known to us as Ricky Blanco. There is one man named Dr. Henri Ahrens claiming to have German diplomatic immunity. We shall see if it holds up. We do have a problem, however. We cannot touch Victor Salvetti for all he has done. He has taken refuge in his country, and we do not have enough proof to be able to extradite him. Does anyone have any ideas on what we can do about him?"

"Leave that one for Ricky Blanco." Said Rick "He will settle the score for all of us; count on it.

Chapter 13

The last meeting of the task force had ended. ACE was going over to the West Wing to brief the president. Audrey had been updated on the fact that Rick Banyan and Ricky Blanco had been one and the same person. Yet the last element to having success was the apprehension of Victor Salvetti for his role in the assassination attempts. He had not broken any Italian laws, and thus could not be touched by extradition, at least with only the minimum evidence they had accumulated.

To this end Rick had pledged to the task force to make that last element happen.

Kevin and Rick met to discuss strategy. Rick's plan from the start was to remove Salvetti from the face of the earth. The United States government could not, and would not, be involved in any way.

"Here's what I've been thinking. If Santanna can be deported back to Italy, then so can Ricky Blanco. Once I'm over in Europe I will use my company's resources to track Victor down. He still has the ability to travel all around Europe to tend to his legitimate business interests."

"He'll be heavily guarded by an entire organization of hoods. He knows that there is figuratively a price on his head. And of course he's aware that the United States cannot be connected to any attempts to bring him down. That's a quandary you have to be able to get around."

"I will find a place where he is vulnerable and take him out. I already know that he has a penchant for erotic sex. Perhaps I can use this obsession to set him up."

"Rick, I'm sure that ACE will be able to get Santanna some sort of clemency for his role in all of this. Right now it looks as if he will be in the hospital until February 28th. I think this offers you an opportunity to get at Victor. I'll ask ACE to provide clemency for both Santanna Santanna and Ricky Giovanni Blanco."

"I understand all the ramifications of any action I take. I want to assure you he will be a non-factor in the future. Now you have a few things to do while I get my people in Europe working on finding him and where he's going to be for the next six weeks. I will submit myself to the FBI for arrest as Ricky Blanco, as soon as Santanna leaves the hospital. That will give you time to arrange for our mutual deportation in lieu of either of us being imprisoned in the local jail."

"What about my niece? When do you think I can tell her parents that she is still alive, and having a baby no less?"

"You must keep a lid on it until Victor Salvetti is no longer a factor. I'm sure that once he's gone, the Camorra, that is, the new head of that group and there are plenty waiting in line to fill his shoes, won't want to chase any of his enemies. I'll call Aldo and let him know what is going on. I have to call him anyway to have him assist in tracking down Victor. When the time comes I'm sure he will be ready to tell your niece and her husband to come on home, but not until we're all assured she's safe."

Upon arriving home Rick called out to the judge. There was no answer. He found him unconscious on the study floor. He called 911 and accompanied him in the ambulance. During the ride the judge became conscious and spoke.

"I never let you know what the real problem was with me when you last took me to the hospital. You see, I…" He passed out again.

After waiting almost two hours a doctor came out to speak to Rick.

"He's conscious again. Keeps drifting in and out. He told me to go out and tell his son what's wrong with him. I didn't know he had a son. There's no easy way to say this. The judge has leukemia. It's the reason why he has resigned his position on the Supreme Court. The recent bout of flu on his frail body brought him closer to the time when we'll be losing him. He wants to see you. Please don't stay too long. When you leave give the nurse your phone number? She has been instructed to call you when it looks like he's going to die."

Rick visited with him for only fifteen minutes, but he was unconscious all the while. He no sooner entered the now empty house, than his cell phone began to ring.

"This is the nurse at the hospital. Sorry to call you, but he's just returned to consciousness. He wants to talk to you."

Rick entered his room. The judge was on his back and the bed was flat, no pillows were propping him up. He was hooked up to many intravenous lines and assorted electric recording and life-saving devices. The nurse told Rick that the judge knew the end is near and wanted the respirator disconnected.

We honored his wish. When we leave, the automatic heart stimulator will also be disconnected, as per his request. I'll leave you alone with him now. The doctor says it won't be very long."

The judge was awake and his skin color was ashen.

"Rick, let me do the talking, please. In the short time that I've come to know you I have learned to love you like a son. I don't have any living family, so tag—you're it. I want to be cremated and for you to spread my ashes in or if that's not possible, then near the Indian burial site in the Idaho countryside. I've left the bulk of my estate in a perpetual bond trust fund that I want you to manage for me by making sound investments. It's to be used for education grants to be awarded to any Nez Pierce tribal member to allow them to attend any college of their choice. Have a group of tribal elder's select those who have the need. I suspect that will be all of the youth living there."

"Judge, I'll do anything that you want. You've been so good to me these last few months. Why didn't you tell me that you had leukemia? Maybe, just maybe, I could have been around more to help you."

"Well, that's all water under the bridge now. So don't have any regrets for my sake. After all, you let me be a part of a group of people who worked to save the life of our president. Now, that's not too bad a way to go out, is it? Have a long full life, Rick. Go marry that pretty gal you introduced me to last Thanksgiving. She sure is a looker."

Rick's eyes rolled back when the judge made the comment. Of course he would not tell him what had happened to her.

Then the judge smiled, and closed his eyes. He was gone.

The judge's lawyer was waiting outside of the hospital room.

"I just heard that the judge was taken here earlier today. I came right over as he had instructed me to do. Is he still with us?"

"No. He just passed away."

"Are you aware that you are the main beneficiary in his will? He has no other living relative to contest it?

"He told me about the bond trust fund that he has established to grant scholarships to members of the Nez Pierce tribe."

"He also left you the town house here in Washington, as well as the car. He said he wanted you to have a place where all the action was. He also said that *Spook's like you should have a place to go to when you need to rest.* Those are his words, not mine."

"How much do you think the place is worth?"

"I'd say at least a million dollars, give or take a few thousand."

"Tell you what, that seems like a pretty fair amount to me. I have considerable funds already from my business interests. I'll be giving you a check for the million. Take your fee out of it, and put the remainder into additional bonds to be put into the trust in the name of the judge. I'll be responsible for all costs associated with the cremation and memorial service."

"Is there anything else I can do?"

"Yeah. I guess that I have quite a bit on my plate. I'd appreciate it if you could prepare a list of the people and their phone numbers that you think the judge would like to attend his memorial service. Then have your secretary or a clerk make the calls. We'll have it in the Supreme Court Chapel next Monday morning at ten. It will be a non-denominational service, and anyone wishing to speak will be allowed three minutes each. I trust that will be enough time to let everyone who wants to speak do so. No flowers please. Let them know that contributions can be made to the National Leukemia Foundation in his name. If you'll excuse me now I have some other arrangements to make."

At nine the next morning Rick used his satellite phone to set up a secure five way conversation with the managers of his four branch office's of The Purple Feather Group. The European contingent was already five hours later into the workday.

"Let me speak first and you will all know what's going on. After that I'd like all of your inputs when I tell you what I plan to do."

He explained everything. Then he received his feedback.

Cameron would be the coordinating point for the plan. Everything would funnel through him. The other three would each construct six weeks schedules of what Victor Salvetti would be doing during the times they could find out. Out of the three sets of inputs they should be able to come up with a pretty comprehensive schedule of all his planned activity. The most important time frame was the fifth and sixth week. This would be when Ricky and Santanna arrive back in Italy.

"Aldo, I want you to give Santanna a full time job as an investigator. Try your best to get him a license. I don't think that the Italian authorities have much on him as all his illegal activity was done in different countries. He can be helpful in tracking Salvetti's activity. And he has a reason to be involved, but keep him out of Victor's sight. Being former soldiers for Victor, who knew too much. He has a hit out on both of us. He's already tried once."

"Why are you doing this for Santanna? I remember that he was the hood stationed outside of the Spanish retreat who was sent there to kill Marta and you." Said Kitty.

"You're correct, but that was a long time ago. Did I mention to any of you that he took a bullet meant for me? And it was not by accident. I owe him big time. In case you're wondering, he will be advised that I am not the Ricky he thought he knew, but an agent of the United States government working undercover."

"You want me to make him a full-time agent?" Asked Aldo.

"That's the plan. I think that with his underworld connections he'll be a real asset to Frondzi Investigations. He's married now to a real nice woman. It's time for him to settle down. Put him and his wife up at my suite in Licata Resort. He can do quite a bit of searching for Victor's whereabouts with a telephone. I'm sure he will need some time to recuperate from his wounds."

"Kitty, you will have to cover Ireland and Scotland, as well as your native country, England. That's a big territory. Use whatever resources you need. This one's important to me."

"Manuela, You have Spain, Portugal and I want you to cover France as well. I think that's all the places in Europe that Salvetti would go. I do know that he had a Dominatrix by the name of Suzette service him when he was in France. We got this information when your man visually tapped into his room. Apparently his addiction to sadomasochism is embedded deeply into his persona. This kinky-sex appetite that he has may be the best way we have of my getting to him. Pay what you have to in order to put him in a position where I can act."

"Remember this gang, I'm only going to have about two weeks at the most to take him out. I can't get to Europe for at least four weeks. At the same time that I make my move on Victor I also must remove myself out of the Camorra's clutches. When I leave Europe Ricky Blanco will be dead. And if at all possible, so will Victor Salvetti. I have a personal score to settle with him. Keep Cameron up to date. We can all get our status reports from him."

Rick no sooner hung up his satellite phone than the regular phone began to ring. It was George Papadopoilis.

"I just received word that Tobias Whitman was found dead in his cell. We had him on suicide watch. It was supposed to look like he hung himself, but his death smells like it has Salvetti's name written all over it. Victor continues to eliminate any evidence against him. God, but I hope that you're successful in getting him brought to justice."

"So am I, George. So am I."

Next on his agenda was a visit to Santanna. He knew it would be difficult. Rick entered the room gingerly. Santanna's wife, Anna Mary, was sitting dutifully at his bedside. She greeted him with a hug and a kiss on the cheek.

"He's been waiting for you, Ricky. He says that he must talk to you. We'll wake him up now. But before we do that can you tell me why the policemen who had been stationed outside of this room since they put him in here are gone?"

"All in good time, Anna Mary, all in good time. Is he still in a lot of pain?"

"He wouldn't let them give him anything until after you leave. He said that he must be alert for your talk."

"Okay. Let's wake him now. I want you to stay and hear all this. You're a part of his life now."

"Wake up now, honey. Ricky's here to see you."

"Hi, Ricky. You don't have to worry about me. I'm not gonna' tell anybody about what we wuz hired to do. We weren't gonna' do anything that you didn't already plan out, were we?"

"You sounding like you think you know something, Santanna. I'm going to tell you everything right now. But before I do that, I want to thank you for saving my life."

"That's okay, Ricky. I had to give you a chance to take him out. It wuz all I could think of. I know that you're not a hood like me. You don't have to be too smart to know when someone is talking bad English to you in order to make you feel good. You got too much class, and it keeps showing. And then there's the way you think everything through, before you act. You keep showing me all the skills you have. I'm not stupid, you know. All I had to do was to watch the way you move."

"I know you woulda' done the same for me. We're buddies, aren't we?"

"Yes, we have grown to be just that. But I haven't always been straight with you. First off, my name is not Ricky Blanco. My real name is Rick Banyan. The man you met back in the Spanish prison was an undercover agent for a secret agency of the United States government."

"I had a hunch, mind you, just a hunch, that you were somebody different. But I never guessed that you're a FED. Does that mean I'm in real trouble?"

"No, actually. It means that you're in pretty good shape. Because I am a FED, as you like to call me, I've been able to pull some strings. Does Anna Mary know about what you were doing for the Camorra?"

"I told her everything before I married her. I had to be straight with her. She really loves me."

"Then what I'm going to tell you both will make some sense. They are going to dismiss all charges against you with a pardon from the president. But you are going to have to pay a price; actually both of you will have to pay that price, but I've tried to soften the blow. Because you are an illegal alien your marriage to Anna Mary does not automatically give you the right to stay in this country. You and Anna Mary, and even me as my alter self, are to be deported back to Italy. I have business over there as Ricky Blanco. It's part of the deal I've worked out for you."

Santanna began to laugh. He laughed so hard that he started to hurt. Anna Mary was smiling from ear to ear.

"Okay. What did I say that is so funny?"

"We were planning on moving to Italy and setting up our home there. The only problem is that a bartender doesn't make much money over there. Do you have any ideas on what I can do?"

"As a matter of fact, I do. I own a private investigations company in Italy. I also have company offices in England, Spain and in New Jersey. All of them are called The Purple Feather Group. Before you ask, I'm of American Indian heritage and the name is sort of a tribal thing. How would you like to work on the right side of the law for a change? The name of the company is Frondzi Investigations. The man who runs the place is Aldo Frondzi. You'll become one of his agents, and even more important is that your first job is to use your contacts to assist in locating the whereabouts of our ex-boss, Victor Salvetti. You remember him, the guy who tried to kill us both."

"Will the police let me do that kind of work? You know, my past and all that bad stuff."

"Wasn't most of that done outside of Italy?"

"Yeah, you're right. I only got into some small trouble back there. When can I start?"

"You got to get yourself healthy and ready to travel. That should be by the end of February. Aldo will meet us when we land in Italy. He'll be taking you to a resort to have a little working honeymoon, on me of course. Just use the phone while you're there and help him to pinpoint where Victor is for me. I don't ever want him to find you two, so I'll be taking care of that little problem, too. That is, once I catch up with him. Just know that I will."

When Rick left the hospital room Anna Mary was weeping tears of joy. Rick caught sight of a tear in Santanna's eye as well.

One week later on Friday Rick checked in with Cameron.

"Only Kitty was able to come up with anything. While spending two weeks in England he remained at the Oxford Arms Inn located on the outskirts of London. She was able to pick up what he did for only the second week of his stay, when she started. He mostly attended business meetings during the day. On three evenings he dined with executives who work for him. On Thursday he had a liaison with a woman know to practice sadomasochism. The session lasted for three hours. He has at least four bodyguards in close proximity to him most times. Only one of these bodyguards stands outside the door to the room while he is engaging in his favorite pastime. She is attempting to find out the bodyguard's names and their rap sheets. Thorough lady, that Kitty is."

"Anything else?"

"Oh yes. Kitty says to be sure to tell you that he almost never forecasts where he will be going next in advance to anyone. However, she expects to find out at least one day before he goes someplace because he has to order plane tickets for his entire entourage. She'll call me and I'll let them know as soon as she has the information."

"Have the others called in yet?"

"You're the last one. Remember they're up earlier than we are. They started calling at four AM. Scares the bejeezus out of me when the phone rings that early."

"Tell you what. Call them back and advise that we'll all be on a secure satellite conference call on Friday's at ten AM Eastern Standard Time. It will provide us an opportunity to discuss different ideas that we will come up with."

The weeks went by slowly for Rick. He spoke to Kevin and found out that the president had agreed to the pardons. He visited with Santanna and found him to be improving daily. He was on schedule for release from the hospital on February 28th. Anna Mary was packing their small belongings for use in their new life. It was agreed that Santanna would turn himself in to the U.S. Marshal's Office directly after leaving the hospital. Rick would turn himself in for processing during the evening of February 27th. They would all be put on a plane leaving for Italy on March 1st. Rick had purchased a ticket for Anna Mary for the same flight.

That afternoon, Rick purchased large gold hoop earrings for himself. He was getting ready to re-assume the role of Ricky Blanco, and he needed his props. When he left the jewelry shop he said to himself: *Sorry, Saila. I've got to become Ricky Blanco again, and that means I've got to look like Mr. Clean for the last time. Promise.*

The following Friday Cameron provided them with an update. They had already been called and told that Victor was headed to Portugal and had booked four rooms, one being the honeymoon suite, in the Hilton Renaissance in Port Alegre for a party of six, five male and one female. His reservation was for six days duration. It looks like he has hired a new assistant. Visits with his company's officers have been arranged. The names of his four-hired henchman are as follows, along with their specialty and other details provided to us.

Georges Pasteanu French National—Cajun Light-Skin-Negro
6' 4" 245lbs
Spent twelve years in Spanish prison—three separate prisons terms. Unable to find the full reasons for jail terms, but murder was included in one charge. Likes to break bones. Enjoys great pleasure in causing pain.

Michael Jones American Fair-Skin-Caucasian
5' 11" 198lbs
Jailed in England for murder, served only 5 years.
Was released on a technicality.
Also spent time in prison in Australia for murder.
Broke out and was never apprehended.

Franky Gumbino Italian/ Irish-Caucasian
6' 1" 190lbs Ruddy Complexion
Never arrested. Formally a Private Investigator.
Holds rank of Lieutenant in the Camorra.
Usually guards Salvetti while he engages in sadomasochism.

Frank Medley German/English-Caucasian
5' 9" 165lbs Light-Skinned
Arrested seven times in four different countries.
No prison time. Witnesses disappeared.
Never made it to a trial.

"Looks like we have the League of Nations to deal with." Commented Cameron. "Log on to my e-mail and we have pictures for you too.

"I think that it's time to let Salvetti feel some heat. Kitty, can you do a job on Frank Gumbino? I'd like him out of the picture for the next three months or so. It's important that we see who replaces him and who gets assigned to guard Victor while he engages in his fancy."

"Not going to be a problem. Consider it done."

"Manuela, I don't want you to miss out on any of the good times, and since Salvetti has left England, I' like your people to handle making Frank Medley disappear."

"With two of his people out of circulation I want you, Aldo, to get the word out to the Camorra in Italy that Ricky Blanco is coming to get him because of what he did to Saila Ewe."

"Are you sure that you want to let him know that you're coming after him?" Asked Kitty.

"That's exactly what I want to do. It will actually put him at a disadvantage, not knowing when or where I'll be attacking him from. Trust me, this is an old Indian trick. He's going to go crazy trying to fill all the gaps that surround him. I'll find the one place he doesn't fill."

Rick left that weekend to take the judge's ashes back to his tribal reservation for dispersion. He arrived in Idaho in the early evening and rented a car to take him out to where his grandfather lived. He was now ninety-eight years old, and was still spry. Rick told him why he was there, and explained the education trust that the judge had established for all the youth of the tribe. Because his grandfather was a

Tribal Shaman he was able to call a meeting of the tribal elder's for the next morning.

It was here Rick was allowed to present his information about the trust, and to pass on the judge's final request. The meeting was held in the largest teepee on the reservation, where they openly discussed what they would be doing. Twelve men of the tribe attended. Two old women also sat in and kept a written record of what was going on. They were not allowed to speak. His grandfather told him that none of them were less than forty-five years old, and two were over one hundred. All of their faces were well weathered.

"It is a great thing this man, who none of us knew, has done for the youth of our tribe. But we have rules. No one but a pure-blood Nez Pierce can be buried in the sacred burial grounds."

"You didn't hear right." Said another. "Your age is getting in the way of all the parts of your anatomy. The man exists only in the form of ashes. What is wrong with allowing his ashes to be placed there?"

"You're splitting hairs. The land is sacred to the Nez Pierce. Outsiders are not allowed to even walk in that area, regardless of what they may have done for the tribe."

And so it went on, back and forth for more than three hours. Rick's grandfather offered his thoughts after the group seemed to be at an impasse.

"Allow my grandson to take the ashes up wind of the Sacred Burial Site to just outside of the area, and let him release them to the winds. The prevailing wind always has access to our dead. Thus the ashes will blow them across the burial site, and the wishes of this noble man will be granted. At the same time we have not allowed anyone to violate our sacred rules."

It was a good compromise, and they quickly agreed.

Rick's grandfather accompanied him to the edge of the burial site. The Shaman said an Indian spiritual prayer for the dead as Rick allowed the ashes to fall from the urn. Rick's own words were somber, yet joyful.

"I offer up your ashes to a world of beloved dead who are now living for eternity with you. They are your new family now. I trust that you will be worthy of each other."

Rick was back in Washington, DC on Monday

On the following Friday, Cameron reported the status of their surveillance.

"Victor left on Thursday to return to Naples, Italy. He is staying in his own home so we don't know how long he will be there. Aldo will have to keep close surveillance on him. He has two new bodyguards, but I'll let the ladies of our group tell you about that. Here are two points of interest. First, he continues to indulge himself on Thursdays. Second, he received the word that an ex-employee has pledged to even a score with him. He just laughed when he heard that one. Ladies..."

Kitty offered her report of happenings first. "Franky Gumbino likes to drink, so I sent Paddy McBride over to Portugal to have a little parting drink with him. He tried to out drink Paddy, an impossible task, and the two of them went outside of the bar to settle up things in a manly way. Needless to say, Franky didn't fare too well. He made the mistake of pulling a knife on Paddy, a stiletto no less. That provided Paddy with a strong reason to take him apart. He did just that. Mr. Gumbino will be in the hospital with a number of broken bones, two of which, won't allow him to walk around for at least eight weeks."

"The only thing that I have to report is that Frank Medley has come up missing." Said Manuela. No one has seen him for three days now. He's really been picked up by the Spanish police; a group of professionals whom I was once one. I checked and found that he had three outstanding warrants. They will be keeping him under wraps for quite a while as they interrogate him about a number of other open cases they have on the books. He's effectively out of the picture."

"Cameron, who's taken over as his bodyguard when he plays his sexual games"

"That would be Georges Pasteanu. He's the big guy."

"That's exactly what I wanted. After I saw the pictures of the four original hoods, I think that I can impersonate him the easiest.

"Manuela, please have your man, Joseph, set me up in France with an appointment with Victor's Dominatrix, Suzette. Tell him to let her know that I'll be willing to pay big money for the right kind of treatment. Set it up for Tuesday, March 5th at nine in the evening at the Le Bourne Hotel. Get me a reservation for room 921. I understand that's Victor's favorite place. If it's good enough for him then I guess it's good enough for me. I'm betting that his next stop will be in France. That's where I'll get him."

"I get the feeling that you're evolving back into the character of Ricky Blanco again. Because Georges has a shaven head. I assume that yours will be that way again."

"Right on, Manuela."

"Aldo, rough up those two new goons that are replacing the one's the gal's had taken out. Let them know that the people who are doing it to him are working for Ricky Blanco. Leave the other guy, Michael Jones alone, for the time being anyway. Looks like we have the beginning of a plan. Be talking to you all next Friday. Cameron will keep us all in the loop if anything changes."

The following Friday Cameron reported that Salvetti was leaving for Paris a week from this coming Sunday. The information became available because he had to tell four new men that he had hired where they would be going and when. There was an increase of two. Victor was becoming nervous, if not actually scared.

Manuela reported. "You have your appointment with Suzette that you requested. Joseph will meet you in the lobby at eight forty-five. He will have all the things that you e-mailed me to get for you. Sure hope that you know how to use that assortment of junkyard garbage. I think you called them accouterments of sexual pleasure. How anyone can get any pleasure out of that beats me."

Aldo was next to report. "Vito, Marta and I will be meeting you and the Santanna's when your plane lands. I've been told that the U.S.

Marshals accompanying you will then give you back your Italian passports. I'll take the Santanna's directly to Licata Resort. You should go to Vito and Marta's home and rest. I'll show Santanna the pictures of all the guys assigned to guard Salvetti. We've got pictures and names of the new ones too. Maybe he can come up with some additional information for us?

The transfer of the illegal aliens with presidential pardons went off without a hitch. They all arrived safely in Italy. Aldo greeted Rick; he was not surprised when he saw his shaved his head again in order to get into his alter self. He was also wearing his new gold hoop earrings.

Marta was starting to show her pregnancy. Rick assured her that it would only be a few more weeks at the most. He then sacked out. The time was close when he would extract his revenge on Victor Salvetti.

Rick received a call from Aldo the next morning.

"Santanna tells me that he knows all about this bodyguard, the one called Michael Jones. The word is that he really works for the man who plans on taking over the Camorra after Victor Salvetti retires or other things happen. The Camorra leadership is all upset about the botched assassination attempt. It has called attention to their other money raising activities. Victor will soon no longer be considered the head of the Camorra."

"Can you set me up to meet this man, Aldo?"

"I can try. Meet me in the bar up the street from Vito's house at nine tonight. It's called the Spazio Casa. There's trouble brewing in the Camorra. I think he will meet with us."

Aldo was able to deliver. They met with Michael Jones and found out that for a price he would be happy to leave the scene when the action started to happen. He was to be on duty Thursday night to provide backup to Georges Pasteanu in the protection of Victor Salvetti. He was only doing what his real boss wanted him to do.

Rick picked up his package from Joseph two days later. He met Suzette in room 921. She was already scantily clad, wearing only her panties, which highlighted her extremely slim hips. She was ravishingly beautiful with bright red hair. By anyone's standards she was a gorgeous-looking woman. Her breasts were medium-large and perfectly formed, yet there were bruised areas showing all over her body.

"Suzette. I'm going to tell you a story and ask you to help me. I have no intention of causing you any pain, either tonight or ever. You will be paid your usual amount for a night's servicing, plus an additional five hundred thousand Francs for later using the equipment that I have brought with me this evening."

"What is it you want me to do to you or for you, Monsieur?"

"First I want you to listen. Then you make up your mind. You have an appointment with Victor Salvetti on Thursday evening at eight."

"Yes, that is so, Monsieur."

"Has he ever hurt you? I believe he has. No Matter. He hurt my woman so badly that he killed her. He was deriving pleasure from using her services much as you have done for him whenever he visits Paris. He decided to use a gun to give her even more pain. He did it for only a minor infraction made on her part. He put three bullets into her stomach and then stood by as he watched her die."

Rick's lying knew no bonds. He was ready to do anything to have her help him. He was telling her the absolute truth, out of context, of course.

"Did you know that he has done this same thing in at least two other places around the world? Have you ever hurt him a little too much? Do you remember his reaction?"

He was on the right track.

"It's only a matter of time before he turns on you. You know that, don't you? And if you help me pay him back, you can get him out of your life forever. And think of what five hundred thousand Francs will do for your future. Why, you can retire from this business altogether, and let those bruises have a chance to heal. Perhaps there is a man that you love. You will be able to love only him. You can marry him if you choose."

'Say no more, Monsieur. What do you want me to do?"

"You do use a chain when you tie him up?"

"Among other things."

"Good. I want you to use my chain, the one I brought with me tonight. I will show you how I want you to tie it. It is much longer than the one you have, and it has special characteristics built into it. Here's how I want you to tie him. I'll be giving you the first half of the money I promised before I leave here. And remember, if you don't help me he will soon try to kill you."

'That's all."

"Yes. Once you have him tied with the chain the way I showed you, knock on the door. When I enter the room with another man, just take your clothing and other paraphernalia and leave. That's all you'll be required to do."

When Rick left the room he knew he had been successful in putting Victor in a place where he was sure he didn't want to be.

* * * *

Thursday evening, eight o'clock. The moment he had been waiting for was upon him. He had the .45 caliber gun equipped with a silencer and loaded with eight bullets in his coat pocket, his bone knife in its scabbard on his leg as a backup, and his special gadget to operate the chain also in his pocket.

He walked up to the door that he saw Victor recently enter, followed shortly after by Suzette. Rick tried to reach past the man and enter the room. The large shouldered man named Georges stopped him from entering. By doing so he was put into a position of being off balance. It was where Rick wanted him.

"Where the hell do you think you are going, Mon? This here's a private party goin' on in dare. You know, you look jus like me, Mon. Except you wear those large earrings. What dey call dem, hoops? Why you want to look like a woman, Mon? I think I break your bones. What you say, Mon?"

The man almost didn't have time to finish his final question, and Rick was behind him and had an arm around the man's neck. A small amount of pressure applied using his other hand to a nerve in his neck brought immediate unconsciousness. He caught the man in his arms and eased him to the floor. Then he dragged his body into an exit doorway and quickly changed clothes with him.

Rick wanted to put his earrings on the man. He found out that he didn't have holes in his ears. He expected that possibility, so he had brought along needles that were treated with a sterilized coagulant. He lanced the ears first, and when he went to put them into his lobes he found he had to push them through in order to hook them. Once through the lobes he played it safe and wiped the metal posts clean with an alcohol pad. *What a waste of good gold,* he thought, as he did his thing with him.

Then came the final touch; he slipped the passport identifying him as Ricky Blanco into the pocket of the coat. He took out the gun and another object that looked like a small transmitter with a switch. He would have to rely on the efforts of Manuela to be able to stop the police from taking prints for identification, in addition to all the other evidence they would find with his body.

He stood in front of the door with his arms crossed awaiting the knock on the door from within. Once he heard it he took out the miniature transmitter and pushed the switch forward. If Suzette had done her job correctly the chain would be wrapped around Victor's chest first then his left wrist, then around his neck and finally around the other wrist, where it was attached with a hook. The small motor on the chain would start to turn and wind a small wire that had been laced through the chain links, and wrapping on the aperture. This would cause the chain to contract and force Victor into unconsciousness. He dragged the hood from the stairwell and stood him in front of himself. Then he pushed the door open. The room was dimly lit. Victor was naked, void of any erection, but not quite out of it yet. His black eyes stared at the apparition sagging in front of him. Rick could see the hatred staring at him.

He barked a quick command to Suzette.

"Take off, Suzette. You'll find your money in a package in the stairwell. Get a life for yourself."

He saw Victor go unconscious and he eased off on the switch, knowing he only had a moment to act. Dropping Georges to the floor, Rick took out his gun, wiped off all prints, and placed it into Victor's hand, and then quickly picked Georges back up and stood behind him. He pushed the lever on the switch backward slightly releasing the tension around his throat.

Victor quickly started to regain consciousness, awakening only to see a blurred and sagging bodyguard, and to hear his antagonist telling him that he was now going to die. Rick pressed the switch forward again on the transmitter and watched the wire slowly tighten as the life was squeezed out of Victor Salvetti. The motor had been placed above the right wrist, and thus the squeezing chain only reacted from a point beyond the hand, leaving the right hand secured by the chain, but not tightening.

Victor started firing the gun as best he could in the direction of Georges. He hit him with four of the bullets, one of them sent into Georges heart, two others into the doorway behind him. Victor tried to draw a last breadth, but failed. He tried to spit at his attacker; he was unable to raise any saliva in his mouth. Next his larynx was crushed, and Rick could see the fear in his eyes heighten. His pain had reached an extraordinarily high level. Finally his spinal cord snapped. He was dead by a slow and agonizing process. It was the way he was told his woman had died. LamieDog's death had been avenged. His Saila could rest in peace.

Rick dropped Georges to the floor for the last time. He quickly removed the extended part of the chain that contained the motor, and pulled the wire out. He wrapped the remains of the chain back around

Victor's now stiffening body. Then he heard the sound of others heading toward the room.

Even in death, Victor still has people coming after me. It was a thought that flashed through Rick's mind, but then quickly rational thought prevailed. Two of the newly hired thugs came charging into the room with their guns drawn to find who they thought was Victor's bodyguard standing over him in what looked like he was attempting to loosen the chain wrapped around him.

"Hey, Mon. Do you see what that she-woman has dun to der boss? I jus cum in da room when I hear di noise. She got him all chained up, and he stil manges to kill da man who want ta kill himself, that he does. We best get out, now. Victor is dead, and we don't want to be around."

Rick pushed past the other two and ran to the elevator. Then he saw that they would be able to catch the same elevator, so as the door opened, he ran to the stairs. They took the elevator. He didn't want them to get a good look at him in the brighter lighting of the hallway.

Two days later Rick Banyan left France's Orly Field. He was wearing a wig that made him look like his passport picture. He carried with him an American English print copy of the Parisian Times. A debt had been paid in full. He would notify Kevin after he returned home; there was no sense in rushing. The headlines were as follows:

> Paris, France (AP) March 8
> VICTOR SALVETTI, INTERNATIONAL MAN OF BUSINESS,LEADER OF THE CAMORRA CRIMINAL ORGANIZATION, HEADQUARTED AND OPERATING OUT OF NAPLES, DIES IN PARIS LUXURY HOTEL IN THE THRONGS OF SADISTIC SEX ACT.
> With his last breath he kills Ricky Gioviani Blanco, a man pledged to destroy him. Blanco was recently deported back to Italy, having been linked to the aborted assassination attempt of the US President.

EPILOGUE

Kevin had the delicate task of telling his brother and ex-wife that their daughter, Marta, who they saw in a coffin in Spain was alive and well. During the trip to Italy he now started to wine and dine them in preparation of the next shocking event he was about to inform them of. He had already tried to explain that their daughter was in great danger of being murdered by an international organization. They had wanted her silenced because of things about them that she knew. It was the reason he gave them to cover the deception he had laid upon them.

By the end of the trip he had explained it as well as he could, and they were buying it, only because their daughter was still alive and that was all that counted. He decided to let them see for themselves what her current condition was, and to learn of her planned marriage to the man who was assigned to protect her. He did assure them that she was in good condition. The latter was said with tongue-in-cheek.

As they walked into the terminal after disembarking from the plane they caught sight of her pretty face that was beaming for joy. Then they viewed her entire body, and said in unison, "what the heck, she's alive and that's what counts". Marta introduced her future husband, Vito. She showed them her engagement ring.

All was happy in the Winslow clan.

* * * *

SIX MONTHS LATER

The place was a remote location in Kuala Lumpur, Malaysia. Three people were in a windowless room. The white walls took on the tint of soft yellowish lights. There were no pictures hanging on the walls. Instead one wall was completely filled with framed diplomas and achievement awards.

The young woman sitting in the wheel chair had beads of perspiration covering her entire body. She was wearing a bright smile on her face. She was wearing what could be described as a jogging suit. She had been able to do something that before today had been impossible.

A man wearing an English-cut three-piece business suit sat almost in a position of attention in his chair. It was obvious that he was on edge as they planned to discuss what had happened to his niece. The air conditioning system purred softly and provided a hum that broke the silence,

A man wearing a long white coat sat behind a large desk. He was an aged oriental with thinning white hair and a long goatee. He too was smiling as he told them he was ready to answer questions.

"But before I do that I want to explain the process that we have followed in order to achieve this goal. As you know the developed countries have in many instances shunned the use of embryo stem-cell development to create clones. We here in this country do not have any rules in place that restrains technological medical breakthroughs. We have taken the product of embryo development and have been able to extract new living cells that we have used to regenerate and grow new spinal tissue. These cells have been placed into Miss Ewe's spine, and have been conditioned to grow new tissue."

"Has this ever been done before, Doctor Zen?"

"Yes, but never as successfully as we have been able to do with her. Today she was able to stand on her own and take three steps, all done under her control. This is a marvelous development."

"Uncle Peter, do you realize that I'm not only going to walk again, but I'll be able to do all the other things that a young woman should be able to do? It's all because you wouldn't let me die, despite my plea's to you to let me expire. I am so thankful to the men in this room."

Then looking squarely into the eyes of the doctor she asked a question, the answer to which would change her life forever.

"When will I be able to resume a normal life again?"

"It really depends on your ability to work your body through the various levels of conditioning that will take place in therapy. To answer your question as directly as I can, it all depends on you, Saila. If I was to venture a guess, I would say approximately a month."

The meeting was ended. Peter Grace pushed the wheelchair containing his niece back to her room in the sanitarium.

"Sorry that I can't stay any longer. I am so glad that you called for me to witness your first steps in six months. It has been a long hard fight for you, but now you're on the mend."

"You haven't told Rick Banyan anything yet, have you?"

"No as we agreed that night while riding in the ambulance, that if you stopped proclaiming your desire to want to die, then I would raise heaven and hell to locate someone who would find a cure for you. You will be the one to tell him, not I."

Later in her room that evening she wheeled her chair out on to the balcony. She gazed out at the beautiful fall sky that outlined the city of Kuala Lumpur, her childhood home. She pulled herself erect, and took three steps towards the rail on the balcony. It was more assurance that she really could walk.

Looking out at her city of life she spoke loudly, but there was no one out there to hear.

"Soon, my darling, soon. I will have you come to me when I have achieved the ability to love you as a woman should love her man. I promise you. It will be soon."

* * * *

Rick had been spending most nights dreaming of the happy times that he was able to spend with Saila. He was using it as a way to keep her memory fresh. But tonight he had a different sort of dream; it was a more troubled sleep. Actually it was a nightmare. His mind raced back to that terrible day when he was told that she had died. He awoke with a start, sweat pouring from his body.

There was a question running through his mind. It had to be answered. He felt his very life depended on it. He asked it of himself.

"Why was I told that they were sending her remains back to Kuala Lumpur to be cremated? Why would they send back a dead body, and not cremate her where she died and have the ashes shipped home?"

Rick would find a way to answer that question.

Finis—No, perhaps a new beginning.

Other Novels by the Author
(James T. Ernst)
Jim Ernst

COINCIDENCE

CASTROPHE

CONSPIRATOR—A Prequel to CLIQUE
Being released as a Print on Demand late in 2003

CATALYST
Look for this one's release early in 2003
Here's a look!

PROLOGUE

The body had been laying face down in the culvert at the side of the road for more than four hours. Even the insects seemed to have had their fill. During the daylight hours many cars passed, but the culvert was below the level of the road. There would be no reason to expect to see anyone out there, much less an unconscious man.

For the past hour he'd been wavering back and forth between consciousness, only to ask himself who he was and what he was doing there. Then, when the mind drew its inevitable blank, he lapsed back into the twilight world of *who cares anyway.* But there was a life that needed to continue and basic survival instincts eventually won out.

As midnight rolled around the urge to relieve his bladder forced him to the slope of the culvert. Unable to pull himself into a standing position using his own strength, and fighting the pain throbbing in his head, he'd made his way to the top of the culvert. Spotting a telephone pole he could use to hold himself up, he started a painful journey on his hands and knees over rocky underbrush, which covered the side of the road for fifty feet. Finally, pulling himself upright and leaning against the pole for support, he reached for the zipper to his fly.

He couldn't find it...But he did find his member, grabbed at it to provide direction away from him, and started to pee. It was then he looked down, and by hazy moonlight could see that he was not wearing any clothes. He felt his groin area. There was no pubic hair in evidence at all. He felt all over his chest. There was no hair there either. He realized he was naked. All he could feel were insect-bites itching, bruises aching from the bones all over his body. He could make out welts that seemed to be all over him. Reaching higher to his head, again finding no hair, feeling only a light-stubble of growth. He ran his hand across his eyebrows. The result was the same. Then he felt the blackness of unconsciousness once again creeping across his hurting body, until it consumed him in its depths.

When he awoke for all he knew a day had passed. It had, in fact, been only two hours. A heavy fog had rolled in, and he could barely make out the outline of a road, only twenty feet away. He pulled himself once again to a standing position using the pole to help him. Then he decided he could not walk that far, and the only way he could make it to the road was on his hands and knees. He fell forward, absorbing a jolt of pain spreading all over his body. He started his journey toward the road, and what he could only hope would be survival. The fog thickened even more.

Finally, he could feel the macadam roadway beneath his hands and knees. It was only minutes that passed, and through the pea soup-like fog he could make out headlights bearing down upon him. The driver must have seen him because the car slowed to almost a crawl. He tried to focus on a plan. His temples pounded as he forced himself to concentrate.

Good, he thought. *The car was moving slowly. That was the only speed I can manage to deal with.*

He stayed to the side almost off the road, lest the car hit him. He decided he'd wait until the vehicle was about to pass him; then he'd hit the fender with his fist, and using all the strength he could muster roll away from the car where he felt he could be seen. His plan succeeded, the car stopped and backed up about ten feet. Headlights bounced back from the fog.

A woman exited the vehicle, her eyes straining through the mist to see what she thought she had hit. He could make her out, standing in the glare created by her headlights. To him she was a beautiful creature. His mind conjured up thoughts that she was an Angel sent to help him. He spoke:

"Help me, help me, please."

His voice was that of a whisper. He was surprised he was able to speak at all.

0-595-25696-1